Eye for an Eye

Eye for an Eye

Dwayne S. Joseph

URBAN
Renaissance

www.urbanbooks.net

Urban Books, LLC
78 East Industry Court
Deer Park, NY 11729

Eye for an Eye Copyright © 2010 Dwayne S. Joseph

ISBN 13: 978-1-60162-226-6
ISBN 10: 1-60162-226-0

First Printing October 2010
Printed in the United States of America

10 9 8 7 6 5 4 3 2 1

Distributed by Kensington Publishing Corp.
Submit Wholesale Orders to:
Kensington Publishing Corp.
C/O Penguin Group (USA) Inc.
Attention: Order Processing
405 Murray Hill Parkway
East Rutherford, NJ 07073-2316
Phone: 1-800-526-0275
Fax: 1-800-227-9604

Acknowledgments

Lisette.

I had to bring her back. Her story wasn't finished. The ride was only half done. I've never done a sequel before. Always said I wouldn't, because once I finish a book, the characters whose lives I toyed with disappear to be quickly replaced by new characters. But Lisette. She just wouldn't leave me alone. She walked up to me two years ago when I was sitting in the café at Barnes & Noble (always to the left of the register, with a cup of tea or a vanilla latte in front of me), and told me that she was a *Home Wrecker*. Then she sat down and refused to get up until her story was told. Well . . . I thought that it had been told. Before she finally got up and walked away, she neglected to tell me that she was going to come back to tell me more.

Lisette.

She's a trip. I have to be honest . . . I missed her. I think she missed me too. That's why she came back to give me the second part of her adventure. She may not admit it, but I think she has strong feelings for me. So there I was at Barnes & Noble again (same side, same drinks) when she walked in, pulled up a chair, sat down, and told me that I was going to need a lot of paper for what she had to tell me next.

Eye for an Eye . . . If you haven't read *Home Wrecker*, you need to. It will make this tale that much more potent. This book was by far one of the most enjoyable for me to write! Readers . . . By now you should be used to the fact that I am giving you darker, more intense, more dramatic, more erotic, and more suspenseful storylines. So you know that before you flip the page to page one, you should be expecting to read *Home Wrecker* on speed, with a side of crazy and deranged. If Lisette was going to come back for you all, there simply was no way for me not to up the ante tenfold. And trust me . . . I have done that!

God . . . you gave me a talent and I will forever be appreciative of it. That's one of the reasons I try my hardest to improve. You want us to strive to be the best. That's why you put us here. We are all indebted to you.

My wife, Wendy, and my rugrats, Tati, Nati, and X . . . Thank you for understanding when I leave the house to go and create! And thank you for being all the inspiration I need. My family (in-laws included) . . . I love you guys! Aleah . . . So great to know that you are a fan! My friends . . . Too many to name, but you know! Marc Gay (You know you want to be a Giants fan)!

To my agent, Portia Cannon . . . Thank you as always for doing all that you do! Let's make that push to the next level. Speaking of which, Victoria Christopher Murray . . . Having your support is an honor. You have no idea how timely our initial phone call was. I thank you from the bottom of my heart for your kind words!

Big thank you to the crew at Barnes & Noble. Kelsey, Sara, Esias, etc. . . . I know mine isn't the prettiest face to see first thing in the morning, but I guess it could be worse! LOL. Thanks for the vanilla lattes, the Mountain Dews, and the hot water refills!

To the readers and book clubs (and, yes, PeaceInPages, this means you!) . . . I cannot thank you all enough for the way you have joined me on this ride. Thank you, everyone, for being behind *Betrayal* the way that you all were. I'm so glad to

Acknowledgments

know that you were willing to accept the change! As for this tale, you all are every bit as responsible as Lisette was for this tale being told. It has truly been amazing to know and hear how much you all wanted her back. There are so many of you to thank that I can't put everyone's name because I know I will miss some (I already had one book club hang me by my toes for that, ahem, PeaceInPages LOL!), but believe me, I am soooo completely appreciative of you all. *Eye for an Eye* is going to spark insane discussions! I can't wait to meet with you again! To my MySpace and FB peeps . . . Wow . . . Thank you for reaching out, giving feedback, joining my fan page, and spreading the word. If I could include everyone's name I would, but again, I need the rest of my toes! But trust me, you all are very important to me. It is truly gratifying to know that my hard work and determination to entertain is felt by you guys. I compete with myself with each novel I do, but part of my driving force is also my desire to give you all something different, something that you can't put down. A million thanks for letting me know that I accomplish that goal. Please keep the messages, wall posts, e-mails, and reviews coming! And be ready . . . I'm bringing more craziness, more darkness, more mystery, and suspense. I hope you all continue to join me on the ride!

To Nancy Silvas, Jocelyn Lawson, Melinda Mooneyhan, Péron F. Long, Portia Cannon, Wendy . . . Thanks for every bit of feedback you gave as I wrote *Eye for an Eye*!

Eric Pete, La Jill Hunt, Péron F. Long, Anna J. . . . . You know we have work to do!

Finally . . . my G-Men. It was a disappointing '09 season, but I know we will be back! Steve Smith . . . I see you on FB, kid! Big Blue for LIFE! Much love!

Dwayne S. Joseph—here still at Barnes & Noble. Come by and have a latte sometime.

Acknowledgments

www.facebook.com
www.myspace.com/DwayneSJoseph
Djoseph21044@yahoo.com

Prologue

"Amado Mio."

Playing from my iPod in the living room.

"Amado Mio" by Pink Martini.

I leaned my head back. Listened to the melody. Felt my skin tingle. The breakdown was coming. My skin always tingled when it did.

"Amado Mio."

Like sex, the song was that good. That sexy. That intense. That powerful. If there were a movie about me, this would be my theme song.

I closed my eyes.

Breathed slowly.

Ran my hands up my thighs, past my stomach, over my erect nipples, to my neck, then back down again.

I was wet from the hot water covering me. I was dripping from the melodic orgasm Pink Martini and their groove had caused. Every woman needs to own a copy of this song.

It was the perfect size. The prefect width. The perfect stroke.

To hell with a dick. Just put this song on repeat.

Ringing.

There was no ringing in the song.

I opened my eyes and looked over to my right. My BlackBerry was on the rim of my tub, ringing softly, the volume set at level two. I sighed. I was in mid-stroke, nearing self-fulfilled ecstasy. I should have turned the damn thing off.

I reached over and grabbed it with my fingers wet from the

water and my pussy. A Friday night, nearing nine-thirty. Aida followed the rules. Only one other person who didn't.

I connected the call and placed the BlackBerry against my ear. "Marlene."

"We have a potential client."

I exhaled. "It's Friday night, Marlene."

"I know I'm not supposed to call."

"Yet you did."

"I'm sorry, but—"

"Friday nights are off limits."

Marlene sighed apologetically. I could see her running her hands through her hair. She said, "I know. I tried not to call, but she sounds desperate. She wants to know if you'll help her tonight."

In the background, "Amado Mio" had finished and was restarting. I'd heard the song thousands of times, but each time was like hearing it for the first time. I hated missing any of the song. "Give it to Aida."

"You've given the last three clients to her."

"And she's done well with them."

"It's been four months since you've taken a client on."

"And?"

"Lisette . . ." Marlene paused momentarily. I could tell she was trying to choose her words carefully. "I know I've asked you this before, but are you sure you're all right? Believe me, you are the strongest person I know, but after everything you went through with Kyra . . . I would understand if you were a bit scarred."

I closed my eyes and shook my head.

That name.

Kyra.

Almost a year ago, she'd taken me to the edge. She thought she'd been on my level. Thought she'd been better than me.

She'd been wrong.

But she had taken me to the edge.

She'd caused things to happen. Things that kept me from getting a full night's sleep. Things that had me on edge. Things that had indeed scarred me. Of course, I would never admit it to anyone. Marlene had seen me at my weakest point and that would be all she would ever see.

I said, "I'm fine."

"Lisette . . . I know you don't like to admit it, but you are human."

"I'm fine," I said again.

Marlene wouldn't let up. "She had you beaten and raped. I don't know anyone who can go through that and remain unscathed."

"I said I'm fine, Marlene."

"Then why haven't you taken on any clients, Lisette?"

I clenched my jaw.

Two years ago, I became a home wrecker: a woman hired by wives to "ruin" their marriages. They sought my services for various reasons. Some were women who'd become fed up with their husbands' infidelity. They wanted evidence to use against them to help garner the best payoff possible. Some women were victims of emotional, physical, or verbal abuse who felt trapped and saw my "expertise" as a means of escape. Other women weren't seeking an escape or a big payday. They just wanted leverage. Something to hold over their husbands' heads so that they could do whatever the hell they wanted to do. Pictures, videos, sometimes the satisfaction of walking in and seeing their cheating bastards in compromising situations—whatever they wanted, I provided.

Marlene had been my first client. A fear of scrutiny from her friends and family kept her hostage in a marriage to a pathetic asshole. I gave Marlene the same thing I gave my clients after her—the very thing that I got off on.

Control.

Marlene and all of the other clients had none. That meant

they had no power. I'd learned a long time ago that life without control wasn't life at all. Life without control was death. Life without control just didn't make any sense to me. Before I helped her, Marlene was weak. She changed when she got control back.

Kyra had managed to take my control away from me. She'd managed to render me powerless. Although I'd never told her directly, Marlene's newfound strength had been what pulled me away from the edge of the insanity I'd been teetering on. Before my services, Marlene had been an acquaintance. Now . . . she was a friend—my only real friend—and despite the fact that I never called her that, she knew it, and I appreciated her for that.

"For the last time . . . I'm fine," I said. "I haven't been in the mood to take on any clients."

"Lisette—"

"Give the client to Aida."

Marlene was silent for a moment before sighing and saying, "OK."

"I'm going to go back and enjoy my Friday night now."

"Are you listening to your song again?"

"Of course."

"Can I ask you something?"

I pressed down on my eyeballs with the middle finger and thumb of my free hand. I exhaled. "What?"

"That song . . . it's about love. Why do you like it so much?"

I opened my eyes and looked toward the living room. The breakdown in the song was coming again.

It was a valid question.

I didn't believe in any of the song's lyrics, yet the song resonated and stoked a fire inside of me more than anything else had. It didn't make sense.

"I don't know, Marlene," I said. "I just do."

"Love is possible, Lisette. I know you're jaded and don't

believe in it, but it is possible. Trust me, after all of the bullshit with Steve, I was prepared to swear off of it forever too, but just when I was ready to do that, Michael came into my life."

I groaned. I really didn't want to hear any of her sappy shit. "Marlene . . ."

"I'm just saying, Lisette, what you do . . . the men you trap . . . not all of them are assholes. There are some decent ones out there. As much as you think there not, if you try to leave your door cracked open just a little bit, you'll see the right guy can come along and it could be a beautiful thing."

I clenched my jaw. Friend or not, I'd had enough. I said, "I don't do love, Marlene," and then I ended the call and turned my BlackBerry off. "Shit."

The bath water had grown tepid. I'd missed another replay of "Amado Mio."

I was irritated.

I turned the hot water faucet on, leaned my head back, closed my eyes, and put my focus back on the song that had no real relevance in my life. At least not in my current one.

"Amado Mio."

A song about being in love forever.

I breathed.

Listened to the song.

And as hard as I tried not to, I went back to a time I'd let go of a long time ago.

Past

1

Love.

It was tried a long time ago. Like *Star Wars*, in a galaxy far, far away. A world very different from the one that existed now. One in which I didn't exist. Only Lisette Jones.

She thought she'd known what it was to be sexy. She thought she'd known about the power of manipulation. She thought she'd had a true understanding of what control was.

But she hadn't known shit. Not the way she needed to. That's why love snuck in through a back door she hadn't closed and tried to fuck up her life.

Lisette Jones was naïve. A young girl living her life the way she wanted to, until one thing eventually destroyed her.

Love.

She'd never really had it.

Her mother had none for her. Her jealousy never allowed it. For as long as Lisette Jones could remember, the only things her mother ever gazed at her with were eyes filled with envy and disgust.

Although she was attractive in a plain, everyday-looking kind of way, Lisette Jones knew that her mother lived with a heart filled with daily contempt because her daughter had the beauty she wanted.

Natural. Exotic. At the age of eleven, Lisette Jones was unknowingly making the boys take notice. By fourteen, she made the teenage boys cum, and unlike her eleventh year of adolescence, she knew full well that she'd been doing that because at age thirteen, manipulation had become the most important word in her vocabulary.

Manipulation.

She learned all about it. Its meaning. Its purpose. Its strength. She learned how to break the word down. Learned to understand that the first three letters of the word were all that mattered.

Man.

At thirteen, Lisette Jones had been shown by her father that she could do and get whatever she wanted. All she had to do was use what she'd been born with. Her eyes. Her lips. Her tongue. Her hips. Her ass. Her legs.

This was the arsenal with which she'd been blessed and at thirteen years old, her father demonstrated to her that this arsenal was more effective than any gun or knife could be.

Her natural assets could render a man powerless and make him do whatever it was she wanted him to do, and it was all because that from the time she began to fill out, her father desired her in the way that he used to desire his wife.

Lisette Jones learned this valuable life lesson every day she spent in her father's presence. And this is why her mother abandoned her. She couldn't compete, and she couldn't handle it. She couldn't deal with the fact that her own daughter was more attractive and more in tune with her own body. She couldn't take the men on the street paying more attention to the child she carried for nine months and labored to deliver for almost forty-eight hours. Most importantly, she couldn't take the cold, hard reality that her husband fucked their daughter visually with his eyes and mentally in his mind, more than he physically fucked the woman he'd exchanged vows with.

Envy became jealousy.

Jealousy became contempt.

Contempt became disgust.

Disgust led to her mother walking out of the house one morning and never coming back.

That was the love Lisette Jones received from her mother.

Left alone with her perverted father, she learned nothing about love, but everything about manipulation and control. She became the master of the home, coming and going as she pleased. Sexy stances, seductive looks, prancing around the house with a towel wrapped around her and nothing on underneath, or in shorts giving visibility to the bottom of her ass, or in low-cut or tight shirts, calling attention to her firm and full breasts—these were her tactics.

Her father had never touched her, but there'd been no doubt in her mind that he'd masturbated daily to the thought of ravaging her young pussy.

Her father. The first man she learned to control. The first man to show her that, despite the thumping of their chests and the dicks they swung as they walked with a pimp's limp, men would never be as powerful as a woman could be.

From thirteen to eighteen, Lisette Jones lived her life according to her own rules. Things and people that had no meaning or importance were used up and then cast off to the side to be ignored completely. People were tools. Men in particular.

She had her father to thank for that knowledge.

Love, which hadn't existed in her world, was never sought, and then Jamil Parker materialized out of thin air to steal her breath, and nearly her life, away.

2

Jamil Parker.

Dead now, but back then, he was the man.

The only man.

Lisette Jones had never known what it was to be weak. Never known what it meant to not be in control. The experience of being powerless had been one she couldn't fathom going through. She'd always had things go her way. Nothing happened unless she allowed it to happen. No one existed unless she wanted them to exist.

Jamil Parker.

He'd gone against the grain. He'd broken the rules.

Freshman year. Art Institute of New York. Second semester. Lisette Jones was having coffee at Chock Express. It was the reintroduction/reinvention of the Chock full o'Nuts coffee chain, which was the original Starbucks before Starbucks came along and moved in on every corner across the free world. That was where Lisette Jones went to study when her roommate was around. She'd wanted a room to herself, but the Institute didn't give freshman those privileges.

Fashion and style had been her passion. Knowing the right colors, the right combinations—Lisette Jones considered herself to be extremely knowledgeable about the dos and don'ts. She'd chosen the Art Institute of New York because she wanted to leave her mark in the fashion world. She always had. The Institute was the best place to be in order to make that happen, and the best was the only thing she would accept. Like it or not, she had to take the good with the bad.

Despite the constant activity, Chock Express became the best place for her to study. The commotion around her became background noise that she would hear, yet not hear at the same time, and that helped her focus.

"The Art Institute, right?"

Lisette Jones looked up from the book she'd been reading, and for the first time ever, her heart skipped a beat.

Denzel Washington had been the Rock, or Dwayne Johnson as he prefers now, at that time. His smile could make women wet. His charm made them shiver. His confidence made them scream and lose their minds. Sean Combs, AKA Puffy, A.K.A. P. Diddy, A.K.A. Diddy, A.K.A. the Shiny Suit Man—he was style ahead of style. Before the shiny suits and the all-white linen parties, before the clothing line and the cologne, he was baggy jeans, sports jerseys, or tank tops, with a black Chicago White Sox hat to the back. His style, along with the ultimate swagger he possessed, made women drop their panties. 50 Cent, or Fiddy, as some call him, wasn't around back then, but a body like his was what women dreamt of touching. The chest, the arms, the abs—they made it easy to bypass the face. That and the money.

Standing in front of her table was a combination of those three men.

More handsome than Denzel with a close-cut fade, as stylish as Diddy in Cross Colours clothing, with wide shoulders and a broad chest, Jamil Parker caused ripples between her legs. The sensation was unexpected and unsettling.

Lisette Jones squirmed in her seat a bit and said, "Yes," and nothing more.

The Denzel-Diddy-Fiddy combo smiled.

Lisette felt a gush.

He said, "I've seen you around. Studying design, right?"

She nodded. "Do you go there?"

"Yeah. I'm in the film and video program. I'm getting ready to be the next Spikeberg."

"Spikeberg?"

"Spike Lee and Steven Spielberg . . . my favorite directors. I'll be making movies like them soon."

"You're pretty confident."

He shook his head. "Nah . . . not confident. Just stating a fact."

"Isn't that being confident?"

He shook his head again. "Being confident means there's room for something to not go your way, but you're just sure that it will. Reality is reality. It just is. I'm going to be Spikeberg. Shit . . . bigger than both of them. There's no room for any other reality."

Lisette Jones nodded and felt a shiver creep up from the base of her spine. She'd encountered guys before who'd stepped to her with lines and the "I'm-the-man" bravado before. Pretty Rickys and sexy thugs who thought that a little smile and a little swag could gain them open-door access to slide into her pussy. But unless she had something to gain by giving them her time and attention, or she had simply been horny, they got about as far as the word hello could stretch, and very rarely would they make it that far.

They may have had the looks, but the looks weren't enough to compensate for what they had been severely lacking. Style. Charisma. True swagger. They were perpetrators.

Most females fell for the bullshit, but that was because most females were either stupid, naïve, or pathetically desperate for a man's attention. Lisette Jones wasn't stupid or naïve and she'd yet to find a man who could do for her what she couldn't already do for herself. But what had never happened before happened with Jamil Parker standing in front of her.

Lisette Jones became intrigued and aroused, and that made her like most females.

She smiled.

So did Jamil, as he extended his hand. "Jamil."

She took it. "Lisette."

"Nice name."

"Thanks."

"Exotic. Like your looks."

"My mother was Puerto Rican and black. My father's from Barbados."

Jamil's thumb lightly moved from side to side against her skin. "Your parents put together one hell of a mix."

Lisette Jones felt hot and cold at the same time. It was an electric feeling.

"So how long are you planning to stay here?" Jamil asked.

Lisette Jones took a slow, full breath, released it slowly, and shrugged. "Not long."

"Want to get something to eat?"

Before that moment, the only answer that existed was, "No."

Before that moment, there would have never been a moment, because the opportunity for the question to have been asked would have never been given.

Before that moment, Lisette Jones had been herself.

Before that moment.

She opened her mouth. Studied his full bottom lip. Imagined herself sucking on it. Then imagined sucking on him. Electric heat radiated between her thighs as she said, "I'm ready to leave now . . . if you are."

Jamil gave a smile that made her heartbeat stutter. He didn't let go of her hand as she rose from her seat.

Lisette Jones was powerless and, for reasons she could never fully understand or explain, it was an intoxicating feeling.

3

Two years.

That's how long Lisette Jones dated Jamil Parker.

For six months, the relationship was heaven. Better than anything she'd ever experienced before. All of the men she'd encountered in the short life she'd lived had all done whatever she'd wanted them to do. They were mindless tools to her that she discarded without a thought or care after their uses were served.

Satisfaction was never something she'd known before, at least not in the truest sense of the word. She thought she'd been satisfied whenever she'd gotten the things she wanted. She thought she'd been pleased when her needs were met. It was only when Jamil came along that she realized that hadn't been the case. Her satisfaction had never been real. It had never been Tom Cruise and Renée Zellweger in *Jerry Maguire*. It had never been complete.

Jamil Parker.

For six months, he 'd the hell out of her emotionally and physically.

For six months, he did things only the men in movies did.

For six months, he was the man who existed only in novels.

For six months, Lisette Jones could spell the word she never believed in, forward, backward, sideways, and in circles.

Love hadn't been real until Jamil introduced it into her world. He did so without being asked. His equal and opposite reaction came before her action. He was considerate, attentive, romantic, and caring in ways that left her stunned. Flowers and cards just because. Phone calls to say hello and to let her know that she'd been thought of. He cooked for her, filled her bathtub with hot water and the right amount of bubbles. He listened when it hadn't been the time to talk, and when it had been time to converse, he genuinely asked about her dreams and her desires. More importantly, he genuinely cared about them.

And then there was the sex.

Lisette Jones had never been religious. She believed in a higher being and had an occasional conversation with Him, but occasional equated to once, maybe twice a year. Religion, something her mother tried to force-feed down her throat before she abandoned her, had never been something she could get into. She never connected with the stories in the Bible. She never had a desire to know anything more than how to recite the Hail Mary. To her, things in life happened, not because of a snake or a bite out of an apple.

Things just happened.

But when Jamil slid inside of her for the first time, at that moment, she fully believed in a higher being, because only a higher being could have created a dick as perfect as Jamil's.

The size, the thickness, the way it moved. Jamil made her orgasm flow from dams tucked far away, deep within the caverns of her pussy.

Sex with Jamil had been like an opera performance. Steady, calm, melodic beginnings. Swelling and rising middles. Powerful, explosive, climactic endings that took her breath away and left her craving more. She'd heard of women becoming dick-whipped before, but as far as she was concerned, that only happened to women who went through life being controlled and never controlling. Before Jamil, the idea of her ever becoming dick-whipped had been an impossibility.

But for six months . . .

For six months, Lisette Jones was hooked. For six months, Lisette Jones was in love. For six months, Lisette Jones lost the absolute and burning need to be in control. For six months, her satisfaction came from not only being satisfied, but also from her wanting to reciprocate freely without a self-satisfying motive. For six months, Lisette Jones lived in emotional and physical utopia.

Then month seven came along and she began to die. Slowly.

4

For the first six months of their relationship, Jamil Parker had been a dream she'd never had. But in month seven that dream became a hellish nightmare that she would awaken from and then revisit time and time again over the course of eighteen months.

Two years total.

That was how long Lisette Jones endured love before she would die and be reborn.

The nightmare first began on a brutally hot Fourth of July. It had been ninety-five degrees without the humidity. With the humidity, it felt like Satan's bedroom. They'd been at a friend of Jamil's for his annual pool party that Jamil had been going to since he'd been a freshman in high school. This was her first time attending. It was also the first time she was going to get to be around any of his friends for a prolonged period of time.

She'd only ever questioned him a couple of times as to why they could never stay long at hangouts or why they always seemed to be going when his friends had been coming. Each time Jamil's response had been the same.

"I hate sharing you with others for too long."

Her vision blurred by love, she hadn't been able to see through the bullshit. Jamil Parker liked to be in control. She'd known it because he decided everything they did and everywhere they went. But the pool party would be the first of one too many demonstrations of the level of control he had to have.

Days before the party, she'd gone shopping for a new swimsuit. She wanted to look good for herself and, more importantly, she wanted to look good for her man. She wanted his friends to envy him. He had what they couldn't. When she walked out in her push-up bikini top and string bottom, heads would turn, women would suck their teeth, and the men would, undoubtedly, call Jamil "The Man."

She wanted that for him and she'd been determined to have that happen. Unfortunately for her, Jamil cared less about being the man and more about everyone staring at her. He hadn't seen the outfit prior to her putting it on, but when he did, all hell had broken loose.

"What the fuck is that?"

They'd been in his friend's guest bedroom, changing. Earlier plans in the day had prevented them from being able to show up already dressed.

"What do you mean?" His harsh tone had caught her off guard.

"What the fuck are you wearing?"

"You . . . you don't like it?"

"You're practically fucking naked."

"Naked? Jamil, it's just a bikini. Relax."

"Relax? With you trying to parade your ass and tits around for my boys to stare at?"

"It's just a bikini, Jamil. Were you blind when we got here? I'm not the only female wearing one."

"I don't give a fuck about the other bitches here!" Jamil yelled, his eyes dark with anger. "You're not walking out that door in some shit like that!"

"But, Jamil—"

"Bitch, what the fuck did I just tell you! Take that shit off. You ain't wearing that."

"But—"

She hadn't been able to say anything else because before she could, she was backhanded viciously across her mouth.

As she stumbled and fell back against the dressing table, Jamil said, "Bitch, don't you know how to follow directions? I told you to take that fucking thing off. I didn't tell you to say shit else!"

Her bottom lip split, she stared in stunned silence as she tasted her blood, while the man she loved stood menacingly, his eyes slit, his nostrils flared, his teeth bared, and his hands balled into tight fists. She didn't know what to say. She didn't know what to think or to do.

He'd hit her.

No one ever had before.

For the first time ever, she was scared and that fear knotted up in the middle of her throat.

Tears began to well up and fall from her eyes as Jamil's chest heaved up and down.

"I can't believe you were trying to embarrass my ass, looking like a fucking stripper."

She shook her head slowly as the tears cascaded down her cheeks. She could barely utter, "I . . . I wasn't . . ." before she was cut off again.

"Get your ass dressed, Lisette, and then go and wash your fucking mouth. We're leaving. And quit with the fucking tears."

Lisette Jones wiped at her eyes and pushed away from the dressing table, but her legs felt like rubber and she had to place a hand down against the edge of it to keep from falling down.

He'd hit her. It didn't seem real. He wouldn't do something like that. He just couldn't.

She gathered her clothes and began to get dressed. As she

did, she trembled, the shocking reality of the situation chilling her to the bone.

He could hit her.

After making a silent and quick exit from the party, they drove home in silence. Without a good-bye, Jamil dropped her off and then drove away, not bothering to make sure she'd gotten inside as he usually did. That night she lay in bed, wondering how she could have been so wrong in the way she wanted to please him.

He'd hit her.

For him to have flipped out on her, she surmised that it had been her fault. It had to be. She cried herself to sleep, certain that she'd lost the only person she ever truly connected with.

But things were different the next day.

They always were.

5

"Baby, please forgive me. I didn't mean to hurt you. I didn't mean to lose control like that. It's just . . . it's just that I love you so much. I've never loved anyone the way that I love you. No one has ever made me feel the way you make me feel. I can do anything with you in my life. Please . . . I'll stop drinking. I'll learn to control my anger. You've got to believe me. You're my world. My everything. I love you with all my heart. I . . . I don't know what I was thinking. I just didn't think.

"I swore I would never be anything like my father. He . . . he used to hit my mom so much. I hated him when growing up. I still hate him. Just give me one more chance to prove that I'm different from him. Give me another chance to show you how special you are. You'll never have to go through something like this again. Let me prove it to you. Let me show how sorry I am. I love you and I need you."

Over the course of eighteen months, those words or different variations of them were spoken to Lisette Jones. It all depended on how Jamil lost control in order to control.

Slaps, punches, kicks, choke holds, verbal abuse. Then came the apologies with roses or expensive gifts, with promises to do and be different.

After that, there was the sex.

Mind-blowing sex. Sex that made her knees weak. Sex that caused God's name to be called over and over. Sex that made her body overflow. Sex that was repeated in multiple positions. Sex that had been better than the time before. Sex that accepted the apologies and made everything all right. Sex that made her believe there would be no next time. Sex made her think that she was special, that he did love her, that he did need her.

Eighteen months.

She was a fool devoted to love and trapped by fear.

She was weak, pathetic, pitiful. Different words, all meaning the same thing. She was a sorry excuse for a woman, controlled by a man who was far weaker than she had ever been.

Eighteen months.

One too many wake-up calls, until one too many became just that.

One. Too. Many.

One night. Lights dimmed low. Luther Vandross, singing "Always and Forever" from the CD player. Lisette Jones died and was reborn.

One too many.

Jamil had been promoted to assistant editor on the set of the soap opera he'd been working for when he graduated. He was still determined to become the Spike Lee/Steven Spielberg love child, but he had to earn his stripes. The promotion had been a very positive step in that direction.

He was thrilled and wanted to celebrate. They'd gone out to dinner. Italian food and red wine. They toasted, talked, and laughed. Love actually felt like it did during the first six months, and for short while, she found herself relaxing ever so slightly. But then they went back to his place. Well, it was their place, but nothing in it represented her. Not unless you counted the toothbrush and tampons in the bathroom.

He put on Luther. It was his favorite singer when he wanted to fuck. They danced, and as they did, Lisette Jones's heart began to race and beat heavily. Earlier that day, Mother Nature had delivered her monthly gift. Before the dinner and the red wine, they'd had Hennessey at the bar, waiting for their table. While Luther sang, they began to kiss, and as they did, she began to shiver. The alcohol fueling his fire, Jamil started to work his hands up beneath the skirt she'd been wearing.

Before he could go too far, she said, "We can't, baby. It's my time of the month. You can't have me that way, but I'll make sure you have a happy ending."

Jamil pulled back and looked at her for a moment before palming her ass. "I don't give a shit about a happy ending. I want my pussy."

He pressed his lips against hers and tried to force his way back up her skirt.

She pushed him away. "We . . . we can't, Jamil."

Her heart was stammering. Anxiety made it difficult for her to catch a breath. She felt the blow before it came, hard across her mouth.

She stumbled back as Jamil told her again that he wanted his pussy. Luther was just reaching the breakdown in the song, holding the word "forever". As he did, everything around Lisette Jones slowed down and then froze.

For seconds that seemed like minutes, she stared at the Denzel-P. Diddy-50 Cent combination, and within those precious seconds, she saw in the highest definition of clarity the monster she'd given her soul to. He'd been the perfect director, who'd had her starring in the perfect horror film for eighteen months.

In that moment of clarity.

Lisette Jones disappeared.

I took over.

I caught my balance and with all of the anger, pain, and

hatred I'd had built up inside of me, I let out a throaty growl and attacked.

I hit him with a solid punch in his mouth, causing his lip to bleed first.

"You fucking bitch!" he yelled out after the shock had worn off.

He swung out and hit me in my jaw. I staggered back. Nearly went down. Lisette Jones would have. But I wasn't her. I wasn't putting up with the shit. I regained my footing and attacked again.

I punched.

I kicked.

I kneed.

I spat.

I attacked him with a rage that Lisette Jones would have never been able to attack with. Everything came out with my fury. The bitterness I held toward my mother and her abandonment. The disgust toward my father and his perverted lessons. The anger I had for the boys and men and their disrespect. The hatred that had been building up inside, for Jamil and his perfect deception, for Lisette Jones and the goddamned weak bitch she was.

Everything came out.

I scratched at his face and dug my fingers into his eyes as he tried to fight me off. We fell down to the ground. I bit at the top of his ear, taking off a piece of flesh the way Mike Tyson had done to Evander Holyfield.

Jamil screamed out and rolled off of me.

I reached out for his paperweight in the shape of a Black Power fist, and grabbed it, my grip damn near strong enough to shatter it.

He called me a "Bitch!" and as he held his hands to his eyes and ear, I brought the fist down on his head over and over and over again, telling him with each blow how much I hated him. How much I hated the sight of him. How much I hated his sound, his scent. His mother for giving birth to him. His father for showing him how to put his hands on a woman. His ex for not doing what I was doing now.

Eighteen months worth of hate.

Two years total.

That night, Jamil Parker died.

As he lay unmoving, I stood up and looked down at him, and wondered how the hell I could have ever fallen for him.

I said, "Direct that, motherfucker," and then let the weight fall to the ground.

I took a breath, held it in, and let the rage simmer down.

I was in control.

No one else.

I exhaled.

Then I called the police.

Jamil's family tried to have me put away in jail. They said I murdered him in cold blood. In court, my lawyer had me play the role and shed tears about the abuse I'd suffered. I deserved an Oscar.

There were more women than men on the jury. They all saw it my way. I walked out of the courtroom exonerated of any wrongdoing.

I've never looked back.

6

Love.

Tried once.

During a moment of weakness.

Never to be tried again.

After Jamil, there were no others. Not out of fear, but rather because of the sheer fact that men and compromising myself in any way, shape, or form for them just simply wasn't an option. Lisette Jones had made that mistake. I never would.

With that distraction dead and gone, I went on to achieve success working for a major fashion company in New York. At that point in my life, I thought I was where I was supposed to be, doing what I was supposed to be doing. I was twenty-six. I held an executive position as head buyer. I was living comfortably, earning well over six figures. The car I drove was a top-of-the-line Mercedes-Benz. Most importantly, I controlled everything and everyone around me, whether they realized it or not.

Lisette Jones.

The lack of respect she had for herself disgusted me. Made me hate any woman like her. On one level or another, most women were like Lisette Jones. Most women sought the company, comfort, and love from a man, as though having that validated their roles as women. The ones who claimed they didn't want or need it were full of shit.

I had nothing in common with Lisette Jones or any woman like her, which is why I never established friendships with them. I had no desire to be around them. I had no desire to bond with them. The drama they endured in their lives would never be something I would have to deal with, because I didn't do relationships. Being completely self-satisfying meant being the fittest one to survive, and survival was all that mattered. Nothing and no one else did.

At twenty-six, my path was laid out before me. Straight and uncompromising. But then I went to Houston, Texas, and the most unexpected right turn appeared on the path I'd been traveling.

I became a home wrecker.

A woman paid to set up husbands, to help wives regain all of the power, dignity, and control that they should have never given up.

The change in my profession had been unplanned, and it had been a destiny that I couldn't avoid.

It started with Marlene Stewart. A successful woman, she allowed herself to be stuck in a marriage to a pathetic joke of a man named Steve. In the lounge of the Sofitel Hotel in Houston, Texas, I came up with a plan to give Marlene the ability to walk away from Steve with all of the control she'd lost long before Steve or her two exes before him. My help hadn't been free and it hadn't been cheap, but Steve's cancerous ways had been killing Marlene slowly, and in order to receive the chemotherapy I was offering to help put her in remission, she was willing to pay me $50,000.

Marlene Stewart.

My association with her should have ended after I helped her, but just as the control had been an aphrodisiac for me, so too had been the money that she'd insisted other wealthy women she'd known were willing to pay for the freedom that I could help give them.

And pay they had.

For two years, the partnership Marlene and I formed

had been a lucrative one, and relatively drama free. All of the clients we dealt with knew to keep the information they passed along to a bare minimum. Or so I thought, until one client who'd received far too much information threatened not only my livelihood, but my life as well.

Kyra Rogers.

She wanted me to trap her husband because she couldn't go through with a deal she'd made. Her husband had her sign a prenuptial agreement, stating that she would receive $5 million for every five years of marriage. She was in year two of the union when she came looking for my services. She wasn't a woman struggling with life with no control the way the other women I'd dealt with had been. She wasn't living with a man whose mission was to conquest as much pussy as he could. Her husband wasn't physically, verbally, or emotionally abusive. He was quite simply a spineless waste of a man with a dick that he didn't deserve to have. Kyra arrogantly offered me $200,000 to get the job done. But despite the amount, I turned her down, because as much as I have no tolerance for women who allow themselves to be controlled, I had less respect for Kyra and her arrogance and greed.

Kyra was used to getting what she wanted though, and didn't appreciate my rejection. She tried to teach me a lesson.

I won't lie.

She almost did.

She'd managed to do what no one else had. Break me down. Turn me into the type of woman I loathed. She'd had me beaten and raped, and I became weak, vulnerable, and insecure.

I didn't have any friends, or so I'd thought.

Fortunately for me, Marlene saw our relationship not as a partnership, but rather a friendship. I tried to fight her and push her away, but despite my best efforts, she wouldn't have it. She helped pull me out of the black hole I was being sucked into. She also helped me realize that while Kyra had broken me, she hadn't won because I had survived.

Kyra thought she'd been better than me, but after Marlene helped slap me back into reality, I showed Kyra that she was nowhere close to being in my league.

Most women would have quit after going through what I'd gone through. Most women would have rationalized that they'd been lucky to survive and that they needed to quit while they were ahead.

But what didn't kill me only made me stronger and smarter.

Home wrecker.

That's who I'd become.

And I enjoyed it.

Present

7

I opened my eyes.

"Amado Mio" was replaying again.

I'd fallen asleep. I don't know how many replays I'd missed, but my bath water had gotten cold. Before Marlene called and disturbed me, I was relaxing. Enjoying Pink Martini's melody, on my way to an orgasm that no one but my song could deliver. I shivered, but not because of the water's temperature.

My past.

That had given me the chills.

Damn Marlene for fucking up my high.

After her call, I closed my eyes and breathed slow, even breaths. Her talk about the bullshit possibility of it had irritated the hell out of me. I tried to focus on the song that I should have detested. Tried to get back to the self-satisfaction I was minutes away from achieving.

I breathed.

"Amado Mio" played.

I went back to the goddamned past.

I shivered again.

Said, "Fuck you, Marlene. Fuck you and love."

Love was for the weak. Love was for people who wanted to live their lives blind to the reality that love was nothing but a lie. Marlene could talk all of the bullshit she wanted to, but my mother, father, Jamil Parker, Lisette Jones, and all of the men I'd dealt with since, have all shown me just how full of shit the word love really was.

It didn't exist.

Marlene called me jaded, but she'd been wrong. I wasn't jaded at all. My eyes were simply open and my heart refused to play tricks on my mind.

"Amado Mio."

I really should hate the damn song.

I exhaled, lifted the stopper to let the cold water go down, stood up, and stepped out of the tub.

Marlene had a potential client. Four months had passed since I'd had one. During that time, I'd worked with Aida, a younger version of me. I'd seen her on the dance floor of the 40/40 club, the night I'd shown Kyra what it meant to truly be in control. She was dancing alone in the middle of the floor, putting on a show for everyone, yet no one at the same time. Men and women watched her, their stares filled with lust, envy, and jealousy, but the attention meant nothing to her. She wasn't there looking for anyone's approval or company. That night, the satisfaction she craved had been to utter a silent "Fuck off" to everyone there.

No one else inside of the club understood that, but I did, because saying "Fuck off" was something I got off on. There's a power to it. An orgasmic feeling to knowing that you are both wanted and hated.

Until that night, I'd never given thought to turning what I did into something that would extend beyond myself. But staring at Aida on that dance floor, knowing that the thoughts she'd read in everyone's eyes, the yearning in their body language, had her wet, made me wet. Never before had I met someone with the looks, the attitude, and the almost full understanding of what control was. It was as though I'd given birth to her.

I approached her because I knew that what I did would appeal to her. She craved control. She liked to manipulate.

I wanted to show her how to master them. I wanted to show her how to truly get off.

As I knew would be the case, Aida had been a natural. Digesting and willingly putting into practice the knowledge I instilled, setting up men became her new form of masturbation. I found great satisfaction in that.

I stepped out of the bathroom and went to the living room. The past three clients had gone to Aida. Now there was a new one. I'd told Marlene to give that one to Aida too, but standing there, unmoving with the love song that excited me like no other, I knew the time had come.

I turned my BlackBerry on.

I didn't believe in love, but I loved what I did.

I found Marlene's name and hit the talk button to connect the call.

When she answered seconds later, I said, "What has her husband done?"

"Not her husband. Her brother-in-law. He's come on to her repeatedly. She's told her sister, but the sister doesn't believe her and now isn't talking to her. She wants proof to help open her sister's eyes. She says money is no object."

"Have her meet me at Barnes & Noble tomorrow at noon."

"OK. Oh, before I forget, someone called yesterday. A former client."

"Who?"

"Rebecca Stantin."

Rebecca Stantin. She'd come seeking my help because her husband, a very well, known pastor, liked to physically and verbally abuse her. I provided very graphic photographs that instantly put an end to the bullshit.

"What did she want?"

"She requested a meeting with you. She says she has something important to discuss with you."

"And she didn't tell you what it was?"

"No. She said she only wants to talk about it with you."

I shook my head. "I don't have time. If she calls again, tell her that whatever she wants to discuss, she'll have to do it with you."

"OK. One last thing."

"What?"

"I have to ask . . . What made you change your mind about meeting with the new client tomorrow?"

I thought about her question for a moment, then said, "My past."

I ended the call and stood still.

My past.

It was history.

Just like Kyra.

Aida was good, but the time had come for me to get back in the game.

8

Barnes & Noble.

At the café.

On the left side, sipping a vanilla latte, venti size. No whipped cream.

As usual, the café was alive with activity. High school students hovered around tables with school books open in front of them and talked about anything but their schoolwork. College students sat with ear plugs in their ears and their heads buried in their textbooks or laptops. Mothers sat with children in strollers or highchairs, waiting for fathers who stood in line to buy sandwiches, cookies, and milk. Wives without their children sat with other wives and enjoyed their few moments of peace, while husbands and single men alike sat together and discussed various topics ranging from politics to sports, as their lines of sight went from one woman's ass to the next, both discreetly and without shame.

I observed it all without paying any real attention to any of it as I waited for Shante Hunt to arrive to discuss why and how she wanted me to trap her brother-in-law.

Women generally wanted their husbands set up for various reasons. Some wanted evidence to use against their men to help them garner the best payday possible as they sought divorce. These women were often physically, verbally, or emotionally abused and felt as though they had no way out. My services helped to empower them so they could take the necessary steps that they'd been afraid to take to seek happiness.

Other women wanted me to provide them with hard evidence, not for the purpose of divorce, but rather for leverage. These clients usually didn't work and were completely dependent on the money and lifestyles their philandering husbands provided. The hard evidence, usually in the form of photographs or videos, gave them the ability to do whatever the hell they wanted. Let's face it, it was easier for their men to allow them to run around and fuck whoever they wanted, than it was to go through with the hassle of divorce, and the money their infidelity would cause them to lose—especially if children were involved.

Empowerment and leverage.

The definition for both was control.

I always gave my clients that.

Shante Hunt would be my first client not seeking it for herself.

"Lisette?"

I'd seen her when she walked into the bookstore. She wasn't there to browse for a novel. She wasn't there to meet friends. Her steps were full of purpose. Her line of sight had been focused solely on the café.

I took a sip of my latte and looked up at her.

She looked biracial—maybe mixed with black and Spanish or Filipino. Her hair was shoulder-length and brown. Her eyes were feline-shaped and hazel. Her nose was thin with a slight ball at the tip. Her lips were thin up top, but full on the bottom. Amazonian in height at about five-eleven, I put her at about 160 pounds, with a set of natural thirty-eight Ds that stood high in a red tank top she had on. Her brother-in-law must have been a breast man.

I said, "And you are?"

She flashed a weird smile and extended a hand. "I'm Shante Hunt."

I didn't have an obsessive-compulsive disorder, but I didn't like to shake people's hands unless I had to. She was there to see me, so I didn't take it. I motioned to the empty seat on the other side of the square table. "Have a seat, Shante."

Shante looked at me momentarily and then pulled her hand back, pulled the chair out, and sat down.

I took another sip of my latte.

Shante said, "Thank you for taking the time to meet with me."

A group of teenagers sitting on the floor to our the left burst out in laughter. Shante looked in their direction, and then looked at the other patrons around us.

I said, "Is something wrong?"

She frowned a bit, and with the volume of her voice dropping slightly, said, "Is . . ." She paused as the teenagers broke out in laughter again. "Is there someplace else that we could talk? Someplace more . . . private?"

I sipped my latte again and looked over at the teens and then back to Shante. "They're talking about their English teacher and his outburst in class when the boy in the blue T-shirt farted out loud during a test. The couple behind us are talking about their son and new girlfriend. Neither one of them likes her. The two women sitting behind you are talking about their girlfriend who's not with them. The girlfriend is having an affair with her husband's coworker and swears she's in love. They know better and are hoping the friend wakes up before it's too late. The employees behind the counter are talking about the classes they're taking."

I paused. Sipped my latte. Looked at Shante.

"No one here cares about what you and I are talking about. This is private."

Shante cleared her throat. "OK."

"So how can I help you, Shante?"

Shante cleared her throat again. "I assume you know why I'm here."

"If you mean about you wanting to set up your brother-in-law, then yes. I do."

Shante nodded. "Well, as I explained to your associate, I heard that you have the, uh, . . . ability to help people with marital problems."

I closed my eyes a bit. I'd gotten all of the information I needed from Marlene, but I asked her anyway. "And where exactly did you get this information from?"

"You helped a friend of a friend of mine about a year ago with her situation. Kelsey Winters."

Kelsey Winters.

A client I'd had before Kyra.

She was one of the wives who never had any intention of leaving her unfaithful husband or the six-figure income he brought home yearly. She just wanted something to hold over him so that she could do whatever the hell she wanted. I provided her with a videotape of her husband eating my pussy.

Kelsey lives it up now and her husband doesn't say shit.

"My friend told me what you'd done for Kelsey. She said that you could take care of this issue for me."

I drank some more of my latte. It was getting tepid. Hot drinks served in cheap cups designed to allow your drinks to go cold faster, which made you get up and spend more money on another hot drink. It was a scam that many cafés participated in. I pushed my half-empty latte to the side. I wasn't getting another cup.

"So why do you want to have your brother-in-law trapped?"

Shante looked around at the people who didn't give a shit about our conversation and then leaned forward. "My brother-in-law . . . He's an asshole. I've never liked him. Not when my sister introduced me to him two years ago. Not one year ago when they got married. And definitely not six months ago when he came on to me."

I stared at her but didn't say anything.

"My sister and I are eighteen months apart. We have different styles, but we've always been extremely close. Growing up, when one of us got hurt, the other knew it. When my sister was thirteen years old, she fell off of her bike and broke her right arm. I was at the store with my father when my left arm started to hurt me so bad that I began to scream and cry. Minutes after the pain started, my mother called my father to tell him what had happened to my sister. That's how things were between my sister and me growing up. You would have thought we were twins.

"Of course we had our share of arguments and cat fights, but nothing was ever that serious. Honestly, I didn't think that anything could have ever come between us. Men, women, children, money . . . nothing. But then she met Ryan. Nothing's been the same since then."

Shante paused as the teenagers beside us broke out in laughter again, and then continued.

"I just knew that Ryan was a piece of shit the moment she introduced me to him. I wasn't fooled by his good looks, his toned body, or his charm. I saw past all of that. I saw in his eyes that he was a jerk. I saw it in his smile. He was a fake. A typical man incapable of having any respect for women."

"Did you say anything to your sister?"

Shante shook her head, frowned, and sighed. "No."

"Why not?"

"Sam's never really had any luck with men. She's chosen great, lifelong friends who compliment the person she is, but she's never been that fortunate with the men she's chosen. For some reason, she's always gravitated toward assholes. Assholes who were abusive. Assholes who liked to control everything she did. Assholes who couldn't keep their zippers closed. Assholes like Ryan."

She paused and drummed her fingers on the tabletop.

I watched her. She had a strong don't-fuck-with-me spirit that I liked. I didn't know anything about her, or anything about the men she'd ever been involved with, but it was obvious that she would never be a woman who needed my services for herself.

"I'm going to get a caramel macchiato. Do you want anything?"

I shook my head.

She got up and went to the counter. Three minutes later, she was back with her macchiato.

She sat down. "I love these," she said, taking a sip.

I sat back in my chair with my arms folded across my chest. "So Ryan's an asshole," I said.

Shante took another sip, wrapped her fingers around the cup, and nodded. "I knew she was heading toward trouble when she said yes to his fucking marriage proposal, which, by the way, was done in front of our entire family. For a full year I watched that smug son-of-a-bitch pull the wool over Sam's eyes as well as the rest of the family. It was a joke. Everyone was blind to him. Blinded by his looks, the money he made, the bullshit personality. Why I was the only one who knew he was full of shit, I don't know. But I knew."

"Yet you didn't say anything."

Shante sighed. "Like I said, the men Sam has been with . . . they've all been such wastes. Without fail, each and every one of them has broken her heart in one way or another. Before Ryan, she'd been living like a nun. She didn't go out, she wouldn't date, and she wouldn't even make an attempt to speak to a man. I swear she was heading straight to the monastery, or into the arms of another woman. But then one day she came over to my apartment and she had the biggest smile on her face.

"That's one thing about Sam. She always had a smile on her face. But as she had bad luck with the men, she smiled less and less, until it finally got to the point where I hardly ever saw her smile anymore.

But that day she came over . . ."

Shante paused and flashed a smile of her own.

"She told me all about Ryan. Where and how she met him. How she couldn't wait for me to meet him. For my parents to meet him. She was so freaking happy. I was too. It was like finally I could have my sister back. But then I met that piece of shit."

"Again you didn't say anything."

"I wanted to, Lisette. Shit, I really did. I knew he was a playa, but Sam was her old self with him in her life, and as badly as I wanted to tell her that I didn't like or trust him, I just couldn't bring myself to do it. After all of the heartache she'd suffered, I just couldn't and wouldn't be the one to bring hurt into her life again."

"So you let your sister date a man you knew would disrespect her?"

Shante frowned. "Yes."

"And then you let her marry him."

A deeper frown. "Yes."

"And now she's not speaking to you."

Shante nodded.

"Guess you should have said something."

Shante sighed. "I just figured if she was happy dealing with him and his shit, then fine. So be it. It was her life. I mean, she wouldn't be the first woman to stay married to a man who didn't give her the respect that she deserved, right? You would have done the same for your sister."

I shook my head. "No, I wouldn't have."

Shante drummed her fingers on the tabletop again, and then lifted her cup to swallow some more of her macchiato, but then put it back down before the Styrofoam hit her lips.

"Six months ago that ass came on to me. We were at my

parents' annual barbecue. I had to use the bathroom. All the ones downstairs were occupied, so I went to use the one upstairs. He was just coming out of that bathroom when I got there. I'd never felt comfortable around him. Always felt like he was looking at me like a piece of meat. Up until that point, looking was all he'd ever done. But with no one around, he grabbed my ass and suggested that we sneak into the bathroom together.

"His advance caught me by complete surprise, and it actually took me a few seconds to grasp what had just happened. After the shock wore off though, I went off on him. Called him all kinds of names, told him that if he ever touched me again I was going to fuck him up and then tell Sam."

"And what did he do?"

"He laughed. Then he said that he knew I always wanted him and that it could happen. That he would never say a word to anyone. You know . . ." She stopped talking again as the teenagers burst out in laughter again. When they quieted down, she continued. "You know, had he only tried it one time, I might have let it go. But he tried it again on two separate occasions after that. It's one thing to disrespect my sister, but I'll be damned if I'll let you get away with disrespecting me like that."

"So you finally told Sam."

"Yes. I love my sister, Lisette, but I'll be honest . . . I told her about Ryan's advances because I wanted her to go off on his sorry ass."

"But she didn't."

Shante let out an angry exhale. "No. That bitch actually accused me of making everything up, saying how I was just jealous of her, and that I was telling her those things hoping she would leave Ryan so that I could have him."

Shante stopped speaking and grabbed her cup. She didn't drink anything this time. She just held on to it.

I watched her. Studied the anger in her eyes as she looked at me. Her sister's actions had really pissed her off. I don't know why though. It was a typical reaction.

I said, "You don't want me to set him up for Sam, do you?"

"I love my sister, Lisette."

"I don't doubt that you do, but, as I said, this isn't about her."

"Does my answer determine whether you'll do it?"

I looked at her.

She looked back at me with nervous, tense anticipation in her eyes.

I said, "I've only ever turned down one client before."

She clenched her jaw. "Why? Wasn't her husband guilty?"

"Her husband was pathetic, but she was a selfish, greedy bitch who didn't deserve my help."

As I said that, Shante's cup caved in. Some of her macchiato spilled over her hand and onto the table. "Shit." She grabbed a couple of napkins she had and wiped her hand and then on the table. "I'm sorry. I didn't realize I'd been holding it that hard. None of it spilled on you, did it?"

I shook my head. "No."

"Good." She finished cleaning up and then looked at me. For some reason, her eyes seemed darker than before. She said, "So how did the woman take it when you told her no?"

I thought about Kyra. Thought about the shit she'd had done to me. Thought about the man in black she'd had pay me a visit. In the midst of a thunderstorm, he'd given me regards from Kyra. Regards that Marlene helped me overcome. I said, "Not very well."

Shante nodded. "And is she still with her husband now? Or did she find a way to get his money?"

Again, thoughts of Kyra ran through my mind. On the floor of a condominium at The Exchange at 25 Broad Street. Her body riddled with pain, she was bleeding, moaning.

She'd just had incredible sex. Sex that she'd been told she would never forget. A fat man named Jim had pulled me out of the thunderstorm the night I received Kyra's regards. In the condominium I gave Kyra my own regards in return. She didn't have a fat man to help pull her out of anything.

I looked at Shante as she watched me, waiting for my response. I said, "She got everything she deserved."

Shante stared at me, her jaw tight, her gaze unflinching. She said, "I want to get what I deserve."

"Are you willing to pay?"

"Whatever it takes."

9

"My services aren't cheap."

"I've already told your associate that money isn't an object for me. I'll pay whatever it costs to get the job done."

"All because you love your sister." She still hadn't answered my question from before. It wasn't an answer that I really needed. I just wanted her to admit the truth.

Shante bit down on her lip, dropped her chin to her chest, and then looked back up at me, her expression colder, her eyes a bit darker. "Ryan thinks he's God's gift to women. I hate people like that. People who think they can do and get whatever they want without regard to other people's feelings. People like that . . . people like Ryan . . . they need to be brought back down to earth. They need to understand that there's a consequence for everything they do."

I stared at Shante. Stared at her eyes. Eyes filled with anger. Her fingers were around her cup again. Looked like she was going to make it spill again.

People like that.

I was a person like that.

I did and got what I wanted.

She hated her brother-in-law. She hated me too. I could see it in those eyes. She hated me, but she needed me, because only a person like that could get the job done.

I said, "Seventy-five thousand. That's what it's going to take."

"And you can guarantee that you can do this?"

"You wouldn't be sitting here if you didn't already know that answer."

Shante nodded. "True."

"Have you thought about how you want this done?"

"I want my sister to see just how much Ryan loves her. I want her to see just how *jealous* of her I am. Bitch. I can't believe she wouldn't take me at my word."

Shante paused and grabbed a clean napkin and dabbed at the corners of her eyes.

"I . . . I'm sorry," she said, tears flowing slowly. "I don't mean to break down like this. I just love my sister. I've watched out for her my whole life. Hell, I practically raised her. I've always wanted nothing but the best for her. How she could ever think that I'd stoop to doing something so low as to make up a story about Ryan coming on to me just so that I could have him for myself, really hurts."

"So now you're looking for a little payback."

Shante shook her head. "No."

I said, "Bullshit. She chose him over you. Don't tell me you don't want her to hurt in any way."

"I . . . I love my sister."

"Why are you telling me that again?"

"Because it's the truth."

"I never called you a liar."

"I . . . I—"

"She chose him over you," I stressed again. "There's nothing wrong with wanting her to hurt a little."

Shante frowned. "I shouldn't want that."

"But you do. Sam should have trusted you enough to believe you, because you raised her . . . gave up your free time for her . . . probably sacrificed relationships to ensure her happiness, without expecting, wanting, or asking for anything in return."

Shante looked at me, her eyes telling me that I was right.

She was pissed. Pissed at her brother-in-law for his arrogance and his false endearments. Pissed at her sister for not valuing all that she'd done.

"This is about you, Shante. This is about payback that you are looking for."

Shante bit down on her bottom lip. Squeezed the cup just a little harder. Her eyes on mine, she said, "Payback. Does that make me a bad person?"

I shook my head. "It makes you human."

Shante nodded.

"Are you ready to pay half now?"

10

She was there!

Rebecca Stantin couldn't believe her luck. Lisette was there in the same place, at the same time. There was no denying it. It was fate. She'd just placed the call to begin her way on the new path she'd chosen, and now she and Lisette were feet apart.

Rebecca's heart beat rapidly. Her right leg bounced like a jackhammer with nervous excitement as she stared at the woman who'd changed her life completely. For $50,000, she'd set up her husband, Bruce. Or, as the people at St. Mark's Baptist Church called him, Pastor Stantin. The good pastor was a charismatic man born with ruggedly handsome good looks and the ability to deliver the Word of God as though the good Lord Himself had delivered the speech to him with instructions to recite His words, word for word.

When Pastor Stantin spoke, he mesmerized, and only when his sermons were over did he release you. He was amazing. And for the longest time, he'd been the most eligible and wanted man in Winston Salem, North Carolina, until Rebecca, who he'd met after service one day, exchanged vows with him on a perfect Saturday afternoon in the middle of fall.

The wedding announcement had caught the entire town by surprise. Rebecca had been twenty, with only two years of college under her belt. She hadn't come from a rich or affluent family. She hadn't been an A student. She'd actually skirted through high school with a C+ average, and was barely getting by with a 2.8 GPA at community college. Rebecca was, by all accounts, as ordinary as they came, but there was one thing that set her apart from the rest.

Blessed with Halle Berry's looks and a body that many swore Halle had been determined to attain after the two met briefly when Rebecca won a beauty pageant at age seventeen, Rebecca was stunning. When the pastor announced their plans to marry, the gasps that went through the packed congregation had been deafening. There were rumors of the two seeing one another from time to time, but there were also rumors of the pastor seeing several other women as well. Although devoted to doing the Lord's work, Bruce Stantin did have a weakness when it came to the opposite sex. But unlike other parishes in which extracurricular activities such as his were frowned upon, Bruce's were practically accepted or ignored because the faith he instilled and the power to seemingly turn sinners into saints made his womanizing unimportant.

The gasps from the church members weren't released because he'd been seeing Rebecca. They were released because no one could figure out what Rebecca had done, said, or promised to get him to commit.

And neither could Rebecca.

The night he'd proposed to her had caught her completely by surprise. They'd just finished having sex, something he loved to do, when he turned to her as they lay naked in her bed, and popped the question. Initially, Rebecca thought he'd been joking. She wasn't naïve to his philandering ways. They actually didn't bother her. The Pastor was indeed a catch, but she was young, and as long as he took care of her, which he did well, then she was fine with being one of a few. She didn't need marriage.

But always the charismatic manipulator, Bruce explained in his deep baritone that God told him one night that the time had come for him to choose a bride, and that the bride he was to choose would be Rebecca. She was the one to complete him. She was the woman to have his last name, and bear and raise the next generation of Stantins who would carry on God's work. His explanation had been so sincere and moving that, with tears falling from her eyes, Rebecca said yes.

The proposal was made in early spring. The marriage took place in the fall. By winter, Rebecca realized that her husband had been an eloquent bullshitter. Bruce wanted to have her for his wife, yes, but not for the reasons he'd stated.

Rebecca quickly found out that Bruce needed to have her at his side. He wanted to move up in the order, and while his delivery and the following and money he'd amassed would help, having Rebecca as his trophy was the last and most necessary rung in the ladder he needed in order to ascend.

Bruce wanted to be famous. He wanted to be the next T.D. Jakes, but bigger. T.D. had the skill, but he didn't have Bruce's looks. Now add to that a woman who every man wanted to see and he had gold. They quickly became the black Brangelina. People adored, envied, and wanted to know about them. Their combined looks, along with his charm and oratory gift, made them marketable, and they soon became the face for a booming religious movement throughout North Carolina. With Rebecca by his side, Bruce became so popular that eventually North Carolina became too small for them, and so they moved to New York City.

To those looking in from the outside, their union was a blessed and devoted one. But Rebecca knew better. While Bruce appeared to be the perfect husband, she dealt with the fact that he had been using her. He'd been as unfaithful as he had been before they'd exchanged vows, if not more so, because he knew that Rebecca wasn't going to leave him. She was the first lady. Her background didn't matter. No one cared about her GPA, and no one cared that she'd brought essentially nothing to the table. She was simply the pastor's adored wife, and all doors were open for her.

Marriage to Bruce was complete security. She wanted for nothing. What more could she have asked for? Just play the good wife, keep her mouth shut about his extramarital trysts, and give him a son to carry on his fucking name.

Those were the things he'd say as he became physically and verbally abusive.

"Enjoy your stature, bitch, because without me you ain't shit!"

Rebecca endured Bruce's punches and kicks below the neckline until she'd become pregnant and then had a miscarriage three months in. Bruce blamed her for losing the baby. He said her ungratefulness brought about God's punishment.

The verbal and physical abuse had been hard to deal with, but the loss of her child—a child she'd seen as a lifeline—broke Rebecca's spirit, and for the next three years, she did as her husband commanded. She played her role. The only order she couldn't follow was to conceive another child—something her husband blamed solely on her.

For three years Rebecca endured. But one day she received an anonymous phone call from someone who said they knew what she'd been going through and that they knew of someone who could help her if she was willing to pay. They gave her Marlene's number, and a week later, after Bruce punched her in her belly because he'd had to make a solo appearance at a speaking engagement, she made the call. Two days after that, she met Lisette. Two weeks after that, Lisette handed her a manila envelope with photographs inside of her husband having sex with her. Rebecca's plan had been to use the photographs to force a divorce, but during their final meeting, Lisette had opened her eyes.

"Your husband's right," she said evenly.

"Excuse me?"

"The life you have, the things you can do. They're all because you're the first lady."

Rebecca slammed her brows together. "I . . . I don't understand."

"What I've just handed you in that envelope is a live grenade. You can use it to get your divorce like you want, but in the process, you'll blow up not only your husband, but you'll blow yourself up as well. Now your husband may survive. He'll probably pull the "Lord has helped me to see the errors of my ways and I'm a changed man now" card. Women will forgive him because they're stupid. Men will forgive him because they're men. Despite the hole you try to bury him in, he'll find a way to climb out. But you . . . While you'll escape the abuse and will benefit financially, you'll lose something that you have that's very powerful. Your stature."

"My stature?"

"You're the first lady. That title gives you a key that only the first lady can hold."

Rebecca held up the envelope. "Are you suggesting that I don't use this? That I just deal with the abuse?"

"No."

"Then what are you saying?"

"Those pictures are power, Rebecca. Power and control. Show them to your husband. Let him know that copies have been made, and that if he lays another hand on you, or says the wrong thing, or even looks at you wrong, that those copies won't be kept private. That a lot of other people will know about his bullshit."

Rebecca's mouth fell open. "Wow."

"You'll be able to do whatever the fuck you want to do, Rebecca, because I guarantee your husband won't want those photos released. Seek the divorce and you throw away your control."

Again, Rebecca said, "Wow."

A live grenade.

As Lisette suggested, she showed Bruce the photographs and let him know that she wasn't the only owner.

"Enjoy your stature, bitch, because if you give me a reason to release them, you ain't gonna have shit!"

Lisette had shown Rebecca what control was. She'd shown what power was, and in doing so, she'd opened a door to a world that fascinated and intrigued her. Lisette had given her a new lease on life and she was enjoying the hell out of it, doing what and occasionally who she wanted. She loved the Lord, but she had needs that the Lord couldn't provide, and every so often, when the itch was there, she sought to have it scratched and she didn't hide shit from her husband. Until Lisette helped her, Rebecca had no real purpose. Nothing really stoked a fire or passion.

Until Lisette, had come into her life. Now she knew what she wanted to do. She wanted to do for others what Lisette had done for her. She wanted to be a liberator, a healer. She wanted to empower women, give them back the dignity that she'd gotten back over a year ago.

She hadn't made the photographs public—and really she had no plans to give away the leverage they gave—but she had officially sought a divorce from her husband. She could do some good as the first lady, but she could do a hell of a lot more as a home wrecker.

Rebecca took a short breath and looked over at Lisette. She was talking to another woman. Rebecca was sure that she was a woman in need the way she'd once been.

Rebecca smiled and waited for Lisette to finish her meeting.

11

Bitch.

Look at her sitting there with her client. Arrogant bitch. She thinks she's so goddamned special. So perfect. I want to go over there so bad. I want to beat on her over and over and over again. I want to cut her and make her bleed. Want to choke her until she passes out. Wait for her to regain consciousness and then beat, cut, and choke her all over again. I want to do it for days. Want that whore, bitch to suffer. I want to make her ass beg for mercy, beg for her pathetic life.

Oh, how I want that.

I can't stop my leg from bouncing. My muscles are taut. They want me to give in. They want me to allow them to function on their own. They want to take me over there so bad. I clamp my hand down around my thigh, right above my knee, and squeeze.

Stop bouncing. I can't do this yet. Not here. Not now. It's not time yet.

I've thought about it night and day for six months. I've gone over the how, when, and where for six fucking months.

Six months of hell.

God, I want to hurt her so bad.

I want her to feel the pain that she's made me feel. The heartache. The emptiness. The loneliness I've had to endure. I want to look directly into her eyes as her life extinguishes the way mine did.

Hell.

Pure goddamned hell.

I squeeze. Feel the ache in my leg. I'm gripping so tightly, I'm causing trauma to the muscle. I'll have a bruise tomorrow. Another one to add to the collection of bruises, cuts, and scars I've accumulated.

I watch her.

I can't hear what she's saying, but I know the words coming out of her mouth are laced with pompous ignorance. Fucking bitch. Fucking whore. Fucking prostitute. She doesn't know how lucky she is. She could die right here and now. But I have to wait and that kills me. Makes me hate her even more. She likes to have everything go her way. I hate making her think that it is. But I have to. Revenge will look, smell, taste, and feel so much better if I wait. If I stick to the plan.

My leg bounces. Says fuck the plan. Do it now.

Now!

I squeeze. My cotton slacks don't prevent my nails from digging into my flesh.

Bitch. I'm going to kill you and it will be all your fault.

God, I can't wait until that moment comes. I'm going to savor it. I'm going to replay and relive it in my mind over and over.

I take a breath, hold it for a moment, and then let it out slowly. Look at her. Arrogantly plotting out how to ruin someone else's life.

You're going to pay for what you've done to me, bitch.

My leg stops bouncing and I unclasp my fingers from around it. My body is in tune with my mind now. It understands that patience is the key to salvation. Patience will deliver to me the freedom that I need to move on. It will be hard, but at least then, without her in the world, I can try. But only when she's no longer a part of this world.

My leg starts to bounce again. I clamp my fingers around it

again and squeeze. My muscles hurt. I wince. But I enjoy the pain. It's sadistic, I know.

I wasn't always this way. Before the pain she'd caused, I was sane. I was happy. I was living a life filled with love. The sun shone and brought heat and light to every one of my days. I looked forward to the beauty of sunrise and the imminence of sunset, knowing that I would be blessed with the magnificence of sunrise again.

But then that bitch took it all away.

She got rid of the sun and brought the cold and the darkness.

I hate her.

I wince and grit my teeth, I'm squeezing my leg so hard. I'm sure I'm going to limp when I leave. But that's OK. I'll squeeze and deny my muscles the pleasure of getting up and ending her life now, because the pleasure will be so much sweeter when the time comes.

Be patient. Breathe and be patient.

Stick to the plan.

She'll get hers.

I promise.

I watch her. I squeeze my leg again. Shit, it hurts.

Fucking bitch.

12

"Hi, Lisette."

I'd just finished my meeting with Shante Hunt and was folding a cashier's check she'd given me for $37,000 dollars. Half now. The rest when she had Ryan Scott by the balls. The sum was commonplace to me now, but the sensation of holding that much money at one time was still intoxicating.

Ruining marriages was a very lucrative business.

I looked up to see Rebecca Stantin standing in front of me. She was the wife of pastor extraordinaire Bruce Stantin. He was a charismatic womanizer and abuser, who had everyone fooled. He preached the Word of God on Sundays, and verbally and physically abused his wife Monday through Saturday.

Rebecca had come to me because she wanted explicit photographs of the good minister committing the sin of adultery. She wanted to use those photographs as leverage to not only get out of the marriage, but to walk away with as large a settlement as well. She was seeking peace and freedom. I'd given her the photos she wanted, but before I let her walk away, I showed her how she could have that peace and freedom while staying in a marriage that had practically given her the key to the city.

I said, "Rebecca."

"Do you mind if I sit down?"

"I'm actually about to leave."

"Please?" she asked. "I promise I won't take up too much of your time. I just have something I want to discuss with you."

I looked at my watch. I met with clients typically no more than three times. The first meeting was to go over the particulars and to collect half of the payment. The second meeting, if necessary or requested, was to provide an update and to finalize how the setup was to take place. The third meeting was the last. I provided the proof they wanted, collected the other half of my payment, and then said good-bye. I never met with them again.

I said, "I have two minutes."

Rebecca smiled and pulled out a chair and sat down across from me. "I appreciate this," she said.

I gave her a half smile. "So . . . how can I help you?"

"Did Marlene tell you I called?"

"She did."

"Oh, OK," she said. "So . . . I saw you sitting with someone. Was she a new client?"

I closed my eyes a bit. "I don't discuss my business, Rebecca. You know this."

She gave me an apologetic frown. "You're right. I apologize."

"So you said you had business to discuss. Is this about your husband?"

"Ex," she said.

"Well . . . soon-to-be ex?"

She held up her hand. There was no diamond on her ring finger.

It surprised me. "You left him?"

Rebecca smiled. "I did."

"And how did he take it?"

"With a tight lip and a clenched jaw. I haven't used the photos, but I told him if he gives me any grief that I will, without hesitation."

"Good for you."

Rebecca smiled and then leaned forward. "Being the first lady was nice, but I didn't want to be the first lady anymore."

"OK."

"Lisette . . ." She paused and looked at me intently, as though she had a big secret she were about to divulge.

I said, "Yes?"

"I want to do what you do."

I cocked an eyebrow. "Excuse me?"

"What you did for me changed my life, Lisette. Before you I was like a zombie, walking around without aim, without purpose. I was dead inside. But when I used those pictures in the way you suggested, and got the results I got, something came to life inside of me. It was like a bulb just came on and brought to light a path I'd been desperately searching for, but had never been able to find.

"What you did was so powerful and so empowering. You helped give me total control. More importantly, you gave me my dignity back. I could pay you from now 'til eternity, and I'd still never really be able to repay you for what you've done."

"And now you want to do what I do?"

"Yes! I want to give women the empowerment that you gave me. I want to give them their dignity back."

I looked at Rebecca with a hard stare. Her eyes were alive with excitement, with passion. She'd been blind but now she could see. And with her eyes wide open, she now wanted to go on a crusade doing what I did.

I shook my head.

I was a home wrecker not because I was on some moral crusade. I was a home wrecker because I enjoyed doing it. I enjoyed playing men. I enjoyed making them bend to my will. Fucking them over the way they fucked over their wives and others pleased me. It wasn't about morals. It was about control. It wasn't about being on a crusade for the sake of womankind.

It was about self pleasure. It was about getting high off of making a man do what I wanted. It was the ultimate orgasm. Women just happened to be helped in the process of my masturbation.

Rebecca had no clue. No fucking idea.

I pushed my chair back and stood up, and looked down at her. I said, "Go home, Rebecca. And don't call anymore," and then walked away.

She wanted to be a home wrecker. That was a joke.

Rebecca called my name. Said out loud that she could do it.

I ignored her and kept walking with Ryan Scott in my sights.

13

Ryan Scott.

Brother-in-law to Shante.

He was perusing a selection of Liz Claiborne dress slacks. He was going back and forth between beige and black, trying to decide which went better with a sepia-colored button-down shirt he was holding.

We were at Nordstrom. His favorite store. He liked to go there at least twice a week. I stood with a bag in my hand, pretending to browse through dress shirts, and watched him. He was about six-five with a gymnast's build. Broad shoulders, full biceps filling out the sleeves of a black T-shirt he had on. His forearms were thick; so were his wrists. His back was wide and trailed down to a thin waistline. He had the perfect V shape up top. His bottom wasn't too bad either, covered by a pair of khaki shorts that stopped just below his knees. He had nice calves. Not thin, but not overly thick, either. They were naturally well defined. He'd never had to deal with anyone accusing him of having chicken legs.

I watched the back of his well-proportioned bald head go from side to side. He was having a hard time with his decision. Style was obviously very important to him.

I'd been watching him for two weeks, utilizing all of the information Shante had given me. Her info had been thorough and incredibly accurate. She knew a lot about him. Almost too much. Honestly, had I not seen the look of disgust in her eyes, I would have surmised that her sister had been right to not believe her.

But I did see the look.

For the two weeks I'd studied him, I'd gotten to know his pattern very well. Shante had called him a creature of habit, and she'd been right. Gym in the morning, then work until lunchtime. Lunch hours were spent with coworkers, usually female. Mondays and Wednesdays he went to the mall around seven P.M. Tuesdays and Thursdays he worked late. On those nights, the same tall, blond female always left the office twenty minutes before he did, applying lipstick, her hair disheveled. On Fridays he did happy hour, and wouldn't come home until three in the A.M.

He reminded me of Marlene's ex-husband, Steve. He was bleeding Marlene dry of her strength and dignity before I set him up. Now Marlene was the one bleeding him dry with child support payments. I was bleeding him dry too, in $50,000 monthly installments. Payments to keep my mouth shut. Stay-out-of-jail money for fucking with the wrong bitch.

Ryan was a lot like Steve. Another pretty boy who thought his dick was golden. The Steves and Ryans of the world were predictable and very easy.

Shante had to go away for a month. When she came back she was going to take her sister out. It was supposed to be an attempt to smooth things over. Dinner and a movie to apologize. She wanted the moment filmed on that night. She was going to call me two days prior to ensure that everything would happen as planned.

I'd spent two weeks watching, studying, learning.

Now it was time to go to work.

I approached him. Stood off to his left shoulder. Said, "You're making the decision too hard."

Ryan turned and looked at me with a set of deep-set, intense brown eyes. They were mysterious. Seemed as though something dark were lurking behind them. He stared at me momentarily before his line of sight dipped down and came back up. I had on a plum-colored sleeveless blouse that hugged my torso like a frightened child, a black mini-skirt that stopped an inch above my knees, no stockings, and black, open-toed sandals with a two-inch heel.

The corner of his mouth rose slightly as he said, "Excuse me?"

I pointed to the brown pair of slacks. "Those are the ones you should buy."

He looked down to the beige pair and held them up a bit. "These? And why is that?"

"They go better with the shirt and that color isn't as secretive as black is."

"Secretive?"

"Black is a concealing color. It's what overweight people wear to make themselves look thin. It's what people wear when they want to conceal flaws. You're obviously not overweight, nor do you have anything that needs to be . . . concealed."

I let my line of sight trail shamelessly down to his crotch.

Ryan narrowed his eyes a bit and flexed his square jaw line.

So easy, I thought.

I added, "I wouldn't lie to you."

"Wouldn't you?" he asked with a cocky grin.

I shook my head. "I don't know you. I have no reason to lie."

He stared at me with his intense eyes and then nodded and put down the black pair of slacks. He extended his hand. "I'm Ryan."

I took his hand. "Lisette."

He repeated my name. "Now you know me, Lisette," he said, his I'm-the-man grin widening.

"I guess I do."

"Does this mean you'll lie to me now?"

"I don't lie, Ryan," I said very honestly.

"Don't you?"

"Lying is for people who have something to hide. I don't believe in hiding anything." Again I dropped my line of vision to his crotch. I could practically see his dick jumping.

So, so easy.

"So . . . Lisette, just how long were you watching me struggle?"

"Long enough to know that you needed my help, Ryan."

"Sure you aren't stalking me?"

I laughed. Not at his comment, which is what he assumed, but instead I laughed at him. He was truly full of himself. If I didn't have to wait until Shante got home, I could have had the job completed before the night was through.

But I had to wait.

I said, "I saw you and I approached you. I don't stalk."

Ryan cleared his throat and cocked an eyebrow. "You're direct. I like that."

"I don't like beating around the bush. And I don't have time for people who do."

"We have a lot in common then."

I looked at him.

He looked at me. Then looked me up and down.

Once again, I thought about how easy this was.

He said, "I'm married."

I said, "I see the ring. And I never asked."

"I just wanted to put that out there."

"I don't know your wife, nor do I want to."

Ryan nodded. "And you?"

"What about me?"

"Is there a husband or boyfriend in your life?"

"I don't do marriage or boyfriends," I said. "I like to come and go as I please."

Had the words come out for him to see, the word come would have been spelled "C-U-M." I'd said it that sexually.

Ryan flared his nostrils. He said, "So, Lisette, do you plan on helping out any other men who may be struggling, or would you like to grab a bite to eat?"

"Isn't your wife expecting you home?"

"I thought my wife didn't matter to you."

"She doesn't," I said. "I just don't do drama."

He shook his head. "There's no drama to worry about."

I licked my lips. Gave him a seductive smile.

He stuck his chest out a bit. Flexed his arms.

His ego was out of control.

Just like Steve.

Just like all of the men.

"So . . . dinner?"

I licked my lips again and then shook my head. "Not tonight. I have some things to take care of."

Ryan clenched his jaw and tried to keep his expression indifferent. He failed, but even if he had been able to, his body language would have given him away. He wasn't used to being turned down.

The tone of his voice edgier, he said, "What about tomorrow night?"

"Possibly."

"How about I call you in the afternoon to see if that possibly has changed into a yes."

"I don't give my number out."

"Well then here . . ." He reached into his pocket and removed his wallet. From his wallet he pulled out a business card and offered it to me. "You call me tomorrow."

"Are you sure you want to give that to me? I could be psycho, Ryan. I could start calling you at odd hours of the night. Your wife might not like that."

Ryan flashed his arrogant smile. "I'm not worried," he said. "Just make sure you call me tomorrow."

"And if my possibly has changed to a no . . . do you still want me to call?"

Ryan shrugged. "I think I'll be able to handle it."

"Are you sure? You don't look like a man who gets turned down too often."

"It happens to the best of us."

"Hmmm."

"I will tell you this . . . If that possibly turns into a yes, I promise you a night you will remember for a long time."

"Is that right?"

"You're not the only one who doesn't like to beat around the bush."

I took the card, slipped it into my purse and said, "If I call, my number will come up as unavailable."

"We have a problem," he said.

I raised an eyebrow. "What's that?"

"My phone doesn't accept calls from numbers that are blocked. You're going to have to unblock your number when you call."

I looked at him as he waited for me to answer.

He gave me an apologetic shrug. "Sorry, but I've had a bad experience before. You know how the saying goes: fool me once . . ."

I nodded and thought about Kyra. Thought about how I'd been burned. I said, "Unfortunately for you, I never unblock my number."

"Not even this one time?"

My turn to shrug. "Fool me once . . ."

He smiled. It was macho and sexy. He held up his hand. "Sure you don't want to give me a chance? I give my scout's honor you have nothing to worry about."

I looked at him as he waited for me to answer. I thought

about it for a fleeting moment. I did have his number. I could call his wife and wreak havoc. But I had a little over a week to get him where I wanted him. And I didn't give in to anyone.

I shook my head. "Sorry."

He frowned. "I had a feeling you were going to say that."

"Fool me once . . ." I said again.

He sighed as his shoulders sagged. "I felt a connection. Would hate to lose it."

I narrowed my eyes a bit.

He sighed again. "Another time, another place maybe?"

I shrugged. "It's a small world."

He held up the beige pair of slacks. "Thanks for coming to my rescue."

"Anytime."

He gave a smile filled with sex. "I'd welcome that."

I turned around and walked away, leaving him hanging without a response. His eyes were on my ass. I could feel it.

He wouldn't care about a blocked number the next time.

14

"I have a new client for you. Have you finished with your other job?"

Aida Restrepo closed the door behind her. She'd just finished giving Edie Blackstone a video confirming Edie's suspicions that her husband, William, was unfaithful.

The video was shot in a hotel room, and unbeknownst to William, it showed him with two females, whose faces were concealed by masks, in a room ablaze with candlelight, engaged in an intense ménage á trois.

Edie cried, gagged, cursed William, blamed herself, blamed God, cursed William and cried some more as she watched the entire sexual episode. Aida watched the tape intently too. Edie didn't know it, but she was one of the females. The other had been a prostitute she'd met at the bar in the hotel lounge. She'd paid her one-thousand dollars for her time.

William was in the entertainment industry and traveled often to Atlanta for business. Edie could never prove anything, but she was certain that he was mixing pleasure with his business. She ignored the uneasy feeling in her gut for a year and a half until she couldn't ignore it any further. That was when she contacted Marlene, whose information she'd gotten from a friend. After giving Marlene all of the information she needed, and paying half of the $30,000 required, Edie prayed that by some miracle the money she'd spent would produce zero results. Of course, that hadn't been the case.

Setting William up had been easy. Aida, who'd flown

to Atlanta and booked a hotel room in the same Marriott William was staying in, approached him by the bar on a Friday night. On Saturday he'd taken her shopping and spent over $600 on her—money that he would say he spent for business. During the shopping excursion, Aida explained how she and her "girlfriend" had always wanted to have a threesome. William expressed that he too had wanted to live out that fantasy. That night, the threesome was on. Aida and her "friend" wore the masks. William brought the condoms. On Sunday, Aida flew home. Monday she collected the other half of the payment and left Edie Blackstone alone, wishing she'd never placed the call to Marlene.

Sometimes the truth was just too bitter a pill to swallow.

Aida walked down the Blackstones' winding driveway to her bone-white Mercedes-Benz. "Just did," she said into her phone.

Marlene said, "Good. I got a call from another unhappy wife."

"Do happy wives exist?"

"Believe it or not, they are out there."

Aida raised her thin eyebrows. That she didn't believe. "So what's the deal with this one?"

"Husband is a womanizer."

"Of course. So what's she looking for?"

"She wants to walk in on you with him willing to engage in the act."

"Willing?"

"She doesn't want to see him doing anything. She just wants to see that he would."

Aida frowned.

Having sex wasn't a necessity for getting the job done, but it was something she enjoyed to do. She may not have been a full-fledged one, but she definitely considered herself to be part nymphomaniac. Had been since her first sexual experience at sixteen. Willing meant no sex. It was a downer.

She said, "OK."

"I've checked out the client and she's legitimate. Housewife, married for four years. Certain he's been unfaithful for three of them."

"And she hasn't left him because . . . ?"

"Because he brings in the money. Plus, she loves him. She just wants to catch him in the act. She's hoping she could use this to her advantage to convince him to seek out counseling instead of her looking for a divorce."

"Idiot," Aida said, shaking her head.

"I set up a meeting with her for Thursday at three o'clock at her home. Her name is Vivian Steele."

"OK."

Aida opened the door to her Mercedes. It had been a present to herself. She'd bought it after the second husband she'd trapped.

Money and power.

Perks of a lifestyle introduced to her by a woman she looked up to.

Lisette.

The only person to ever truly "get" her.

She had a mother, but she felt more of a kinship with Lisette, who she'd only known for six months. She and her birth mother were just never close. She understood that a man and woman each had a role in the home, but she'd always hated that her mother acquiesced to her father's every need. Yes, he brought the money into the household as a construction worker for the city, but that didn't give him the OK to be verbally and, at times, physically abusive. Aida and her older sister grew up watching her mother take her father's shit, and because of that, Aida grew up being very distant from her. She wasn't close to her sister, either, because her sister had followed in her mother's footsteps with her own husband.

Lisette didn't take shit from anyone, and that was something Aida had great respect for.

She'd been at the 40/40 club enjoying herself when she met her. She'd been alone, not because she had to be or because she didn't have friends to hang out with. She just wanted to be. Her friends never got that about her. They never understood her need to be alone. Her need to not compromise—something they all felt had to happen in life.

The only person who had, had been Lisette, who within a matter of a few minutes broke Aida down. No one—not even her own mother or sister—had ever done that. No one knew her. She'd been called selfish and narcissistic, but only Lisette had known that had never been the case. Lisette broke her down, left her alone for an hour, and then came back and presented her with an enticing opportunity.

If you want to make money . . . call me.

She'd left her phone number, along with a promise of truly being in control and then walked away again. Aida called her the next day, and the rest is history.

Money.

Power.

Sex.

Lisette taught her what power was—something Aida thought she'd known all about—and then showed her how to use that power to make money. The sex was just an added bonus.

Aida got into the car and started the engine. She listened to the Mercedes hum quietly. Her mother and sister thought she made money from modeling. It was an occupation Lisette had instructed her to have to help explain where her income was coming from.

If they only knew.

She said, "Just e-mail me the info."

Marlene said, "It's already in your inbox."

"OK."

Aida ended the call, hit play on her CD player, put the car in drive, and pulled off slowly.

In her rearview mirror she watched Edie Blackstone's home fade away. William was in for one hell of a surprise when he got home.

Aida laughed.

She was so born for this.

15

It was coming together.

Slowly but surely, that bitch is going to get what is coming to her. She is going to pay for the pain she's caused me. I hate her so damned much. She took away my happiness. The only true happiness I've ever really known. I press on my left eyeball. I feel a slight relief from the dull migraine causing me pain behind it. But it's only slight. I know the pain won't go away completely until she's gone.

Bitch.

I've searched for balance and joy for so fucking long. Since my teenage years. Years filled with frustration, confusion, denial. I hated those fucking years. I spent so much goddamned time pretending to be something and someone I wasn't.

I press on my left eyeball and then dig into my temples with my index and middle fingers. My migraine is getting worse as I try not to remember how much I hated myself.

I was a coward.

Afraid to live. Afraid to be.

So many times I just wanted to go to sleep and never wake up. I prayed for death at night, but my prayers were never answered. Eventually I got tired of praying, and attempted to take matters into my own hands by slicing my wrists, but just as I could feel death coming, I was found and taken to the hospital. My life became hell after that as I was forced to go to a psychiatrist.

Dr. Elanore Livingston. Old and white with gray hair always

worn in a bun, with small eyes I just didn't trust hiding behind wire-rimmed glasses. She tried to get me to talk. Said opening up and expressing the things I was feeling inside would make me feel better. That my healing would begin when I released the pain I had. Stupid, dumb bitch. She didn't know shit.

I look down at the scars. If only I'd used a sharper blade. If only I hadn't been a coward.

But of course, if I hadn't, I would have never been around to eventually find my happiness. My love. Love that that arrogant bitch took away from me.

"I'm going to make her pay," I say out loud. "I'm going to make her suffer."

Slowly but surely.

I press on my eyeball and dig into my temples again. I hate being patient. Hate that I can't just say to hell with the plans that I've been formulating and putting into place. But I have to wait. In order for the revenge to be sweet, I have to wait. I have to let everything systematically unfold.

Slowly but surely.

I look up and stare at my reflection in the spider-webbed mirror above my bathroom sink. It's spider-webbed because I've pounded on it. Cold, dark eyes stare back at me.

"Be patient," I say. "It will happen. And when it does, it's going to feel so, so fucking good."

I smile and then pick up a razor blade sitting on the sink just beside the hot water faucet. It's never been used. I place it against the inside of my forearm and drag it across horizontally, being careful not to go too deep. I don't want to die. Not anymore.

I get the chills as blood starts to rise. I imagine that it's her forearm I've sliced. I imagine that it's her blood that's flowing like a slow stream. I take a deep breath, exhale slowly, and give her another slice. The cold eyes distorted in the cracked glass watch me.

Revenge. A dish best served when cold.
Whoever said that must have killed someone.
Her blood runs. It splatters into the sink.
Soon. Very soon.
But not yet.
There are still things that need to be done.

16

Rebecca Stantin sat at the corner of the bar and watched. Her eyes were on a man sitting toward the middle of the bar, sipping on a bottle of Dos Equis. He looked like Maxwell without the unkempt Afro. Twenty minutes had gone by and he'd had no one join him.

She was in the lounge at the Hilton hotel. She was there to prove to herself and to Lisette that she could trap a man.

She'd been in the lounge for a half hour watching various men come and go. Her eyes went to their ring fingers right away. She'd seen numerous men without rings. This didn't necessarily mean that they weren't married, but she ignored them anyway. She'd seen others with rings, but they'd had female companions either with them or join them. Whether they were wives or not, Rebecca didn't know.

She'd chosen the hotel for her test because there was always a married man who traveled to be found, but after thirty minutes, she'd given up hope of finding one, and asked the bartender to close out her tab.

That's when Maxwell's older twin walked in.

He was dressed in a black pinstriped suit, his tie loosened, the top button of his white shirt undone. He'd come to the bar, sat down, and flagged the bartender with his left hand. A silver wedding band adorned his ring finger.

Rebecca's heart beat as she watched him. This was what she'd been waiting for. When the bartender handed her the check, she'd paid the bill and then told him to bring her another apple martini. With her drink in front of her, she watched as the gentleman sipped on his beer and watched the NBA basketball game being televised on a flat screen television in the upper corner of the bar. Lakers vs. Magic. Twenty minutes and two beers later, and not a single visitor, Rebecca was sure he was the one.

She took a final sip of her drink, then rose from her stool sat down in an empty barstool beside him.

He looked over at her as she sat down, his eyes lingering on her momentarily. The long gaze hadn't surprised her, though. She was wearing a black, sleeveless, stretch-knit, body-hugging dress that was accented with a square neckline. She may have been a first lady for a few years, but she still knew what sexy was and how to pull it off.

She smiled at him. He smiled back.

"What's the score of the game?" she asked. The way to get to a man was either through his stomach or by talking sports. Luckily for her, although she didn't play, she was a basketball fanatic.

The man said, "The Lakers are up by five."

Rebecca hmmedd and then looked back up at the TV screen. "I wonder if they'll meet in the Finals again."

The man took a sip of his beer and shrugged. "The way both teams are playing, it's a definite possibility."

"Well, hopefully Dwight Howard shows up this time if they do."

The man smiled and nodded in agreement. He turned to her. "Sounds like you know the game."

"I have to thank my father for that. He had me watching games with him ever since I was a child. I'm a big Bulls fan. You have to blame that on M.J. I've been following him ever since he went to U.N.C."

"Ahh . . . I thought I caught a southern accent. Is that where you're from?"

"Born, raised, and still a resident."

"Nice. So what brings you here to New York?"

Rebecca let out a well-practiced sigh. "Business conference."

"Who do you work for?"

"Mary Kay."

"OK."

"What about you? I see the shirt and tie, so I'm assuming this is a business trip for you too."

"You assume correctly. I flew in from California this morning."

"Yuck. The jet lag must have you exhausted."

The man looked at her and with a subtle dip in his tone said, "Traveling is second nature to me, so jet lag is never much of a problem. I was actually looking to get into something tonight."

"This is my first trip to New York. I was planning to make the most of it myself."

The man smiled and extended his hand. "I'm Cole."

Rebecca took his hand. "Destiny." She'd chosen the name because she felt as though she'd discovered just that the day she realized what her mission in life was to be.

"Nice to meet you, Destiny."

"Likewise, Cole."

Cole held her hand for a second or two longer than was necessary before he let it go. "Can I buy you a drink?"

Rebecca nodded. "I'll have an apple martini."

Cole got the bartender's attention and ordered her drink along with another beer. "So, if you don't mind my asking," Cole said, his attention back on her, "are you here alone?"

Rebecca said, "I am."

"Husband couldn't make it?"

Rebecca laughed. It was a genuine one. "Husband? Ha. That's definitely not something I plan on having again."

"Sounds like you've had a bad experience."

Rebecca thought about her ex-husband and the trauma he'd put her through. "You could say that," she said, forcing him out of her mind. "And that was enough. I'm strictly all about being single now."

"That's a shame," Cole said. "I'm sure there are plenty of men out there who would love to have you on their arm."

Rebecca raised her eyebrows and turned her palms up toward the ceiling. "Well, they can have me on their arm, but only for one night. Two if they're lucky."

Cole laughed as the bartender brought their drinks.

Rebecca took hers and took a sip. "My turn to ask. What about yourself? I see the ring. Is the Mrs. upstairs or is she at home eagerly waiting for your return?"

Cole shook his head. "The Mrs. is definitely not upstairs," he said his eyes on her intensely. "And as far as being at home waiting for me goes . . . she's probably laying out on the beach right about now."

Rebecca hmmedd. "After these meetings I've had today, I could go for some time on the beach right now. Maybe a nice long stroll at night."

Cole smiled. "I've had about as equally exciting a day as you have. I might have to join you on that stroll."

Rebecca looked at him with a slight smile. "I don't know if your wife would like that."

"Well . . . I didn't have any plans of telling her."

Rebecca took another sip of her martini and raised the corner of her mouth. "You're bad," she said.

Cole laughed. "I'm not bad."

"Sure, you aren't."

"Really. I'm not. I just believe in enjoying life. I mean, we only get one shot at it, right?"

"That we do."

"Right. So why not make the most out of every opportunity that presents itself."

"Hmmm . . . I guess, since you put it that way, a little company might be nice."

She took another sip of her drink. For some reason, she'd had the notion that trapping a married man would have been, in some ways, harder than going after a single man. That their moral code, their promise to love and to hold through sickness and health, 'til death did they part, would have provided more of a challenge for getting them to dishonor their vows. Her thoughts went back to her ex-husband as she wondered if it had been this easy for Lisette to trap him. Had he fought the temptation at all, or had she simply walked up to him and said, "Fuck me now" to which he answered in the simplest of voices, "OK"?

"So how long are you here for?" Cole asked.

"Two days. I fly back to North Carolina on Saturday morning."

"Too bad you couldn't stay through the weekend. There's a lot of sightseeing you'll be missing out on."

"Well, I'll just have to make sure I stay longer next time."

"You should let me know when that next time comes up," Cole said, his eyes on hers, unblinking.

Rebecca smiled. "Maybe I should."

Cole's eyes took in her body again, only this time his perusal wasn't as subtle as when she'd first sat beside him.

Goosebumps rose on her skin.

Her last encounter with Lisette hadn't discouraged her, but it had put a shred of doubt in her mind as to whether she really could do this. But now, sitting there with Cole in front of her, the doubt was gone. She could do this, and although she knew she still had things to learn, she was certain she could do it well. Before the weekend was through, she was definitely going to call and request a meeting with Lisette again.

"So, Destiny, why don't we go up to my room to finish

off our drinks and watch the rest of the game?" As fluidly as he'd asked, it was obvious he was used to having these sorts of encounters.

Rebecca's heart thumped in the pit of her stomach. She'd hired Lisette to set up her husband. She'd wanted pictures of the good minister in a compromising position. She'd known on some level that the pictures were going to be bold, but she hadn't expected them to have been as graphic as they were. Without question, she'd gotten what she'd paid for.

She looked at Cole as his appearance morphed from attractive man to wolf.

Lisette had sex with her husband and had everything captured on camera, because it had been what she, the client, had requested. The request hadn't bothered Rebecca at all. She wasn't the one taking part in the act with a man she'd just met, so morally, she really wasn't doing anything wrong.

Cole smiled.

Somewhere in California, his wife was there waiting for him to get home. Where she was waiting didn't matter. Only that she was.

A second had passed since Cole's invitation, but to Rebecca, that second felt like minutes stretching into hours as her mind processed the moment that had come.

She wanted to be a home wrecker. That's what she'd said. She wanted to do what Lisette had done for her. Lisette had given her freedom when she'd given her the photographs. She'd given her peace of mind that she couldn't find before. She'd given her happiness. Some women may not have agreed with the tactics Rebecca had employed to attain that freedom, but those women could never truly understand what she'd been going through. The hell her life had been.

But there were a lot of other women in the world who could identify with her, and those women were the ones Rebecca vowed she wanted to help. Women like Cole's wife, who would never know about her husband's casual stroll or meaningless fuck in a hotel room.

Rebecca took a slow breath. She didn't have to go upstairs, but if she was serious about realizing what her mission was to be, and if she'd meant what she'd told Lisette—that she could, in fact, do this—then she had to go all the way. The time had come. It was now or never. It would just be sex this time. But the next time it would be liberation for someone. It would be the ultimate payback.

You vowed 'til death did you part, asshole, Rebecca thought. Then she said, "That sounds like a good idea."

Cole smiled, left two twenties for the bartender, and stood up.

Rebecca rose from her stool a second later.

Cole stepped to the side. "After you."

"Such a gentleman," she said, moving past him. She made her way to the elevator, and as she did, she swore that the next time, somewhere a wife would be waiting for a set of photographs of her own.

17

"Lisette?"

I turned around. It was Friday night. Nearly midnight. The witching hour. S.O.B.'s in SoHo. Wyclef Jean was performing. I was standing by the bar, moving to the rhythm with a cosmopolitan in my hand. People danced, jumped, and whined to the Caribbean fire Wyclef was spewing. Haitians were inside and frenetically waved bandanas with their country's flag printed on them. Other islands were represented as well. Trinidad, Barbados, Jamaica, Puerto Rico, St. Thomas. The crowd was young, hip, dressed to impress, sweaty, drunk, and having a damn good time.

I looked at Ryan Scott as though I'd never seen or talked to him before. I'd walked by him minutes ago, making sure to brush by him as I did. I'd given him five minutes. He approached me in three.

Above Wyclef's orders for the crowd to "Wave ya rag!" Ryan said, "Ryan . . ."

I gave him another who-the-hell-are-you look.

He said, "From Nordstrom's. You rescued me with my slacks."

I gave a nod of recognition. "I remember now."

He took a step closer toward me. A few inches away now. I could smell the cologne he wore and the alcohol on his breath. "You never called."

I gave no apology as I looked at him. "My possibly turned into a no. There was no reason to call."

He frowned. "Wish you would have called to tell me that."

"Didn't think you could handle the rejection."

"I'm a big boy."

I licked my lips suggestively. He was wearing a powder blue polo that fit tightly around the biceps, with black slacks, and black leather shoes. I said, "I'm sure you are."

Ryan clenched his jaw as his eyes traveled over me. I had on a white, button-down shirt with thin, black stripes that hugged my torso and accentuated my C cups. Black pants covered my legs. Black stilettos, with three-inch heels, were on my feet. I was all business and damn sexy.

He said, "I guess it was good for you that you didn't call."

"And why is that?"

"Because I have an uncanny ability to turn noes into yeses." His tone was serious and thick with arrogance, as was the look he gave me.

I said, "Is that right?"

"Definitely."

"And you think your abilities would have worked on me?"

He shrugged. "Women just seem to be powerless when I turn on the charm."

I cocked the right corner of my mouth upward. "You're a cocky son-of-a-bitch, aren't you?"

He shook his head. "Not cocky. Just confident."

I smiled. "Well, I'm not like most women."

His turn to smile. "That was obvious the first moment I laid my eyes on you."

I took a sip of my cosmo.

His smile widened. "I can't believe I ran into you again."

"It's a small world."

"I think it's fate."

"Fate? And what makes you say that?"

"This is New York. Small world doesn't apply here."

"I see."

"I think someone has it in for us."

I cocked an eyebrow. "Someone like who?"

"Someone who knows we'd make beautiful music together."

I looked at him.

He looked at me.

Wyclef was insisting that everyone "Jump and wave!"

I said, "And what about the music you make with your wife? Isn't that beautiful?"

The corners of his mouth dropped a notch. "Our notes have fallen flat," he said.

"So now you're looking for a new instrument to make music with?"

"I wasn't looking for anything before. But now that fate has put us together again . . ."

"You're a bold man."

He shrugged. "You get nothing in life if you don't go after it."

I nodded. Drank down the rest of my cosmo. Said, "True."

"Can I buy you another?"

I thought about it for a moment, then said, "A Mojito."

"I'll be right back."

He made a move to walk past me, but before he did, he stopped and without warning or hesitation, leaned forward and pressed his lips against mine.

It was a smooth move and caught me completely off guard.

I could have pulled away. Could have adjusted my stance, squared my shoulders, and hit him with a right cross—something I was trying to get the women in my Wednesday night kickboxing class to perfect.

But I didn't.

Instead I opened my mouth to accept his tongue, which he slid in deftly.

As Wyclef continued to make the crowd party as though

they were parading up and down Eastern Parkway in Brooklyn on Labor Day, Ryan and I kissed as if we were fucking.

Ravenous.

Forceful.

Deep.

Our tongues were out of control as though they were following Wyclef's orders.

Marlene had told me once that her ex, Steve, fucked as if he'd invented the act. She'd almost been right, but Kyra's ex, Myles, could have given Steve a tutorial. I didn't know how well Ryan could fuck, but if it was anything like his kiss, then he deserved a medal.

It had been awhile since I'd been fucked. More than six months to be exact. Before Kyra. Before the lesson she'd tried to teach me. The lesson that fucked with me more than I'd ever admit to anyone. One that I barely admitted to myself.

The crowd in S.O.B.'s went wild suddenly. Shakira just stepped onto the stage to perform her record-breaking collaboration with Wyclef, "Hips Don't Lie."

The volume grew.

People screamed.

Ryan kissed me. Demonstrated what his tongue could do to me. He threw his arm around my waist. Pulled me into him. Pressed his dick against me. It was hard. So fucking hard.

More than six months.

My pussy was wet. Dripping. In need of being pounded.

Ryan's dick throbbed to Wyclef and Shakira's rhythm.

I pushed against it, my hips refusing to lie, letting him know they wanted to be held firmly.

Wyclef and Shakira made the revelers inside of the club lose their minds.

My pussy gushed liquid fire.

Wyclef and Shakira were at the breakdown now. Wyclef

was rapping. No one inside of the club was standing still, save for two people fucking with their lips.

As Wyclef finished his rap and Shakira began singing again, Ryan pulled away suddenly and looked down at me. His eyes were intense, dark, filled with promise and purpose. He said, "Do you still want that drink?"

I looked back at him. My pussy throbbed. Erupted again.

Wyclef and Shakira said, "No fighting."

No fighting.

I was on the job and I wasn't going to fight it.

I said, "Let's go."

Ryan smiled arrogantly. It turned me on.

I turned and headed for the exit.

Ryan was a step behind.

18

At S.O.B.'s.

Standing beside the bar.

Lip-locked while Wyclef and Shakira made everyone's hips move, while theirs told no lies.

Ryan and I were oblivious. To the revelers. To the sounds coming through the speakers. Oblivious. We were going at it, our tongues acting out pornographic scenes we created in our minds. At S.O.B.'s it wasn't real. Wasn't tangible. We were just kissing. Just mentally fucking.

Now, in the middle of the king-sized bed in the closest hotel we could find, the fucking was very, very real.

I was on top. My heels were flat on the mattress. My knees were bent at ninety-degree angles. My fingers were clasped around the headboard. I wanted to feel each and every thrust in the worst way.

I flexed my quadriceps, pushed myself up to the tip of Ryan's latex-covered shaft, and dropped myself down. Hard. I was in control. Taking it the way I wanted it. Taking it as deep as I needed it. I flexed my quads again, pushed myself up, and slammed myself down.

Ryan said, "Shit," as I tightened my walls around his deliciously hard shaft. He said, "Shit," again as I bore down and moved my hips counterclockwise.

"Shit."

He clamped his hands around my hips, his fingers digging

into my flesh, and thrust upward, trying to send his dick into my abdomen. It hurt. Gave me the chills.

I looked down at him. Beads of sweat glistened on his bald head and over his sculpted chest. I said, "Do it again."

His ego stroked, he did. Harder this time.

It hurt even more.

I loved it.

I constricted the walls of my pussy. Felt his shaft pulsate.

His eyes closed to slits as he bit down on his bottom lip. I could see it in his eyes and in the tightening of his jaw; his release was coming.

So was mine.

Bumps rose along my arms as I pressed down on him and rocked my hips back and forth. The friction made me moan. Made me "Oooh." Made me close my eyes. Made me arch my back, raise my chin to the ceiling. My hands were still fastened around the headboard as I moved faster. My breathing quickened. My heart beat heavily.

Ryan said, "Goddamn . . . goddamn . . . shit . . . shit . . ."

I turned the speed and intensity up a notch. Ryan had been keeping up with me, but now I was in a gear that didn't exist.

He couldn't handle it.

He said, "Shit, Lisette. Shit. I can't hold it."

I moaned.

Increased my speed even more.

Ryan said, "Shiiiiit!" and bucked upward as he exploded into his condom.

His thrusts made me gasp. Made me grit my teeth. Made me release the headboard and place my palms on his chest, as lava erupted from deep inside of me.

It felt . . . felt . . . felt so, so fucking good.

I dug my nails into his skin.

Ryan bucked several times and cursed again.

I worked my hips until my gushing ceased, and then sat still.

My heart was pounding as I took slow, deep breaths. Ryan looked up at me and smiled. "So . . . was it good for you?"

I looked down at him. I could have told him that he'd been impressive. Could have said that he and Myles were neck and neck. But I'd stroked his ego enough.

I slid off of him, rose from the bed, and pointed to his pecs. There were scratches where my fingernails had been. "The Mrs. won't be too happy about those."

He shrugged. "The Mrs. has no sex drive. She'll never notice."

I cocked an eyebrow. Whether his wife had a sex drive or not, Ryan was a natural-born womanizer. It didn't matter how good the woman was. It didn't matter how potent, sweet, tight, or wet her pussy was, men like Ryan—men whose dicks couldn't be kept in check—they could never be satiated. For them, cheating wasn't about the act. Cheating was just about the need to feed their ego. There was a power to being unfaithful. They were taken men, yet with their looks, their virility and their charm, they had the ability to make a woman say to hell with her wedding rings and the fact that they would simply be regarded as just the other woman or in many cases, just an easy lay. The Ryans of the world got off on that.

I stared at Ryan as he lay back on the bed propped up by his elbows. Tall, chocolate with a sculpted physique. His sister-in-law had claimed that his body and his I-love-me-some-me attitude had no effect on her. That she'd never given in to any of his advances. Shante was either an in-the-closet lesbian or she'd flat-out lied.

Marlene had said that there were still good men in the world. That not all of them were lying, unfaithful, or abusive assholes. Not all of them were Ryans. I know there was truth to that. After all, one good man had rescued me from a rainstorm and saved my life. But as far as I was concerned, men like that were few and far between.

I said, "Too bad for her."

He shrugged again. "It's her loss and your gain."

"My gain? Are you implying that I'll want more?"

Ryan gave my naked body the once-over, bit down on his bottom lip a little as his eyes narrowed into an animalistic glare, and gave me a Terrance Howard–laced smile. "You're forgetting about my uncanny ability."

Ryan had game. I would give him that.

Lisette Jones would have fallen for the arrogance. She would have found the smiles, the looks, the style, the body, and the very good dick appealing and addictive. Ryan's game would have roped her in and then fucked her whole head up.

Ryan looked at me as though I was as pitiful as the long dead and buried Lisette Jones or the countless other pathetic women he'd played before. He looked at me as though I'd already been caught up in his web. He had game and uncanny abilities, but I had them too. And my abilities were going to cost him.

I bent down and picked up my matching black Victoria's Secret thong and bra, which had been discarded hastily along with the rest of our clothing as we'd made our way to the bed.

"You're leaving?" Ryan asked.

I slid into my thong. Put my bra on. Grabbed my white shirt and black slacks. I said, "Yes."

Ryan frowned ever so slightly. He was trying to hide his disappointment. He'd thoroughly expected there to be a round two before we parted. "I was hoping you'd stay for a little bit."

I put my shirt and pants on, then went to the mirror across from the bed. "I have somewhere to go."

"At one-thirty in the morning?"

I looked at Ryan through the glass. His eyes had taken a

darker turn. I said, "I'm not sure who you're talking to, but your frigid wife is at home." My tone was sharp, biting, no-nonsense.

Ryan's eyes softened. "I'm sorry," he said. "I just thought that what happened between us was damn good. Though, it was something we could and, shit, should do again. You may not want to admit it, but I know you do too."

I pulled out my Lipglass, not lipgloss, from my purse. Wet, Wild, Wonderful by M•A•C. Bronze gold in color. My favorite one in their collection. I turned and faced him.

Tall. Chocolate. And a very good dick.

He was right.

The sex had been damn good.

I thought about feeling it again. I still had a few days before the ruse ended, and I would fuck up his world. Still had a few days to be pounded, to be fucked. Not a necessity, but a perk.

I let my eyes roam over his defined chest, his thick arms.

I thought about it.

But again, I had game too, and part of my game was to make them yearn for more.

I said, "Another time . . . another place."

"Do you still have my card?" he asked, his voice heavy with disappointment.

No need to lie. I said, "I do."

Ryan smiled. "Good. Use it this time."

I gave him a smirk. "Maybe."

"Just like the possibly?"

"Possibly turned into a no," I said. "This time I'm saying maybe."

He nodded. "I'll accept that."

I looked at him for a moment and then without saying anything, turned and left.

Game.
He had it.
But his skills were no match for mine.

19

She was late.

The meeting was supposed to have been for three o'clock, at her home, but the meeting place was changed last minute to Starbucks. It was now twenty minutes to four. Aida took an angry sip of her iced caramel Frappuccino and set the cup down hard. It was hot and humid outside. Ninety degrees, but with the humidity it felt like ninety-five. It was the kind of mid-July weather Aida loved. Hot sun, high temperatures accompanied by humidity that clung to the skin like a sleepy child demanding to be held. Most people hid when the weather was like this. They stayed indoors bathing in air conditioning or locked in their cars doing the same, burning gas. They didn't want to sweat or mess up their hair.

But Aida didn't mind at all.

She liked the heat. She liked the cotton-thick humidity. Her hair was long, hung down to the middle of her back, but she never cared about it getting messy. She had no problem with sweat. Truth be told, there was something sexy about it to her. On the days when the heat index was high, Aida wore as little as possible. Short shorts. Tank, tube or bikini tops. Flip-flops, never sneakers. She wanted as much of her skin as legally and morally, possible to be exposed to the heat. She liked when sweat ran down her body. She felt it added to her sex appeal.

She wanted to be out in the heat now, enjoying the day, enjoying the ogling that she always got. Her occupation afforded her a lifestyle in which she didn't have to be stuck slaving away in an office as a peon or standing on her feet eight hours a day working retail somewhere. Her occupation gave her freedom from having to deal with bullshit.

Today she should have been out, sweating, getting tan, but instead she was sitting at a square table that wobbled, wearing a chic red blouse, a pair of stretch jeans, and black pumps, sipping on a Frappuccino, waiting for another desperate housewife in need, who couldn't show up for her fucking appointment on time.

Aida took another swallow of her drink, slammed the cup down again, and then pushed her chair back.

"Fuck this shit."

Patience had never been a friend of hers. She'd waited long enough. Vivian Steele would just have to deal with the bullshit until she was ready for help—if ever.

"Aida?"

Aida was just about to rise out of her chair. She looked up to see a pair of apologetic, almond-shaped, brown eyes staring down at her. Aida looked her over. Attractive with thin lips, a slender but pronounced nose, shoulder-length brown hair with blond highlights, and bronze-colored skin from over-tanning. Her upper torso was thick, but curvaceous. She was a B cup, with wide hips and short, thick legs. She looked Greek or Italian. Aida couldn't tell which.

Aida said, "Yes?"

The woman put her hand to her chest. A gaudy wedding ring encrusted with diamonds glinted in the café's light. "I'm Vivian Steele. We have an appointment."

"Yes . . . for three o'clock," Aida said, refusing to conceal her annoyance.

Vivian nodded. "Please forgive me for being late. My husband had a last-minute trip and needed to have some shirts ironed. It took longer than I thought it would."

Aida scowled slightly. She'd set up a meeting to have her unfaithful husband trapped, yet she was bending over backwards to iron his goddamned shirts.

Idiot, Aida thought.

She said, "No problem."

Vivian Steele sat down. "Have you been here long?"

"Since three o'clock."

Vivian looked at her watch. It too was riddled with diamonds. It looked very expensive. She frowned. "I'm sorry," she said again. "I'm usually not one to run behind."

"It's fine," Aida said. "I usually give clients a thirty-minute grace period anyway."

"Thanks for giving me an extra ten minutes."

Aida nodded.

Vivian stared at her long and hard for a few seconds. It was intense and made Aida slightly uncomfortable, though she didn't really know why.

"You're Puerto Rican?" Vivian asked.

"Yes," Aida answered, wondering what that had to do with anything.

"I can tell by the accent. And your looks, of course. I've been there a couple of times. Beautiful island. Were you born there?"

"Yes," Aida answered curtly.

"I've thought about living there. Had to be great to have grown up there."

"I moved to New York when I was four."

"Oh."

Aida cleared her throat. "So, tell me why you're here." It was time to get down to business. Enough of the small talk.

Vivian sighed. "My husband, Griffin, he . . . he . . ."

"He . . . ?"

Vivian sighed again. "He's unfaithful. Well . . . he's having an affair."

Aida nodded. "And how do you know this?"

"I found text messages and pictures in his phone. He was taking a shower when a text came through. His phone's usually off. He has two cell phones. One is for personal use. The other is for business. He travels a lot, working for the government. His business phone is for international calls. When he's home, which is once or maybe twice a month, he usually has it off and just uses the personal one. I don't know why he had it on this day. Well . . . I do know why."

"What did the texts say?" Aida asked. It wasn't really pertinent information that she needed. She was just being nosy.

Vivian frowned again. "It said 'Hi, sexy. I'm missing you and those kisses of yours already. Hurry back here.'" Vivian paused and dug into her purse, a Coach bag, and removed a travel pack of tissues. She pulled one out and blotted her eyes, which had begun to water. "I'm sorry," she said. "I swore I wasn't going to cry. After I saw the text, I went through the phone and found pictures of him with another female. I think she's from the Philippines. He goes there a lot. In some of the pictures, they were kissing."

Aida nodded. "And did you confront him?"

Vivian shook her head. "No."

"Why not?"

Vivian dabbed at her eyes again. "I . . . I don't know."

"So what did you do with what you found?"

"Unfortunately I never got a chance to do anything."

"Why not?"

"Before I could even think about what to do, he turned the shower off. I panicked and closed the phone and put it back down where it was quickly before he came out of the bathroom."

"OK. And did you get another chance to go through the phone after that?"

Vivian nodded. "I did."

"And?"

"And the pictures and texts were all gone."

"Did you check the phone completely?"

"Yes. The inbox, the outbox, the draft folder. Everything was gone. Well, everything not work-related."

"And you never said anything to him?"

"No."

Aida shook her head. She never understood women like Vivian. "So basically, you have no proof that your husband has been cheating?"

Vivian frowned. "No."

"My associate says you think he's been cheating on you for a few years."

"Yes."

"Have you found pictures or texts before?"

Vivian shook her head. "No. This was the first time. But I've smelled other women on him. Well, other women's perfume. And I've found strands of hair that were completely different from mine."

"And you've never called him out before?"

"No."

Aida gave Vivian a hard look of disapproval mixed with disgust. She wasn't supposed to show her clients that she thought they were fools for allowing themselves to be disrespected. She was supposed to keep her expression impartial. But she couldn't help it. Her mother dealt with bullshit and disrespect and so did her sister. She was damned if she'd deal with it too.

"What are you here for, Vivian?" she asked, her tone curt.

"I . . . I want you to set Griffin up."

"Are you looking to divorce him?"

"No."

"Are you seeing someone else? In other words, are you

looking to have something to hold over his head so that you can be free to do what you want with who you want?"

Vivian shook her head. "No," she answered again.

"Then what are you looking for exactly? If not divorce or a fuck-who-you-want pass, what is it you're looking to accomplish?"

Vivian wrung her hands as her eyebrows—too thin from over-plucking—bunched together. "I don't know."

"You don't know?"

Aida rolled her eyes and let out a breath of air filled with irritation.

Vivian frowned and wiped at her eyes with her tissue again. "I love my husband," she said.

"OK."

"I don't want to leave him."

"Ok. So you'd rather be his fool?"

"No."

"You're not looking for a divorce and you're not looking for something to hold over him. Vivian . . . you called us."

Vivian crumpled up her tissue. "I know. I just . . ."

"You just what?"

"I love him, despite what he's done."

"Yes, you've made that clear."

Vivian sighed and grabbed a fresh tissue from her pack. She wiped her eyes and then looked at Aida. "I . . ." She paused, clenched her jaw, and shook her head.

"Yes?" Aida said, the pitch in her voice indicating to Vivian that she felt as though her time was being wasted.

"I can't leave Griffin."

Aida closed her eyes a bit. "Why not?"

Vivian's shoulders slumped. "I haven't worked in over four years. The last job I had was working for a cleaning company. I have no other experience to put on a resume, and I never went to college. I hate to admit it, but I need to stay with Griffin. I need the security that he provides."

She stopped speaking and wiped at her eyes again. Aida sat back in her chair and tried her best to not tell Vivian how pathetic she was with her eyes and body language. She wasn't very successful. She looked at her and thought about her mother and sister, and countless other women she knew who were just as pitiful. Just as dependant.

Thank God for Lisette, she thought.

"Are you sure you should be here, Vivian?"

Vivian nodded and wiped her eyes yet again. "Yes."

"Why?"

"Because I need your help. I need you to help me save my marriage."

"Save your marriage?"

"Yes. You asked me if I wanted to have something to hold over his head."

"Yeah."

"I . . . I guess I do, because I want you to provide proof that he's cheating, or at least that he would cheat."

"And this is going to save you marriage how?"

"I'll use the proof to force him to go to marriage counseling."

"And that's going to save your marriage? That's going to solve your problems?"

"Yes. It has to."

"And what if it doesn't? What if the counseling doesn't work and he still fucks around on you? Or what if he says he won't go to counseling?"

Vivian shook her head. "He won't say no."

"How do you know? A lot of men refuse."

"I've been with Griffin since before he started making the money he's making. He wouldn't want to give me half of what he earns. Plus, everyone in his family is married or has been forever. Griffin hates to fail. Failing at marriage wouldn't be an option for him."

Aida took a sip of her Frappuccino and then wiped her lips with the back of her hand. She looked at Vivian for a long second, then said, "Do you have a picture of your husband?"

Vivian nodded, reached into her Coach bag, pulled out a 5x7 glossy photo, and handed it to her.

Aida took it and looked at the photo and felt herself get warm. Griffin, wearing a black tank top and shorts, was damn sexy. Bald head, chocolate skin, wide shoulders, and thick arms. His chest seemed to be well defined, and she figured he had a six pack hidden beneath the top. Damn sexy. Looked like he could fuck. Aida licked her lips, then said, "OK. How would you want this done?"

"I want to walk in on him about to have sex with you."

"About to, as in . . . ?"

"As in I want both of you to be naked and on the bed. But I don't want you doing anything."

Aida gave her a twisted look of confusion. She thought about what Vivian Steele wanted: her naked on the bed, with Griffin and his nakedness beside her. Nothing more, nothing less. Then she thought about what Vivian Steele didn't want: Her naked on top of Griffin, riding him, or laying beneath him as he pounded her. She said, "You want to walk in and find us on the bed, but you don't want us doing anything?"

Vivian shook her head. "No. I couldn't deal with that. I'll barely be able to handle seeing him naked with you, but I need to catch him that way. He needs to be caught like that."

Aida thought about Marlene's ex, Steve. Lisette had told her how they'd set him up. How Marlene had walked into her home and found Lisette riding him. She'd had a friend with her. Someone to witness the act of infidelity.

Aida looked down at the picture. "You're going to need a witness," she said.

"A witness?"

"Yeah. Someone to catch him with you. That way there's no room for any kind of his word against your word bullshit."

Vivian nodded. "I hadn't thought of that."

"Definitely something to think about."

"I guess I can walk in with my friend or my sister."

"Sister . . . friend . . . who you choose doesn't matter to me. Just make sure they're with you."

"OK."

"I guess you want this to happen in your house?"

"Yes."

"When?"

"Would two Saturdays from now be too soon? Or would you need more time?"

"No. That's not a problem."

Aida took a sip of her drink and looked down at Griffin's photo again. "Have you discussed the pricing with my associate?"

Vivian nodded. "Yes. Forty thousand. Half now, correct?"

Aida nodded. "That's right." Her expression was all business, but on the inside she was smiling. $40,000 to set up a man. $10,000 went to Lisette. The rest was hers to keep.

Strippers showcased their bodies in front of horny-assed-single, and, more often than not, married men day in and day out. Some made a few thousand a week—the ones working in high-class clubs. The majority of the "dancers" made a few hundred. Just enough to pay the bills, buy food, and keep a roof over their heads. They would be dancing on poles for years to make any real money.

Prostitutes sold their bodies to horny and, oftentimes, dirty, perverted, and yes, married assholes looking to bust a quick nut or do shit, or have shit done that they couldn't do or have done at home. Some made good money, but ninety percent of them didn't.

In both cases, the strippers and whores had to bust their asses figuratively and sometimes literally to make the money that Aida was going to make off of Vivian alone.

She looked down at the photo of Griffin one last time. Vivian wanted to catch them just about to have sex. She thought about that.

Just about to.

She took a breath and wondered if Griffin was as big as he looked. As thick. She thought about feeling him inside of her.

Just about to.

Aida laughed on the inside heartily.

She was going to fuck Griffin and make $40,000.

To hell with the "just about to" bullshit.

20

"Lisette, can we talk?"

Crossing the parking lot. Headed to my car. I'd just finished my weekly kickboxing class. I had thirteen people in my class. Eleven women and two men.

Four of the females were in college. They were fit, thin with damn near zero percent body fat. Looked like they could have been contestants on the next season of *Survivor*. They came to class in tight Spandex and sports bras, revealing belly rings and perky breasts. They threw punches and kicks with vigor and attitude. They had the bodies and the youth that everyone else wanted and they knew it.

Six other women were housewives who used the class as a weekly escape from the husband and kids. It was also their hardworking attempt to burn off the extra fifteen to twenty pounds they'd put on after giving birth. They smiled and played nice, but each one of their punches and kicks were directed at the college girls and their pre-baby bodies.

The two men in the class were life partners who saw the class as a way to learn to protect themselves. It also gave them quality time together, as they both worked long hours as lawyers. The taller of the two was six feet three inches, in his forties and was the "woman" in the relationship. The shorter partner was five feet five inches and had one hell of a Napoleon complex. He clearly ran the show. I allowed them to take the class only because of their sexual preference. They were loved by all of the women.

My last participant in the class was the star. A woman with a mean right cross, a nasty uppercut, and a knee thrust that I wouldn't want to be on the receiving end of. She gave me a run for my money in the stamina department, some days daring me to work her and the rest of the class harder. Her three kids were grown and had families of their own, and her husband of fifty years had passed away two years earlier. There are a few women in life who I admire. Michelle Obama for being the most powerful woman in the country. Oprah for being second in line. Queen Latifah for her talent. Sharon Stone for revealing her pussy in the interrogation room scene in the movie *Basic Instinct*, with a big "Fuck all of you" in her eyes. That was powerful.

My last class member may not have been in as powerful a position as the first lady, nor had the money that Oprah had, nor the acting and singing/rapping ability that the Queen possessed. She may not have even had as tight a pussy as Sharon Stone. But one thing my seventy-five-year-old star had was spunk. I could only hope to be as energetic when I reached her age.

As usual, I'd run the ladies and men through an intense hour and a half. They came to work, to release, to sweat, and I made sure they di,d in abundance. Ryan had been on my mind during class. My punches and kicks were backward and forward thrusts. Hard. Intense. Kicks meant to be felt. Punches meant to cause eruption. I'd been thinking about Ryan since our night together at the hotel. His dick had left an impression. One that I wanted to feel again. I hadn't pulled his card out and called him yet. I wanted to make him wait. Just as he had with me, I know I'd left an impression too, and I knew that his desire to feel me again was strong. It didn't matter if I made him wait a day, a week, or a year; he would beg to be inside of me regardless of the lag of time.

My plan was to conduct the class, go home and shower,

and then call Ryan and arrange a meeting for later that night. Tomorrow I would call Shante with an update as she'd requested.

Seeing Steve, Marlene's ex, was not part of the plan at all.

I looked at him and balled my fists. We were at the scene of the crime. A little over six months ago, he'd paid me a visit here. A visit I would never forget.

I said, "What the fuck are you doing here?" My tone was harsh, biting, and promised violence.

Steve wisely took a step back and put up his hands. "I just came to talk," he said.

"You wasted your gas. We have nothing to talk about."

"I just need ten, fifteen minutes of your time."

I squared my shoulders. Planted my hips. Tensed my muscles. "The only thing you need is to get the fuck away now and make sure my money is deposited."

"That's why I'm here," Steve said. "I need to talk about the money."

Weeks after Steve's visit, I paid him a visit he'd never forget. One that placed his balls in a very uncomfortable vice.

In this parking lot. In the midst of a rainstorm. Steve had attacked and then raped me. I'd put up a fight. Would have kicked his ass had I not slipped in a rain puddle and fallen backward, hitting the back of my head on the concrete. I was dazed and barely conscious as Steve got on top of me, gave me regards from Kyra, forced my sweats down, and proceeded to drive his dick into me while he pressed his forearm down against my throat to keep me from screaming. His clothing had been black and he'd worn a black ski mask.

The rain had fallen in torrents that night, and because of my semi-consciousness and the rain drops, I'd been unable to focus on his voice as he'd whispered to me, or his eyes as he stared down at me.

But I'd caught his scent. His cologne. Contradiction for

Men by Calvin Klein. I'd smelled it on him two times before under very intimate circumstances. Circumstances that I'd made happen as I was in the process of setting him up for Marlene.

Steve had left me bleeding and barely cognizant on the ground of the gym's parking lot. I would have probably died had it not been for a stranger—a man I would forever be indebted to. He took me to the hospital where the doctors took care of me and the police collected sperm that Steve had left inside of me. The police had asked me question after question in an effort to find the person who had attacked me. The only name I had to give was Kyra's, but at the risk of giving up my profession, I gave up no information.

For three weeks after the incident, I was in a daze. I said to hell with the world and had even started saying to hell with myself. I'd never had control taken away from me in that way before, and it got to me. I stayed in my condo for three weeks, trying to hide myself from the reality of what had happened.

Three weeks would have been longer had it not been for Marlene and her insistence to bring me back to the land of the living. She'd forced me to accept reality. She'd forced me to realize that Kyra had given me her best shot and had failed. I was still standing. Still breathing. I was still me.

On that day, I recalled the scent of the man in black.

On that day, I realized that it had been Steve.

I paid him a visit weeks later and with my visit, I fucked him in way he had fucked me, only instead of shoving something up his ass, which is what I would have loved to do, I fucked him where it truly hurt him.

$50,000 a month.

I went to Steve's office and gave him that ultimatum. $50,000 a month or I would go to the police and give up his name. The move I would or wouldn't make was up to him. Knowing that he wouldn't choose jail time over my silence, he

signed over a check for the first monthly installment before
I left.

In six months' time, he'd paid me $300,000. I turned over
more than half of that anonymously to numerous rape and
abuse clinics. I took Steve's money not because I needed it,
but rather as a reminder. I wanted him to remember each
and every month when he signed that money away that he'd
chosen the wrong bitch to fuck with.

Steve said, "I . . . I can't afford to pay that amount anymore.
I lost my job." He looked at me with eyes pleading for
sympathy.

I asked, "Am I supposed to feel sorry for you?"

Steve sighed and clenched his jaw.

I readied myself in case he decided to be stupid.

There were no rain puddles this time.

"Lisette . . . shit. My company went under when the economy
tanked. I'm looking for work, but investment banking isn't
exactly a booming field right now. The money I'm paying you
is bleeding me."

Again I gave him a look devoid of sympathy. "You raped
me, Steve," I said.

Steve dropped his chin to his chest for a moment before
looking up at me. "I know," he said, his voice low. "It's
something I truly regret."

I narrowed my eyes. "I bet you do."

"What happened that night, Lisette, I swear it wasn't me."

"That's not what the sperm sample the police have on file
says."

"Lisette . . . shit . . . can't we come up with another
alternative?"

I thought about it for a moment. "Cutting your dick off
would be the only other alternative."

Steve frowned. "Come on," he said, "There's got to be
another deal we can make."

I looked at him. His forehead knotted together in the middle. His jaw was tight. His shoulders were slumped. Desperation reeked from his pores.

It gave me the chills to see him so defeated.

"Please, Lisette? I still have Marlene to pay."

Shit.

I'd helped Marlene come up with a way to become unforgettable to Steve too by instructing her to become pregnant. She did and six weeks after that we fucked up his world. In addition to paying me, he was also paying a hefty amount in child support for their son, Benjamin. I was Benjamin's godmother. Didn't ask to be. Marlene had just given me no choice.

Benjamin.

He looked nothing like his father. Lucky break for him.

I had no kids and didn't want any, but I loved the little man, despite where half of his DNA had come from.

Shit.

I glared at Steve.

Asshole.

Fucking asshole.

I'd gotten past the incident, but the level of my contempt for him hadn't dwindled.

"I could just go to the police," I said, meaning it.

"Please, Lisette—"

"Stop begging me, asshole."

He opened his mouth and then closed it.

"The police have your sperm." I stopped talking and looked at him intensely as he stared at me. "Today, I don't feel like going to them. Tomorrow I may. Or maybe the day after. Possibly next month. You think about that shit, Steve. Think about it every fucking day."

Without another word to him, I walked past him and headed to my car.

When he came at me before, he'd attacked me from behind. I didn't worry about that this time.

21

Soon.

So very soon that bitch is going to get it.

Everything is falling into place beautifully. Of course I knew that things would because I put my plan together meticulously. Ts crossed. Is dotted. This is going to be the perfect revenge. When it all blows up in her face, she is going to shit herself. It's painful having to wait everything out. Painful in so many ways.

Bitch.

Look at her. She thinks she's so goddamned tough with her kickboxing. Bitch. She can kick and punch all she wants . . . that shit's not going to help her. Nothing will.

I scream out and slam my hands down on my steering wheel viciously to release my pent-up anger and hatred. As perfect as everything is going, my control is still threatening to slip away.

I stare at her as she talks to Steve, and strangle my steering wheel. I can't hear what she's saying but she's obviously talking down to him.

What a coward.

Be a real fucking man and put her in her goddamned place. Pussy. Weakling. Just like everyone else, he plays into her hands. People just don't get it. She's not that damned good. She's not untouchable. She's not invincible. She can be brought down and brought down hard. I'll show them. All in due time. And that drives me fucking nuts!

I scream out and rattle my steering wheel this time.

"Breathe," I tell myself. "Goddamn it, will you just fucking breathe. You can't act now. You can't open the car, run over to her, and make her bleed. You can't make her look you in the eye as she dies. But soon you can. Soon you can reveal everything to her just before she takes her last breath."

Soon.

But until then, just breathe. Just calm the fuck down.

I scream out again. Rage rides the wave of my hot breath. It's a good thing no one is around. They'd think I'm crazy, psycho. Some kind of nut. They wouldn't understand my pain, my suffering. My need for retribution. People see me breathing, moving, walking, talking, but they don't really see me at all. If they did, they'd cry out and run away from me. They'd see the horror. They'd see the zombie that I am.

Oh, so very fucking soon.

I let go of my steering wheel and shove my hands in my hair and grab a handful of it in both hands. I pull. Wince and smile as I do. It hurts and feels good at the same time. Pain and pleasure. Pleasure and fucking pain. They go hand in hand like life and death. Like her death and my life. Her death is going to be my rebirth. Until that moment, I'll just continue being the walking dead. Plotting. Waiting. It's all going to be so worth it. That final moment. I've relived it over and over in my mind and my dreams.

Bitch.

I stare at her. She's still talking down to him.

"Hit her, you fucking coward!"

I growl and pull harder on my tufts of hair. My scalp stings and itches. It almost feels like I've made it bleed.

"It's coming, you whore!" I say, screaming the last word. "Do you hear me? Your time is coming!"

I scream out once more and lash out on my steering wheel again. One, two, three, four, five times.

I'm breathing heavily. I'm on the verge of hyperventilating.

I really need to get it together. I know this. There are things
that still need to be done. Chess pieces—pawns—that need to
be moved. Before I can yell out check-fucking-mate. I need to
get a grip.

I look at myself in my rearview mirror. Cold, brown eyes
stare back at me with satisfied approval.

You're doing a good job, they say.

Keep it up.

*The moment is coming. That bitch and everything around her is
going to come tumbling the fuck down.*

Just make your moves.

I give my eyes a nod and then look away and put my
attention back on her. She's walking away from Steve now.
I momentarily look from her to him. He's standing like an
old man. Shoulders dropped, back bowed, head hanging low.
Christ he's soft.

I look back at her. She walks to her car as if she's the queen
of the fucking world. Arrogant, narcissistic bitch. I can't wait
to bring her down.

I reach for my cell phone and press speed dial number two.
My eyes are on her as I wait for my call to be answered, which
it is after the second ring.

"Hey, you."

I ask, "Did you deliver the package?"

"Hello to you too."

I roll my eyes. "Did you deliver the fucking package?"

"Not yet. I was waiting for word from you."

"Deliver it tomorrow."

I end the call and toss my cell on the passenger seat and
watch her drive away in her fancy car.

"You took everything away from me and I'm going to
return the favor twentyfold, you bitch."

I put my hand to my head and run my hand through my

hair, massaging my scalp. When I pull my hand away, spots of blood are on my fingertips.

It's going to be her blood soon.

Very, very soon.

22

Asshole.

I should have reared back and leveled him just for the hell of it. Should have sent his balls up into his throat. Put his dick on a long if not permanent vacation. Ass. If it weren't for Benjamin, Steve would have had to resort to selling drugs or his ass to make money to pay me to keep my mouth shut. I still should have made him do that. Still should have made him sink as low as he had to just to save his sorry ass.

I left him standing in the parking lot with homicidal thoughts running through my mind. I felt like whipping my car around to run his ass over before I exited the lot. Wanted to make him be the one lying bloody and in pain on the concrete. After all, turnabout was fair play.

But as bad as I wanted to, I didn't.

I just kept my fingers tight around the leather of my steering wheel, kept my foot pressed down on the gas, and forced my eyes to remain focused on the road in front of me.

Forward ever. Backward never.

An old saying I'd heard a former coworker from Trinidad say just before he quit without giving two weeks' notice.

Forward ever. Backward never.

Steve was behind me.

Fuck him and the piece of shit that he was. He'd wasted enough of my time. I wouldn't let him waste any more.

Banishing him from my mind, I set my sights back on Ryan

Scott. In a few days I was going to fuck things up for him. But before then, I had time to put in.

I drove home with my thoughts back on the hotel room and the sex we had.

The intensity.

The heat.

We taught one another a lesson as we fucked. Did our damnedest to prove a point.

Each time Ryan drove up into me, he was telling me that he hadn't just been all talk. That he was the motherfucking man. That no matter how hard I tried, I was going to remember his Mandingo dick, just like they all did. And just like the others, I was going to go back for more, because he was long, strong, and could go all night long.

I rode him, contradicting his every thrust. He wasn't the man. I just let him think he was. It wasn't that I wasn't going to forget his dick, it was that he wasn't going to be able to get my sweet, black pussy off of his mind. He may have been long and strong, but each time I pushed down and worked my hips, I showed him that there was no way in hell he was going to be able to keep up with me.

It had been a fiery battle of wits.

And we were going to go at it again.

It was all part of the job.

Something I needlessly told myself when I pulled into the underground garage in my condominium complex, when I rode the elevator fifteen flights up to my floor, when I washed off the workout sweat, and one final time when I pulled Ryan's card out of my purse and dialed his cell.

This was work.

This was my job.

"Hello?"

"I thought your phone didn't accept calls from blocked numbers."

"I changed my settings since we last talked."

I nodded and hit play on my iPod. Pink Martini began to play. Some people were addicted to drugs. Some to alcohol and cigarettes. I was addicted to Pink Martini. Had to listen to them multiple times daily. Had to have my fix.

I walked into my bedroom as they played. I was naked. Air drying. I stepped into my walk-in closet and said, "That was a smart move."

Ryan said, "I like to think I'm a smart man."

I smiled. He was witty. Quick on his feet.

I rummaged through my clothing, looking for an outfit. Something sexy, chic. I said, "Is the ball and chain locked around your ankle tonight?"

"Shouldn't I be the one asking you out?"

"I never asked you out."

"You got me there."

"And so the answer to my question is . . . ?"

"My answer is . . . I have a skeleton key."

I removed a strapless red dress from the hanger rack. I'd worn it once before. A year ago. Used it to entice a politician who loved to put his hands on his wife. Red had been his favorite color. Had no doubt his color of choice had since changed. I put the dress back and said, "I'm hungry."

"I could go for a bite myself."

"Just a bite?"

"Trust me," Ryan said, his voice cocksure, "It would be one hell of a bite."

I smiled.

He was very quick on his feet.

I said, "I'm feeling Mexican."

"Have you ever been to La Esquina in Little Italy?"

"Once or twice."

"They have great food, great ambiance."

"Yes they do."

'I'll make reservations."

"I'll be there at nine."

He said, "I'll be there at eight-thirty."

I ended the call and settled on a pair of tight jeans. I bought them the previous week at the National Jean Company. It was a bargain at $260. I looked through my tops and chose a black halter top. A pair of black sandals with a four-inch heel completed the ensemble.

I stepped out of the closet and laid the outfit on the satin sheets of my bed. I loved the feel of satin on my skin as I slept naked at night.

Ryan Scott.

He ran through my mind as Pink Martini played.

I wouldn't feel satin on my skin that night, but I would feel something else.

For the job.

Only for the job.

23

"You give the word 'sexy' a run for its money."

Standing in front of La Esquina. People sat in simple chairs at round, red tables in the street-level taqueria, eating fish tacos and Mexican tortas. Some were dressed up, but many were in shorts, T-shirts, and flip-flops, sipping Coronas and Budweisers.

To those who'd never been there, La Esquina looked like nothing more than what it appeared to be—a hangout spot. A place to unwind and relax and chill with friends. A place to grab a quick bite to eat before club hopping began, or the last place to go to once the club hopping ended.

If you were looking for a fancy restaurant to dine in and you didn't know anything about the well-known establishment, you'd most likely walk or drive right past it without giving it a second glance. Out-of-towners never ate there unless they were taken there, or enticed to go there by a guide book. But if you were a New Yorker—a true New Yorker—then you knew all about La Esquina and the thirty—seat café with shelves lined with books and old vinyl. You also knew about the hidden passageway that led to an elaborate underground, dungeon-esque restaurant and lounge accessible only through a back door. You had to have a reservation to get in, and flip-flops and shorts weren't allowed.

I'd taken the subway to get there. Didn't feel like driving. Just hopped on the 6 to Spring Street.

I looked at Ryan.

He was dressed in stylish, loose-fitting blue jeans, a white V-neck T-shirt, sand-colored blazer on top, with brown, square-toed, leather shoes on his feet. He looked like an A-list actor dressed casual cool for a night out on the town.

I said, "Thank you."

He gave me the once-over again. "Damn. It's very nice to see you again." He gave me his Terrance Howard smile and then leaned toward me to give me a kiss. I pulled back before he could. We looked good together, but we weren't an item.

Surprise and disappointment flashed in his pupils momentarily.

I said, "Did you make the reservation?"

"I did."

"Lead the way."

His line of vision went up and down on me again before he said, "Follow me."

We made our way through the taqueria to the back door, confirmed our reservation with the hostess, and were taken to a table in the middle. As it usually is, the restaurant and lounge were packed with well-to-do twenty-, thirty-, and forty-somethings all out having a good, sophisticated time.

Our waitress, a svelte Latina with attractive eyes, sexy lips, ample hips, and full, firm breasts, took our drink orders—a sangria for me, since I was feeling Mexican, and a Corona for Ryan—and walked away.

Ryan knew the right moves to make.

Had I been a man looking to impress a woman, the restaurant, with its dimmed lighting, Mexican murals on the wall, and Latin music playing, would have been the type of place I would have chosen too. Had I not been on the job, I would have been impressed.

But I was on the job.

"So, how many women do you bring here a week?"

He laughed. "You say that as if I'm some kind of playa."

I cocked an eyebrow and said don't bullshit me with my eyes. "Aren't you?"

"I'm no saint," he said. "But I'm definitely not a player."

I couldn't help it. I laughed.

Ryan said, "I'm serious."

"So your coming on to me—"

"Was strictly because I felt an immediate connection with you. And based on what happened the other night, you obviously felt it too."

"How do you know that I wasn't just horny?"

"Because you used my card tonight."

"Maybe I just needed to have my itch scratched one more time."

Ryan looked at me. His eyes intense, focused. He said, "And maybe you're just scared to admit that possibly, for the first time, you've met your match."

I looked at him as he watched me with an I-dare-you-to-counter-that gaze.

Very quick on his feet, indeed.

The waitress returned with our drinks and asked if we were ready to order. As neither one of us had bothered to look through our menus, we told her that we needed a few additional minutes. The waitress walked away. Ryan's eyes trailed behind her.

"Thinking about passing her your card?"

Ryan smiled. "Just admiring her outfit."

"The hostess has the same outfit on, but you didn't give her a second glance."

Ryan took a swallow of his Corona. "The hostess is over two hundred pounds," he said.

I thought about Fat Jim. He'd rescued me after my encounter with Steve. I rewarded him by presenting him with a lucrative modeling contract from a former celebrity client of mine. Bryant "Big Man" Drew. He'd launched his own very successful clothing line for plus-sized men. Fat Jim became the face of the line and was now a very rich man and a catalyst for making the Big Man the "It" Man. He was also one of the nicest, most genuine persons I knew. He, along with Marlene and Aida, was a friend.

I said, "She could be one of the nicest people you ever meet."

Ryan said, "She'd still be over two hundred pounds."

"You're ignorant."

"I'm honest. Something most people aren't."

"You're still an asshole," I said, meaning it.

"And you're sitting with me," he countered.

"I should call your wife."

"If you do that you won't be able to have that itch scratched anymore."

"I assure you . . . I could find another scratching post."

"Maybe so. But it definitely wouldn't be as good."

"You should tone that confidence down a notch. You could get your feelings hurt."

Ryan smiled. "You used the card. I don't have to take it down at all."

I closed my eyes a bit.

Thought about why I was there with him.

Shante Hunt. His sister-in-law. She hired me to bring him down because he was an arrogant son–of-a-bitch who'd come on to her. Her brother-in-law. It was complete disrespect that she'd turned down and then told her sister about. Her sister, disbelieving or denying the truth, lashed out at Shante and now they weren't speaking. Shante wanted proof that Ryan couldn't be trusted to give to her sibling.

That's why I was sitting in front of Ryan Scott.

It had nothing to do with the fact that other thoughts had been on my mind when I'd used his card.

Nothing at all.

The waitress returned. We still hadn't picked up our menus. We had her wait as we did.

I looked at Ryan.

He looked at me.

Sex hovered between us.

Thick.

Raw.

Food was the last thing on our minds.

"Are you still hungry?" Ryan asked.

I swallowed down my sangria. Licked my lips. Nodded. Said, "I am."

He clenched his jaw, then looked up at the waitress. "We'll take the check."

A half hour later, we were at the Mercer hotel in SoHo. It was a hotel his company used often to put his "clients" up in.

We were in the loft-like room fucking on a chaise. My legs were wrapped around his waist. My pussy constricting around his shaft as he jackhammered in and out of me.

He was scratching the hell out of my itch. Showing me just how ignorant he could be.

I used the card for the job.

That's what I told myself between each deep and painfully pleasurable thrust.

For the job.

For the job.

For the . . .

Shit it was so good.

So hard.

So deep.

So goddamned deep.

I dug my nails into his back. Left marks there to match the ones I'd left on his chest. I bit down on my bottom lip. Shivered.

I tightened my walls.

Felt his shaft pulsate.

Made him say, "Shit, I like that."

Then I spread my legs.

Made him say, "Goddamn that's good. Open them wider."

I did.

Ryan pounded me even harder. Went deeper.

I erupted as he slammed into me. Felt like a geyser shooting hot water into the air.

I moaned.

I gasped.

Demanded to be fucked harder.

Told myself again that I was there for the job.

For the . . .

I arched my back.

Cursed as he pounded against my pelvic bone and came.

He collapsed on top of me and told me not to move as he bucked several times.

I lay still, my heart beating heavily, my pussy electric, throbbing, on fire.

For the job.

That went through my mind as we fucked again before going our separate ways.

24

"Excuse me, can you give me a spot?"

Aida gave Griffin Steele a smile and then added, "If you're able to I mean."

They were at Gold's Gym. The free weight area. Aida had spent the last half hour working up a generous sweat on the treadmill in the Nautilus equipment room. The room was packed with fit and toned men and women determined to keep their lithe and sculpted physiques intact. It was also packed with middle-aged men and women trying desperately to lose pounds that refused to be lost.

Aida ran at level ten speed. She wanted to sweat, to get her muscles pumping. She ran on the treadmill nearest to the main door of the room. From that position she could look straight through the door's glass to the main entrance of the athletic facility, which was just yards away. Five minutes before she'd arrived for her workout, Griffin Steele had walked in for his. Aida ran, her eyes focused on the entrance, watching all of the comings and goings, and made sure that Griffin didn't leave.

Satisfied that the sweat she'd worked up had created an alluring sheen on her skin, she ventured downstairs a half hour later to make her move on the man whose wife had claimed was a sucker for an athletic female.

Griffin looked up at her and smiled. Beads of sweat ran down his forehead and over his well-defined arms. He was working his chest, and had just completed three sets of dumbbell chest presses. Aida had watched him perform his sets and wondered how it would have been to have him lift her up and down as she sat atop him as easily as he had handled the eighty-five-pound dumbbells.

He said, "If I weren't able to, I'd find a way to be."

The corner of Aida's mouth rose. It was a weak line, but she'd liked it. She flipped a strand of her hair behind her ear. It was subtle, sexy, and extremely flirtatious. She said, "I appreciate that."

Griffin rose from the workout bench. He stood a full foot taller than Aida. She loved tall men.

"I'm over here," she said.

She turned and headed to a bench a few feet behind him to his left.

"Bench press?" Griffin asked.

"Yeah. This is my chest day."

In a not-so-subtle way, Griffin's line of sight trailed down to her breasts. She had on a hot pink sports bra that hugged her full breasts. Breasts were his body part of choice—more pertinent information from his wife.

Griffin brought his eyes back up to hers. "It's my chest day too."

Aida took her line of sight to his pectorals, pumped beneath a tight black tank, looked back at him and said, "Sorry to bug you, but my partner flaked out on me."

"Not a bother," he said. "Too bad she had other plans."

"He. And if by 'other plans' you mean another bitch to fuck, then, yeah, that jerk had other plans."

Her tone was harsh and rough around the edges. Her natural tone before Lisette had come along and smoothed her out.

"Damn," Griffin said, taking a spot at the top of the bench.

"Sorry. Didn't mean to go off like that."

"It's fine. I'm just sorry to hear that he's cheating on you."

Aida straddled the bench slowly, almost suggestively, and sucked her teeth as she lay back. "Yeah. He thinks he's so slick. Thinks that I don't know."

Griffin's crotch hovered close to her mouth. An explicit thought ran through her mind.

"Did you step to him about it?" Griffin asked.

Aida shook her head. "No. And I'm not going to, either. It and he's a waste of my time." She grabbed the barbell, her hands shoulder-width apart. "Oh, well. It's his loss."

"Someone else's gain," Griffin said, his eyes going over her again.

Aida looked up at him. Spoke sex with her eyes, and said, "It could definitely be someone else's gain."

She tightened her fingers around the steel bar.

Griffin clenched his jaw and flared his nostrils.

"I'll need help when I reach seven," she said.

"OK."

Aida counted, lifted the bar on three and brought it down to her chest in one smooth and controlled motion. She did the first five repetitions easily, struggled on the sixth, and just before the seventh rep said, "OK. Now."

Griffin gave slight assistance and helped her raise the bar as he encouraged her. "Push it. That's it. Don't stop! Two more. There you go. Push it! Push it!"

Aida grunted out the last two reps and then set the bar down. She was breathing heavily, not because the weight had been particularly heavy, but rather because with each up-and-down motion of the barbell she imagined moving her mouth up and down on Griffin's penis as it hovered above her.

She sat up, turned, and faced him. "Sorry you had to give me so much help," she said. "My focus is a little jacked up right now."

"No apologies necessary. My focus would be off too."

"Thanks for the help."

"Not a problem. Just let me know when you're ready to do the next set."

Aida let out a dramatic sigh. "That might be my last set. I just don't feel like working out anymore."

Griffin frowned. "I thought you said it was his loss."

"I did. And it is."

"Then why are you letting him get to you?"

Aida ran her hands through her hair in an exasperated motion. "It's not so much that he's gotten to me," she said. "Honestly I'm more pissed off than anything."

"Then say something to him."

"He's not worth it."

"Then do another set."

"Aren't you just the slave driver," she said with a smile.

Griffin shrugged. "Just trying to keep you focused. You're far too sexy to let a guy who doesn't appreciate you stress you out."

Aida smiled again and flipped a strand of hair behind her ear again. "Thank you. Your woman's lucky to have you."

Griffin shrugged. "Apparently she didn't think she was lucky enough. She's dating my best friend now."

Aida opened her eyes wide. "Damn!"

"Yeah. I guess the six-bedroom house, the Benz, and the weekly spa appointments I provided for her weren't enough."

"Wow. That would damn sure be enough for me."

Griffin shrugged again. "Like you said . . . her loss."

"Someone else's gain."

Griffin looked at Aida with lustful promise in his eyes. "Definitely," he said, the volume in his voice down a notch, the timbre deeper.

Aida smiled.

God, I'm good, she thought.

She said, "You know, it just hit me that we don't know each other's names."

Griffin nodded and laughed. "This is true." He extended his hand. "I'm Griffin."

Placing hers in his, Aida said, "Aida."

"Nice to have met you, Aida."

"Likewise, Griffin. Honestly, it doesn't feel like we just met."

Griffin agreed with a smile. Her hand was still enclosed in his. "There does seem to be a familiar connection there."

"You always come to the gym at this time?"

"I usually come in the morning, before six, but I had a late night last night. I couldn't drag myself out of the bed this morning to get in here."

"Late night, huh? Guess she wore you out."

Griffin laughed. "Yeah. Work usually does."

Aida gave an I-see nod. "Are you a workaholic?"

Griffin raised one shoulder this time. "I've been known to put in an hour or two of overtime."

"All work and no play?"

Griffin tightened his jaw. "I'm all about business, but I make sure I get the play in there, too."

Aida cleared her throat. "That's good to know. So, if you don't mind me asking, what do you do?"

"Don't mind at all. I work for the government."

"Doing?"

"IT consulting."

"Sounds interesting."

Griffin shrugged dismissively. "It's OK. Boring, really. Only perk is that I get to do a lot of traveling."

"Mmmm, I love to travel."

"Do you?"

"Yeah. I've been to a few places. A few islands. Puerto Rico, Trinidad, Bahamas, Jamaica."

"You're young to be so seasoned."

"I'm twenty-six. Been holding things down on my own

since I was seventeen. I've done a decent job saving money, unlike a lot of people I know. Most of them don't do shit. I figure you only have one life, so you may as well get out and enjoy it before your time is up."

"Good philosophy. You never do know when it could be your time to go."

"The only place I haven't been to that I really want to visit is the Philippines. I've heard it's beautiful over there."

Aida stared at him. Watched his eyes intently.

Griffin nodded, his eyes giving away his thoughts. "I've been there," he said.

"Really?"

"Several times. It's one of the places the job sends me to frequently.

"Is it really gorgeous?"

"It is."

"Filipino women are beautiful."

Griffin agreed. "Yes, they are. You would fit in over there."

"I'm not Filipino."

"Trust me, you don't need to be."

Aida gave him a smile. *He is a charmer*, she thought. *A very sexy one.*

She let her eyes roam without shame over his sculpted arms. She loved thick, well-defined arms on a man. Loved they way they held her firmly in the fits of hot sex.

Enjoying her ogling, Griffin crossed his arms across his chest and flexed.

Damn, he is a cocky son of a bitch. Engreido.

She had no doubt in her mind that he could fuck. Vivian was pathetically insecure and dependant, but Aida was sure that Griffin's dick had a hand in her not wanting to let him go.

Her eyes went from his arms to his chest. It was still swollen from his workout. She imagined running her hands over his pecs while she sat on top of him. She ran her eyes down his chest and paused briefly on his midsection, before going down to his crotch. She wondered about his size, his girth. He was a very well-groomed man with his faded moustache and goatee. She wondered if he kept his penis groomed too. Her blood pumped as she grew hot and wet beneath her thong.

She pulled her eyes away from his crotch, just knowing that she was going to have it, and brought her eyes back up to his.

One corner of his mouth was raised into a you-like-what-you-see smirk as he stared back at her. "So," he said, machismo in his tone, "are you ready to do another set?"

Aida smiled. "I'm still not in the mood to work out anymore." Her tone was even, but her eyes were saying a hell of a lot more.

"So what are you in the mood for?" Griffin asked.

Aida looked at him.

He looked back at her.

People around them continued with their workouts, oblivious to their conspicuous sex talk.

Aida said, "So . . . no girlfriend?"

"Told you she left me high and dry."

"No wife?"

Without hesitation. "No."

Son of a bitch, Aida thought. *(I'm going to fuck you and then fuck you over) Te jodere y entonces te jodere otra vez.* She said, "You don't swing both ways, do you?"

Griffin laughed. "Definitely not."

"Just checking. You never know these days."

More laughter. "That's true, but I'm definitely not playing for both teams."

Aida stared at him. Focused on his full lips before going over his torso again.

Griffin ran his eyes over her. "So no other set?"

"Nope."

"And you don't want to call your boyfriend up? Maybe lay into him? Maybe work things out?"

"I was single as of an hour ago. I'm definitely not working anything out."

Griffin looked at her, his stare deep, intense. "Want to go out for a drink?"

Aida flashed a smile. "I was just waiting for you to ask."

25

Vivian Steele didn't want her to do anything with her husband, because she couldn't handle walking in on them having sex. She was barely going to be able to handle seeing them naked on the bed together. She was paying $40,000 for visual proof of her husband about to cheat so that she could use that to force him to go to marriage counseling.

What-the-fuck-ever.

If that was what she wanted, then fine: Aida would give the client what she'd paid for. But that moment was days away, and before then, Aida would be damned if she didn't get as much of Griffin Steele's dick as she could.

Which was what she was doing now.

In the back of Griffin's jet-black Cadillac Escalade, on his cream-colored leather seats, Aida rode him fiercely.

They were in the parking lot of the gym. The sexual tension between them had been too high to wait to be released. The Escalade idled while the air conditioning blasted. The sun had gone down, but the humidity was still suffocating.

Aida leaned back and grabbed the driver's side headrest. "Fuck," she said. "Goddamn, baby. Give it to me."

She loved this shit.

Loved fucking.

Loved being fucked.

She dug her fingers into the leather and pushed her hips down. She wanted to feel Griffin deep inside of her. He was so big, so thick. It was more than she'd imagined. Shit. He was perfect.

Griffin clamped his big hands around her waist, held her firmly, and drove up into her.

Aida cried out. "*Cono.* Again, baby. Do that shit again!"

Griffin did as commanded.

Spanish flew from Aida's lips. She was loud. Could have been heard, but the parking spot around the back to the left—a spot where few members parked their cars—was perfect for their pornographic activity.

Aida sat up, pushed her sports top down, palmed her breasts, and squeezed her very erect nipples as Griffin palmed her ass. She moved her waist back and forth. Made Griffin's swollen member nearly slide out of her each time before swallowing it up again.

Her blood pumped. Bumps rose on her slick skin. She got the chills, it felt so good.

Sex.

From the first time she'd ever experienced it, to now: it was something she craved, needed, had to have. She'd never found the act unenjoyable. She'd never been disappointed by any partner. Not because all of the men had been perfect lovers, because they weren't, but rather because she never allowed them to make the experience a bad one. If they didn't know how to move, she moved for them. If their dicks weren't fulfilling enough, she adjusted her pussy to compensate for their shortcomings. If they came too quickly, she didn't care: she finished the job her damn self. She never had sex without having an orgasm. She didn't believe in that. If it was on, then it was on, and one way or another, she was going to explode. And explode she always did. In spurts. In gushes. In tidal, wave eruptions. Sex was her drug and she couldn't and wouldn't go through withdrawal.

Aida moaned out loud, then leaned forward, wrapped her

Griffin clenched his jaw again, and then said, "Will do."

Aida leaned toward him and planted a kiss against his cheek. "Mmmm . . . salty."

She left Griffin smiling and stepped out of the Escalade. With a wave, she turned and headed to her car. A few seconds later, Griffin's Escalade started and then, with a quick honk of the horn, passed by her.

Aida smiled as the SUV disappeared. Griffin Steele was a good fuck. She looked forward to round two and possibly a round three.

More importantly, she looked forward to collecting the other half of her money.

hand around the back of Griffin's sweaty, bald head and drove her tongue into his mouth. She kissed him ravenously as he thrust up into her. Aida moaned again, forced her tongue deeper, then pulled back after a few seconds of hard kissing and stared into Griffin's eyes as he stared back at her.

The synchronized fucking never missed a beat.

"Your . . . your boyfriend's an idiot," Griffin said, squeezing her ass harder, pushing himself deeper. His breaths were heavy, short.

Aida bit down on her lip. He'd gone damn deep. Breathlessly, she said, "Ex. And it . . . it's his loss . . . remember?"

Griffin flashed a naughty smile and thrust up again. "You're going to have to introduce me to him."

Aida cringed. Pushed down to make it hurt more. "Oh, will I?"

Griffin nodded. "Yeah. I need to thank him."

He thought he was so good. Thought he was the sole star in the play, giving the performance of a lifetime. He knew his lines and delivered them easily without hesitation.

Aida laughed.

He had no clue. As big a role as he had, her role was even bigger.

She said, "I'll see what I can do about that."

Griffin nodded and ravaged her pussy with a series of fast, deep thrusts. "I appreciate that."

"Do that again," Aida said. "Harder."

Griffin pushed up. "You want it to hurt?"

Aida pushed down. "You can't hurt me."

Griffin slapped her ass. "You say that now."

Aida leaned forward and bit on his earlobe. "You haven't got the balls to hurt me."

Griffin flashed an almost sinister smile, then smacked her ass again, harder this time. "Better watch what you say."

Aida's turn to smile. She loved having her ass slapped, her hair pulled. She loved when it got rough, uninhibited.

She leaned back, wrapped her arms around the headrest again. Pushed down and moved her waist like an erotic dancer on her knees, leaning against a steel pole with her legs spread wide, performing in front of horny men whose eyes expressed how badly they wanted to taste, touch, smell, lick, suck, bite, finger, fist, and fuck her shaved pussy.

Her skin felt prickly. Her body temperature rose. Her explosion was coming and it was going to be powerful, electric, intense.

She bit down on her lip again.

Arched her back.

"Oooh."

Griffin's pace increased. His door was opening too. He dug his fingers into her waistline. Said, "Shit! Shit!"

"Ohh. Right there!"

"Goddamn!"

"That's it, *papi. Jodame.*"

"Shit! Can't hold . . . going to . . ."

"Give it to me, baby. *Damelo.*"

"Love that Spanish shit," Griffin said. He dug his fingers deeper and let out a growl. "Shiiit!"

He bucked powerfully.

Made the walls of Aida's dam crumble into pieces.

Aida came and smiled as she did. "Aye, Griffin! Shit! *Cono!*"

Griffin bucked a few more times before he fell back against the seat.

Aida let out a long exhale and sat up and stared at him. Sweat ran in rivulets down from the top of his head. The air inside of the Escalade was musty and reeked of salt and sex.

The windows were nearly illegally tinted, so in the darkness no one had seen what had just occurred. But the SUV wasn't soundproof and if anyone had walked by, they would certainly have been witness to every stroke, just from the sounds alone.

"Should we give our exes a call now?" Griffin asked with a sly smirk.

Aida laughed and slid him out of her and sat beside She raised her sports top back over her breasts, and pu thong and shorts back on. "We should have called the minutes ago."

Griffin peeled off the condom he was wearing, ope passenger door, and threw it outside. "That," he said, the door, and then pulling his boxers and sweats around his ankles, "would have been hilarious."

"Next time," Aida said.

Griffin nodded. "Definitely next time."

"Maybe we can let them watch."

"Or participate."

Aida smiled. "Even better."

Griffin had a sneaky glint in his eyes. She didn' but it gave Aida the chills. "So . . . are you still drink?" Griffin asked.

Aida closed her eyes a bit. "Sure you're still me? I mean, you did just get the cake."

Griffin smiled. "I'm a hungry man. One bi not enough."

Aida laughed. "OK. But I need to go ho first."

"I need to do the same." Griffin reached and grabbed his cell phone. "What's your call you in about an hour."

Aida shook her head. "Had drama in th out my cell."

Griffin clenched his jaw. "OK. Well, he a card from his wallet and handed it to h is on there. Call me when you're ready."

Aida took it and put it in her pocke hand around the latch and opened the my number is going to come up block answer it."

26

"So how are things going?"

I wiped sweat away from my forehead. I'd just finished running a few of the gym's employees through a hard kickboxing workout. I don't usually run the class for the employees, but the regular instructor—a Billy Blanks wannabe with half the size and double the amount of hair—had been robbed and broke his ankle in the process. The manager called me, since I was the only other kickboxing instructor the gym had, and begged me to run the class. I had nothing going on for the evening, so I agreed to do it.

I push the gym members hard during every one of my classes. They were there to get results and I took my job of helping to produce those results very seriously. I pushed the employees ten times harder because it was all about setting the example. As far as I was concerned, you shouldn't work at the gym if you weren't in shape or weren't determined to be.

I wiped away sweat again and stepped outside. It was nighttime. Approaching nine o'clock. For the first time in four days, the humidity wasn't suffocating. It was still warm though at about eighty degrees.

Walking to my Mercedes-Benz E-Class coupe, I said, "Things are going fine."

I was going to call Shante Hunt with my update when I got home, but changed my mind and called as I left. Home was for a hot shower, some Pinot Noir, and Pink Martini on repeat. Home was about pleasure.

Shante said, "I guess you've made contact with the son-of-a-bitch?"

I thought about the nights out with Ryan. The nights of sex.

Contact.

Yes. There had been plenty.

I said, "Yes."

"He's an arrogant asshole, isn't he?" Shante asked, her tone biting, laced with disgust.

I paused as a car slowly turned in front of me and headed down an aisle to the right of where I was parked. A woman was driving the car. Didn't know why, but it almost seemed as though she'd been staring at me.

"Thinks he's God's gift to women," Shante added.

I nodded as I approached my Benz. "He is sure of himself," I said.

"I can't wait for this to happen. I can't wait for him to get his."

"Have you and your sister spoken yet?"

Shante sighed. "No. She still won't talk to me."

"The plan is for you to take her out and then bring her home so that she can walk in on Ryan and me correct?"

"Yes."

"Well if she's not talking to you, how are you going to make that happen?"

"My sister is just being stubborn for the sake of being stubborn. Trust me, all I have to do is show up at her house. She won't say no to going out."

"OK."

"Has . . . has he come on to you?" Shante asked, her tone indicating that she didn't want to know the answer.

I said, "Yes, he has."

"Have you . . . have you responded?"

I was at my Benz now, opening the door. "I've done what's necessary to ensure that you get what you're paying for."

Shante scoffed. "What I'm paying for. I still can't believe I've had to resort to this just to open my sister's eyes."

"Sometimes people need to be forced to accept reality."

"Yes, they do," Shante said.

"Are you sure this is something you want to go through with?"

"I'm very sure," Shante replied. "I wish I were home to make it happen now. I hate having to wait. Piece of shit. Pathetic joke, pathetic excuse for a man." Shante paused and exhaled heavily into the phone. "Sorry," she said, her voice softer, but the edge still there. "I . . . I tend to lose it when it comes to him. He just gets under my skin. Have you ever dealt with someone like that? Someone who just makes you lose your center, lose your control?"

I thought about Kyra for a moment. Thought about the control I'd lost. Thought about the way she'd gotten under my skin. The way she'd almost won before I found my center again.

I said, "No."

"Guess you choose the right people to deal with."

I wiped my forehead again. Update given, it was time to end the call. "OK, the day after this is finished we'll meet at Starbucks. Make sure you have the check for the other half with you. You won't hear from me again after that. And I don't expect to hear from you."

"OK."

I ended the call before she could say anything else.

I got why she was irritated and pissed off about Ryan, but something about her and her outburst bothered me. As much as Ryan's attitude and dick intrigued me, I was looking forward to not having to deal with Shante Hunt anymore.

I threw my gym bag onto the passenger seat and was about

to get in when I sensed someone behind me. I spun around, my hands balled into tight fists, the muscles in my legs taut and ready to swing out at whoever was there.

But I froze.

Standing in front of me was a ghost. A devil. A figment of my imagination, which must have certainly gone fucking wild.

I stared.

Didn't want to believe what I was seeing. Couldn't believe it. Refused to believe it.

I stared.

Blinked. Barely breathed. My heart beat heavily. Thudded beneath my chest. Echoed in the caverns of my ears. Nothing around me moved. Sounds disappeared.

I stared.

Felt myself teeter off center.

Standing in front of me was a person I never expected to see again. A person who had ceased to exist a lifetime ago.

My mother.

I stared at her.

Her hair was still long and curly, brown, though peppered with slender streaks of gray. Her eyes were still almond shaped, still sad, with crow's-feet at the corners. Her mouth hadn't changed. Her lips were still full, still succulent, despite the deep frown she wore. She wasn't overweight, but she'd put on size with age. Her waistline and hips were wider. Her legs and arms thicker. She'd probably put on a good twenty-five to thirty pounds.

My mother.

Still attractive after all these years.

Years.

All of them.

I said, "What are you doing here?"

"I . . ." she paused, fidgeted with the bottom of a yellow top she had on. Yellow had always been her favorite color.

I didn't own any yellow clothing. She opened her mouth. Struggled to find her words again, before letting out a sigh and saying, "Hello, Lisette. It good to see you again."

I closed my fists tighter. Wished she was an assailant that I could hit. I said again, "What are you doing here?" My throat was raw, dry.

"It's been so long, Lisette."

"Goddamn it. What the hell are you doing here?"

My mother opened her mouth to say something else, but then frowned and reached into her purse, hanging over her shoulder. She removed a white piece of paper and what looked like a newspaper clipping. She extended the papers toward me. "I received these in the mail two days ago."

I looked at her skeptically with a raised eyebrow for a long moment, before taking the papers from her.

I looked at the newspaper clipping first.

"What the . . ."

What I was holding didn't make sense to me. I looked at it for a long, tense couple of seconds. I said again, "What the . . ."

Kyra Rogers. In black and white with a smile spread across her face. She stared up at me. Above her head a caption in black letters read:

WOMAN MISSING. WHEREABOUTS UNKNOWN.

Below her picture, handwritten sloppily in red marker diagonally across the words of the article, was:

Your daughter knows what happened to her.

I went from the clipping to the folded piece of paper. I unfolded it. On it, in the same red ink, written in the same unkempt handwriting, was my home address, along with the address for the gym with the date and time of the kickboxing class I'd just finished instructing. I looked at the piece of paper for a lingering second, then looked back to the clipping.

Kyra.

Fucking Kyra.

I looked over my mother's shoulder, then turned my head left and right, and then looked behind me. I ran my eyes over every fucking car, every fucking shadow, before focusing back on my mother. "Who sent you this?"

My mother shook her head. "I . . . I don't know."

"Don't bullshit me!" I snapped. I was trying to remain calm, trying to keep my composure, but it was hard. Damn near impossible. Someone said I knew what had happened to Kyra. Who?

There were only three people besides myself who knew what had happened to her: Three thugs, all paid more than enough to keep their mouths closed. I didn't worry about them talking about Kyra's last night of existence. A night in which I'd given her my regards before she'd taken her last breath.

"Who sent this to you?" I demanded again.

"I don't know," my mother insisted again. "What does it mean? Who is that woman?"

I crumbled the papers in my hand and looked around the brightly illuminated parking lot again. Various people walked from the gym to their cars, or went in the opposite direction to get their workouts in.

I looked from one person to the next. Wondered if any of them had sent the papers. I studied them with a scrutinizing eye. Tried to X-ray vision my way through car windows and windshields, tinted or not.

Someone knew and they knew about my mother. Knew how to get in touch with her. Had told her how to get in touch with me.

"Lisette, what's going on?"

I turned and looked at my mother. She'd abandoned me. Left me with my pervert of a father. Left me to fend for myself. She stood in front of me, saying my name and asking me questions as if she had a fucking right to.

"When did you say this came?"

"Two days ago. Lisette—"

"And you don't know who sent it?"

"No. Please, Lisette, what's going on?"

I closed my hand tighter around the papers. Looked around the parking lot again.

Who?

I shook my head.

My mother called my name again. "Lisette . . . are you in some kind of trouble? Who is that woman? What does the message mean?"

I clenched my jaw. Her voice was like fingernails on a chalkboard. "Shut . . . the . . . fuck up," I said my voice tight with anger.

My mother frowned as her eyes welled with tears. "You're angry, and you have every right to be. I know I owe you an explanation for what I did, the way I left."

"I don't want to hear this bullshit," I said.

"Please, Lisette. Just let me explain. I've missed you. I've—"

"Missed me? Bitch, you abandoned me."

"I know. I swear to you, I regret that decision. I was young. And you were so . . .so . . . manipulative."

"I was a fucking child."

"I know. I just didn't know how to deal with you. I made a bad decision."

"A bad . . ." I closed my mouth and shook my head again. I didn't need this shit.

Someone knew.

They knew my address.

They knew I'd be instructing the class that night, which meant the other instructor's robbery hadn't been random.

I looked around again. At people. At cars. At darkness, and shadows in the light.

Someone knew and they'd sent my mother. The woman who didn't mean shit to me.

I looked back at her. Closed my eyes to slits, and in a voice as tight as a wire on the verge of snapping, said, "Thank you for bringing these to me. Now stay the fuck out of my life."

Without another word, I climbed into my car, slammed the door shut, started the engine, and pulled away.

I never looked in my rearview mirror.

My sights were focused intensely straight ahead.

The white piece of paper with my home address and the newspaper clipping were still crumbled in my hand.

Kyra Rogers.

Someone had brought her back from the grave.

I had to find out who.

27

I'm laughing.

I can barely contain myself. She looks like a fucking bobblehead doll the way she keeps looking all around her.

Feeling paranoid, bitch? Are you racking your brain trying to figure out what the fuck is going on? Are you trying to figure out why the hell your mother is there? Well, I did some investigating. I spoke to some of the people from your past. People you went to school with. Surprise, surprise, you weren't very well liked. It didn't take much money to get just enough information of your background from them to use to my advantage. I found out all about your screwed, up family life. The people I spoke to all called your father a pervert. The females all claimed that he looked at them in inappropriate ways. Some said he tried to touch them once or twice. I bet he did some nasty things to you. I tried to reach him, but he's been dead for five years. Heard you didn't go to his funeral.

And then there's your mother. Heard she left one morning and just never came back. Some said there were rumors of physical abuse from dear old Daddy. Others said you drove her away just so you could have your father to yourself. Sick, bitch. Really sick. She was easy to find. She lives literally three hours away. Remarried now with two twin daughters, three years younger than you.

Keep looking.

"Nah nah nah nah nah."

You'll never find me, you cunt. But I found you. And I'm under your skin, eating away at you slowly.

I'm laughing so hard my sides hurt. Good thing I parked

far enough away so that she can't hear me. I wish I didn't have to though. I wish I could have pulled right into the parking spot beside her car instead of passing by slowly.

Better yet, "I should have run your ass over, you whore. I should have put an end to you. But I would have been cheating myself, and after all of the plotting, preparation, and execution I've done to snuff out your pathetic life right now, it just wouldn't have been fair to me, and it wouldn't have been fair to Kyra. Kyra," I say.

Shit.

I'm fucking crying now. I shouldn't have said her name. It's hard enough hearing her voice and seeing her in my dreams and thoughts every fucking day. I haven't spoken her name in months. Saying it is just a painful reminder that, for as long as I live, saying her name out loud would forever go unanswered.

Kyra. My sweet, loving, tender, soft Kyra. My tears are flowing now. I miss her so damned much. It's not fair. She was everything to me. She was my beginning, and she was supposed to be my fucking ending.

I wipe tears away with the back of my hand, then slap my open palm down on my thigh and squeeze. I need to stop. I need to put my focus back on that bitch. The one responsible for Kyra never returning my calls, or coming home.

"Focus."

But it's so hard.

I scream out, punch my thigh, hit my steering wheel, grab handfuls of my hair and pull. I try to make the stinging in my scalp keep my mind from going back to the past. Back to a time when life was good, with promises to only get better.

"Focus," I say again as I pull. "Goddammit . . . focus!"

But I can't. My eyes are staring at that bitch through my salty waterfall, but my mind has already drifted. I'm no longer in the car. I'm back in the past, in the club where Kyra and I first met. I'm back smelling smoke and sweat mixed with layers of cologne and perfume. Music is blasting. The DJ's on some shit. He's like a fucking aerobics instructor, playing shit that's guaranteed to make us lose weight.

I'm alone, walking around, watching people dance to the techno hip-hop that's thumping. The club's on fire in a blaze of dark red lighting. Strobe lights flash every couple of seconds like lightning, giving glimpses of the people who are packed like sardines on the dance floor. Each flash shows a different face. A new pair of eyes closed and lost to the rhythm. I've seen the faces before. They're the same goddamn faces I always see.

I'm sipping a Corona, watching them, and while I do, I think about moving to a new place so that I don't have to see the same goddamned people anymore.

And then I see her.

She's not dressed weird or differently. Her hairstyle or color doesn't separate her from the rest. She's the same average height as everyone else. She's in the middle of the floor, alone, moving to the music just like everyone else, but she sticks out. There's just something about her. Something as entrancing as the thumping bass and electronic chords in the music.

I'm glued where I'm standing, unable to take my eyes off of her. I'm a fucking voyeur enjoying the show that she has no idea she's putting on. Goddamn she's sexy. Great curves, great ass, nice, full breasts. Shit, I'd like to get my hands on them. I was already sweating from the temperature in the club, but I'm sweating even more now. I haven't been turned on like this in a long time. Not since my ex, who'd broken my fucking heart.

What's her story? Which way does she roll?

I'm wondering that as I stare at her. I take another sip of my Corona. I want to step to her. Want to ask what her name is. I think about it. *Be bold and walk right up to her*, I say to myself. *Don't think.*

I take another sip of my beer and then nod. I'm going to do it. I'm going to make the move. But just as I lift my heel, someone steps in front of her.

A fucking man. And he's holding two drinks in his hand.

"Fuck."

I put my heel back down, close my hands tight around my beer, and just watch as she takes the drink from him and smiles. The man leans forward and plants a kiss on her lips. It shouldn't, but that shit pisses me off. It doesn't make any sense, but I feel like those are my lips that asshole is kissing.

But they're not.

I take an angry swallow of my Corona and am about to say, "Fuck it," and keep it moving when I notice something. When he'd kissed her on her lips, his mouth had lingered there for a few seconds, but there'd been no emotional reaction from her.

"Shit!"

I watch her intensely. I pay attention to her body language as her date wraps his arms around her and pulls her body against his. He kisses her on her neck, whispers in her ear. She smiles as if what he'd said had been pleasing to her.

But she's faking it.

No one else can see it, but I can. She's not into him. And it's not that she's not into him, it's that she's not into *him*. She's not into his kind.

The untrained eye would never have caught it, but I'm not untrained. I can see it in her eyes. She might be doing the "right" thing by being with him, but she clearly wants to be with someone who understands her. Someone who feels what she feels. Someone who desires the things she's longing for.

I sip my beer and stare. The longer I stare, the more I see how uninspired she is. I watch her for three more songs before she excuses herself from her date and heads to the bathroom. Her steps are unbalanced, which means she's feeling nice.

They always say that the truth comes out when you're feeling nice. I drink the rest of my Corona, and this time I say, "Fuck it." I'm going to find out.

I make my way to the bathroom, watching her ass switch as she walks a few feet in front of me. What I'm going to say exactly, I'm not really sure, but I'm going to say something.

We're a few feet away from the bathroom. I don't usually give a damn about people, but I don't want anyone in my business. If I'm going to step, then I need to step now. And that's what I'm about to do when the unexpected happens.

She turns around and looks at me and says, "You've been watching me."

I'm shocked, almost speechless. It takes me a few seconds, but I get myself together. "How do you know?"

She smiles. It's sexy, seductive, naughty. "Because I've been watching you."

"You have?"

"Yes."

"I didn't catch that."

"You weren't supposed to."

I'm looking at her curiously. "You're not in the closet or confused?"

She shakes her pretty little head. "No."

"So what are you doing with him?"

She laughs. Up close and personal, the laugh is sexy as hell. "I'm playing him," she says.

I look at her with a raised eyebrow. "Really?"

She holds up her left hand. A diamond is blinging from her ring finger. "We're getting married next week."

"You are?"

"Yes. I'll stay with him for about a year and then I'll divorce his ass and take half of his money."

My eyes snap open. "Are you serious?"

"Very."

"Damn."

She laughs.

I say, "So, do you always tell random strangers your business?"

She smiles again. "No."

"Then why did you tell me? Or are you just bullshitting me?"

She takes a step toward me. There's a look in her eyes that's lustful and dangerous. It gives me the chills, it's so fucking sexy. She's inches away from me. So close I can smell the alcohol on her breath.

"You're sexy," she says.

"So are you," I reply. My heart's beating as heavily as the bass in the club. I know what's about to happen, yet can't believe it's about to happen. "Aren't you worried about your fiancé seeing us?"

"He's fifteen years older than me and is as blind as a bat without his glasses. He never wears them when we go to a club because he says he looks old with them on. And he can't wear contact lenses. He's not seeing anything."

She leans forward and puts her lips against mine and kisses me hard and forceful. Her tongue knocks and I part my lips to let it in. The music and everyone in the club disappears as we kiss as though we'd kissed before. It was natural, familiar and so fucking good. So fucking right. We kiss for a few more intense seconds and then she pulls back. The music, the people inside return.

I put my hand over my mouth. "Wow."

She smiles. "I'm Kyra."

"I'm Vivian."

"I felt something when I saw you Vivian."

I nod. "I felt it too."

"I couldn't keep my eyes off of you."

"You obviously saw me unable to keep my eyes off of you."

"There's something between us, Vivian. Something that just feels meant to be."

"I was jealous when I saw you kissing him."

Kyra smiles. "I like jealousy. It turns me on."

We talk for a few more minutes and then, after another delicious kiss, go our separate ways. I'm hers and she's mine when we do.

For five years, we loved one another and scammed pitiful, unsuspecting men at the same time. We took turns playing the "good wife." Those times were always torture for me because we couldn't be together. We would take some time off every now and then to have our time though. I loved those times. I miss them.

Five years.

We were beautiful together. A perfect match. Yin and fucking yang. I did any and everything for Kyra and she did the same for me.

Five fucking years.

I'm back in the present now, tears still running down my face. That bitch is going off on her mother now.

I pull on my hair. "You took her away from me, you cunt. But you're going to get yours."

Through tears I watch her look for me again before she says something else to her mother, and then gets in her car and pulls away. "I know how you think," I say with a smile. "I know where you're going next. But I've already beaten you there."

I look in my rearview mirror and make eye contact with Myles Rogers. He was supposed to have been the big catch for Kyra and me. The husband who was going to take us over the edge. We were going to retire after we got Myles's money. We were going to let our love be free. No more pretending. It was just going to be me and Kyra against the world, living in peace, love, and lesbian bliss.

Myles looks at me, his eyes wide with fear. Duct tape covers his mouth and is wrapped tightly around his wrists and ankles. I used a taser gun on his ass to render him fucking immobile. He never saw it coming. He's sweating like a fucking pig now.

"She's going to try to see you," I say. "She wants to know if you sent her the article. Too bad you won't be there to answer her questions."

Myles mumbles defiantly. Sounds like he cursing at me.

I turn around and hit him over and over in his face. "Shut the fuck up!" I hit him again. "Kyra's dead and you're going to pay for it. All of you are. And that bitch is going to pay the worst of all. An eye for an eye."

I hit him, spit on him, and then turn and start the engine.

Soon, you goddamned whore. So very soon you will pay for what you did.

28

Two minutes out of the gym's parking lot, I was on my BlackBerry. My right hand was clenched tightly around my steering wheel, while my left hand found Marlene's number and hit the send button.

My heart beat heavily. Beads of sweat ran down my forehead. Stress. That's what the sweat consisted of. Stress and anxiety.

Someone knew. Someone had sent my mother. Who? Why? More importantly, how? How in the hell could someone have known?

I just made it through a yellow light, then ran a red. To hell with the traffic ticket if it came. I opened and closed my fingers around the wheel. Marlene's phone rang once, twice, and then another time before she answered.

"Hey!"

My godson was crying in the background. Screaming actually.

I said, "My mother . . . she was here. Someone knows about Kyra. Do you know who? Did you have anything to do with this?"

Benjamin screamed out. Heard him stomp his feet. Marlene tried to calm him down. Told him to, "Hold on, sweetie. It's coming." She must have given him his milk because the wailing stopped instantly. "OK," Marlene said, her attention back on me. "Now what are you talking about, Lisette? Your mother? Kyra? Did I have anything to do with what?"

I clenched my jaw, and took a slow, deep breath. I'd

rambled. Something I never do. I needed to get a hold of myself. Needed to calm down. I came to a stop at a red light. "My mother came to see me at the gym tonight. She had a newspaper clipping about Kyra's disappearance on it. Written in red across the article were the words, 'your daughter knows what happened to her.'"

"What?"

"She also had a plain piece of paper with my home address along with the gym's address and today's date and time of the kickboxing class I just finished."

Marlene said again, "What?"

"Someone sent the clipping and the piece of paper to her."

"Your mother? I don't understand. Why? I mean, you haven't spoken to her in years."

One night over drinks, I'd confided in Marlene the story of my mother's abandonment. It had been one of Marlene's rare free nights. Steve had actually picked up Benjamin for his appointed weekend, and Marlene wanted to get out of the house and get some dinner and drinks. We went to Publics in Nolita. Marlene had grilled kangaroo on a coriander falafel with red wine. I had pan-seared Tasmanian sea trout with my never-fail drink of choice–cosmopolitan.

I hadn't planned on opening up about my past, but for some reason that night, I did. I blamed it on the humidity of the evening. Marlene said that whether I wanted to admit it or not, she'd broken through my very hard shell and had become something I'd never had–a girlfriend.

I said, "I know."

"Who else knows about her?"

"No one."

"So then how did someone know how to get in touch with her? And they sent her information about Kyra?"

"Newspaper clippings."

"And the gym's address?"

"I was subbing for our instructor who just happened to get robbed and had a few ribs and his ankle broken."

"And your mother was given today's date?" Marlene said. "Jesus," she whispered.

I made a right turn on Lexington Avenue.

"The robbery was no coincidence," I said. "Someone set this up."

"But . . . but who? And why? Jesus, Lisette, what the hell is going on?"

"I don't know, Marlene. That's why I'm calling you. Someone knows I had something to do with Kyra's disappearance."

"Christ, Lisette. I don't even know what happened."

I'd never told her how I'd given Kyra my regards. All she ever knew was that I'd gotten her back for ever thinking she was better than me, and that was all she needed to know.

"I don't know who the hell this person is, but I need to know ASAP."

In the background Benjamin began to whine again. Marlene grunted. I could tell she'd picked him up. "All right, sweetie . . . just close your eyes," she said in a soothing tone, before saying to me, "What do you want me to do?"

"Call your friend Lisa. Ask her again about her association with Kyra."

"OK, but I don't know how much information I'll get. She swears that she didn't give the number to Kyra directly. She said she gave it to a friend, and that friend gave it to Kyra."

"Find out who the friend is."

"I'll try."

"Don't try, Marlene. Find this person. Tonight."

"OK. But what if I can't find out anything?"

"Then call all of our clients. Ask them if they knew about Kyra. And if they didn't, then ask if their friends did."

"OK." Marlene hushed Benjamin again as I made a left onto 123rd street. I was in Harlem, driving with intense purpose.

"Lisette . . . what if none of the clients know anything? Who else is there?"

I sped through a red light. Ignored blaring car horns as I did. "Myles Rogers," I said. He didn't know what I'd done, but if anyone, other than Lisa, her friend, or my three thugs, could say anything about my relationship with her, it would be him.

"That makes sense," Marlene said.

"Get Benji to sleep and then make those calls. Call me when you have something."

I ended the call, tossed my BlackBerry onto my passenger seat and gritted my teeth as I raced through a yellow light.

Myles Rogers.

Last time I'd seen him, I'd thrown his laptop into the middle of the street.

Myles Rogers.

He could talk, but I'd saved his ass. I doubted he'd give me up to anyone, but I needed to know for sure.

29

Aida was the one who was late this time, purposefully. It was another hot day—about eighty-five degrees. The humidity was back after having taken a couple of days off, and made eighty-five feel like ninety.

Aida had plans for the day. She was going to wash her car, go to the mall to buy a new string bikini, and then hit Victoria's Secret for something special to wear later that night when she saw Griffin again.

She'd spoken to him earlier in the day, not because she had to or needed to, but instead because she wanted to. When they spoke he told her that he couldn't stop thinking about her. That he'd been having dreams about her. Hot dreams. Intense dreams. Dreams that consisted of them being naked and intertwined.

Aida had masturbated while they'd talked. The sound of Griffin's voice, the memory of the sex they'd had in the back seat of his Escalade a few days earlier, and then in a hotel room later that night, still very fresh in her mind. She moaned loudly, breathlessly, as she fingered herself deeply to the rhythm and deep tone of Griffin's voice as he told her all about the things he'd done to her in his dreams. Things he promised he was going to do to her next time. Rough things. Deep things. Fast, slow, potent things. Things that made Aida squirm as she lay back, planted her heels on her Tempur-Pedic mattress, and spread her legs wide.

Aida's fingers dove deep into her warm pool of ecstasy

between her legs, making her catch her breath. Griffin coached her as she played. He had her go faster, deeper. Told her to put as many fingers as she could inside. Ordered her to taste herself and describe her sweetness to him. Aida rocked her hips from side to side. Allowed her fingers to become Griffin's dick. Let them pound her the way he had. The way he would have again, had he been there. She cursed, squealed, called his name, told him how good he felt. Told him that she had to have him again. That she needed to feel him again. Her hips rose off of the bed and her legs shook as she came to the suave and sexy sounds of Griffin's commands. It wasn't as good as the real thing, but, shit, it had been a very close second. Before the phone call ended, they made plans to see each other later that night.

Aida knew Griffin was a dog. A man who had absolutely no respect for women. He was narcissistic to the 9th degree. Had Jesus not done it already, he would have claimed walking on water as his feat alone. He was a self-satisfying, selfish, insensitive bastard. He was the kind of man Lisette and Aida enjoyed taking down. Yet as much as she knew she shouldn't have been, Aida was finding herself getting hooked. So much so that she began to wonder is she was going to be able to let Griffin become nonexistent after the job was completed.

Lisette would be thoroughly disappointed.

The freak in her was beginning to cloud her judgment, and she knew that she had to get a grip. This was a job and when the job was over, she had to move on.

Aida told herself that as she'd washed her car, as she shopped for the new string bikini, and as she stopped in Victoria's Secret and bought a matching red lace bra and panties. Do the job, get that money and keep it moving.

She could handle it.

Lisette had chosen her because she'd expected her to.

She could handle it.

She would handle it.

Aida told herself that as she stepped into Starbucks. She was there because earlier in the day, Marlene had called her and told her that Vivian Steele requested a meeting.

"Meeting? For what?"

"She wants an update."

"And this can't be given over the phone?"

"I told her that you said things were going well, but she wants to hear it from you in person."

Aida rolled her eyes. She'd planned to lie out in the sun later that day, enjoying the heat and humidity before she met Griffin. "Fine. Whatever she wants. What time?"

"At two-thirty at Starbucks."

"Again?" Aida sighed. "OK."

Aida looked down at her watch. She was thirty minutes late. She looked around and spotted Vivian Steele sitting at a table near the back. She rolled her eyes. Vivian annoyed the shit out of her. She had no backbone and therefore allowed her husband to walk all over her. What's worse, she was completely dependant on him. Griffin may have deserved what was coming to him, but as far as Aida was concerned, Vivian Steele deserved to be disrespected. Aida could never understand women like Vivian. Women like her mother and sister.

"Hello, Vivian," Aida said, approaching her at the table. "Sorry for being late."

Vivian looked up at her and for a split second, Aida thought she saw a flash of anger in her eyes. But then Vivian smiled. "That's OK. I know I kind of sprung this on you."

Aida sat down. "Yeah. I did have some things I was taking care of today."

Vivian frowned. "I'm sorry," she said again. "I promise not to take up too much of your time."

"So, my associate says you're looking for an update?"

Vivian nodded. "I was just wondering how things were going."

"Things are good."

"Did you approach him at the gym?"

"I did."

"And was he . . . receptive to you?"

"He was."

Vivian frowned.

Aida said, "Didn't you expect him to be?"

"Y . . . yes."

"So why the disappointment?"

Vivian sighed. "I don't know. I guess there was a part of me that just held out hope that my husband wouldn't respond, even though I knew he would."

"Your husband's a womanizer, Vivian."

"I know."

"He's not going to change."

Vivian's frown deepened. "I just had to try something."

"OK. So you try this, you get him to go to counseling and nothing changes. Then what?"

Vivian shrugged. "I don't know," she said, her voice defeated. "I haven't really thought about that."

"Don't you think you should?"

Vivian wrapped her fingers around her cup of coffee as her shoulders dropped.

Aida shook her head. *So pathetic*, she thought. "Anyway, is everything set for next Saturday?"

"Yes. I've told him I'm going to visit my sister for the weekend. She lives in Virginia with her husband and three kids. He says he has work so he won't be able to come. He never got along with my sister so his excuse doesn't surprise me."

"OK. As you've requested, you'll walk in and find us on your bed. I'll make sure we're both naked."

"But not doing anything."

"Right. Not doing anything."

"OK."

"We'll meet here the next day to settle our agreement."

"OK."

Aida pushed her chair back. She was annoyed. The "update" could have been done over the phone. "Well . . . until next Saturday."

She stood up and was about to leave when Vivian spoke again.

"Aida, I have one question before you go."

Aida looked down at her. "Yes?"

"You . . . you haven't slept with him, have you?"

Aida thought about being in the back seat of Griffin's Escalade, and then being with him later that same day in a hotel room in the city, where they'd fucked just as intensely as they had in the gym's parking lot. Griffin was well endowed and knew how to use his tool. Over the phone he'd promised to reenact the scenes from his dreams. Aida felt herself growing wet as she shook her head and said, "No."

"Are you sure? I mean, my husband's an attractive man. I wouldn't be surprised if—"

"We haven't," Aida said curtly.

Vivian gave a half-hearted smile. "OK. Thank you."

Aida walked away before Vivian could ask anymore pathetic questions. *I should have said yes,* she thought. *Yes, we fucked, and we're going to fuck again.*

Next Saturday the job would be done.

Aida thought about Griffin and couldn't help but wonder if she would be.

30

Since my unwanted reunion with my dear old mother, I'd made changes. I'd had to. Someone knew about Kyra, and he or she had my home address. Going back to my old condo ceased being an option the minute I left the gym's parking lot.

I'd had my home invaded one time. By Kyra. She'd broken in and ripped up my furniture, clothing, and shoes. She destroyed my electronics equipment and shattered my CDs. Then she called me to gloat. She wanted to get a rise out of me. Wanted to have me flustered. Wanted me to be scared.

But she was stupid.

Had she been smart, she would have never contacted me. The move I made this time, I would have had to have made back then too. It would have been unavoidable. But Kyra had been in over her head. She didn't know who she was fucking with.

The person who had sent my mother my information was no fool.

He or she had made the move and remained silent. Remained hidden in the goddamn shadows. I didn't want, to but I had no choice but to move. I also ended my membership at the gym.

After hanging up with Marlene, I went to Myles's luxury penthouse in Harlem. I hadn't spoken to him, but I'd kept tabs on him. He hadn't moved after Kyra disappeared, and he'd kept his routine pretty much the same. The spouse was always suspect number one, so I'm sure his movement or lack thereof had been an effort to keep the police from breathing too hard on the back of his neck.

I could have called and asked him if he'd given my personal information to anyone, but I needed to see him answer the question. There are people in the world who are paid by the government to be human lie detectors. They can tell by a person's change in speech, breathing pattern, and posture whether he has been lying. They can tell by the eyes, the muscles in their jaws, the sweat that trickled down their brows. It takes years of intense and thorough training to become that astute. The money spent, the time invested to acquire that skill, would be a complete waste of time when dealing with Myles. If the fate of the world relied on him being able to tell the whitest of lies, then we'd better pray for another big bang somewhere down the line.

I wanted to look Myles in the eye and have him tell me that he didn't know what I was talking about. That, other than Kyra herself, he'd never brought my name up to anyone.

I waited for three hours in the lobby of his building, having the doorman call him every twenty minutes. I even had him go up to Myles's floor a few times to knock on the door. Unfortunately, there was never a response. I hated waiting that long, but someone knew where I lived and they knew about Kyra, and I had to make sure that Myles wasn't that someone.

After three hours of wasted time, I left and went to his second home: Starbucks. He had a gambling problem and every day, rain or shine, Starbucks was where he went to sit with his laptop and place his bets. I'd thrown his laptop into the middle of the street, not to cure him of his problem, but rather because he'd annoyed me. Myles allowed Kyra to wear the pants in their household. I didn't care one way or the other who ran things in his home, but because I hated the bitch, his deference to her pissed me off. I waited at the café for an hour, but Myles never showed.

Frustrated, I left and got a penthouse suite at the On The Ave Hotel across from Central Park. I called Marlene as I stood on the balcony and looked down at the park.

"What did you find out from Lisa?"

I was doing my best to remain calm, remain collected, but it was a challenge. There was a certain level of control that I'd lost with someone knowing the things he or she knew, and that had me uneasy. I never liked not having absolute control. Kyra had taken it away from me once and I swore that wouldn't happen again. Now there I was on the balcony at a hotel instead of being at home on my couch, listening to Pink Martini.

Marlene sighed through the phone. "I've called her over and over, and left numerous messages, but I can't get her, and she hasn't returned my calls."

I slammed my hand down on the balcony's rail.

"I know that's not what you wanted to hear, Lisette, but it's the only thing I can say."

"Did you try her house number?"

"Yes, of course. And I got the same result. I tried mutual friends, too, but none of them know where she is either."

I ground my teeth together as car horns cursed for me from the busy streets fourteen floors below. "What about our other clients? Have you called them?"

"Yes."

"And?"

"None of them had ever heard of Kyra."

My turn to curse this time. "Shit."

"Did you get anything from Myles?"

"Not yet."

"Where are you, Lisette?"

I looked out past Central Park, across Madison Avenue.

New York City didn't have bright stars in the sky to admire the way states in the South and Midwest did, but what it did have were lights and sounds. From cars, from buildings, from people. There was a soul to New York City. A soul different from any other city in the world. On The Ave boasted about the panoramic view in their brochure and on their Web site. It was a major selling point. Had the night been different, I would have stood naked on the balcony and enjoyed the sights and sounds of a city unmatched. Of course, had the night been different, I would have never been here.

I clenched my jaw. I said, "I'm at a hotel in the city."

"Are you sure you're safe there? You can come here if you want."

"I'm fine," I said.

"What are you going to do?"

I took a breath and exhaled slowly, trying to find my calm. What was I going to do?

Someone connected to Kyra was out there. What was he planning? Was she bluffing? Just playing some kind of twisted joke? Did he or she really know something?

Was this about money?

Did he really know something, and if that was the case, was this his way of getting me to keep what he knew a secret? However much that may have been.

What if it wasn't about money?

This person claim, to know about my involvement with Kyra. Was this about revenge? Was that what he or she was gunning for?

Revenge like Steve.

My mind went back to the gym when it had been raining. Revenge had been the fuel for Steve's fire then. I'd humiliated and screwed the hell out of him. There were plenty of other Steve's out there. Plenty of others who'd had the scales unbalanced in their ex's favor.

I was a home wrecker.

It was a lucrative occupation.

The potential for danger was always there, but the way I operated and conducted my business kept the danger level low. Steve had been the only problem and that had been because of Kyra.

She was an anomaly.

And she was gone now.

Marlene wanted to know what I was going to do.

I wanted to give another answer, but at the moment I had no other answer to give. I said, "I don't know yet."

"Jesus, Lisette," Marlene whispered, her voice thick with worry.

"Keep trying Lisa," I said.

"I will."

In the background, Benjamin made a noise, a soft whimper. Marlene shushed him softly.

"Marlene . . . has anything suspicious happened on your end?" I hadn't thought about it until that very moment. Someone was quite possibly gunning for me. If that were the case, to what means would this person go?

A second or two of silence passed before Marlene answered. "No. Lisette . . . do you think Benjamin and I could be in danger?"

I frowned and, as reassuringly as I could, said, "No. Whoever this person is, they've made their move. This person is out for me alone."

"Are you sure? I . . . I have Benji.I If I need to leave—"

"You and Benjamin will be fine."

"What about Aida? Should we warn her about what's going on?"

"No. This all happened before her. She doesn't have anything to do with this."

"OK," Marlene said, doubt in her voice.

I needed to get off of the phone. I needed to sit and breathe. Talking to Marlene was stressing me out. I said, "Call me as soon as you hear from Lisa. She's the key to this."

"Lisette, I know this is something you've never done, but do you want me to contact Shante Scott and cancel the arrangement? I mean, with all that's going on, I don't see how you can really focus on getting this done right now."

"I'm not canceling anything," I said with an edge. Her question irritated me. It reminded me again of the control that I could feel slipping away.

Marlene wouldn't give up. "But, Lisette, I just—"

"I said no, Marlene. Whoever this person is, I'll find them and deal with them. In the meantime, I have a job to do, and it will be done."

Marlene sighed. She wanted to protest again. I could hear it in the way she breathed. But she knew better. Conceding, she said, "OK. Just . . . just be careful, Lisette. Oh, and Rebecca Stantin called again. She's asked to meet with you again. What did she want?"

I frowned and shook my head. "To waste my time," I said and then ended the call.

The next day I rented a new condo on the Upper West Side of the city. I paid a moving company extra to pack up my things and deliver them that same day.

Two days had now passed, and Marlene still hadn't found Lisa, while I still hadn't found Myles. I was frustrated and, as much as I hated to admit it, I was on edge.

I looked at myself in my bedroom mirror. I was naked, letting the air dry off the beads of water from the hot shower I'd just taken. Pink Martini played softly from my iPod in the living room. My song on repeat.

BlackBerry in my hand, I dialed Ryan Scott's cell number. My secret admirer would have to take a back seat. I had a job to complete.

"Hello?"

"Hello, Ryan."

"Lisette? Wow. It's been a couple of days."

"I've beenbusy."

"I'm glad you haven't forgotten about me."

"Haven't forgotten," I said. "Just a lot going on."

"Care to tell me about it over dinner?"

My mother's unwanted appearance. A secret admirer who brought Kyra back to life. Lisa and Myles—both still missing.

I said, "I don't want to do any talking tonight."

Ryan said, "OK."

"On The Ave Hotel by Central Park. Get a room. A penthouse suite. I'll meet you there."

I hung up the phone and looked at my body. Tension had my muscles tight. Frustration and irritation had my blood on fire.

I hadn't been able to enjoy the view last time. Tonight I wanted to release on the balcony with the sounds of New York as the backdrop.

31

On the balcony of the On The Ave Hotel.

Naked.

Sitting on top of Ryan.

My hands were pressed down on his chest, the tips of my fingers touching tiny bits of scab from when I'd dug in with my nails and had drawn blood. Ryan's hands were clamped around my ass, his fingers squeezing my cheeks, as he drove himself into me. Hard, deep thrusts.

I bit down on my bottom lip. Took short, quick breaths. Beads of sweat trickled down my forehead, trailed down from my neck, past my breasts to my stomach.

Ryan looked up at me and smiled. I could tell by the overconfident glint in his eyes that he thought I was sweating, biting my lip, and inhaling and exhaling quickly because of the sex. Because of how he was thrusting back and forth. Because of how he rotated his waist to the right and then to the left.

The sex.

The other times he'd been inside of me that had been the case. I'd sweated because of the physical workout. I'd bitten down on my lip because of how deep he'd gone. I'd taken quick breaths because of his back and forth motion.

The other times.

But not this time.

On my mind, refusing to leave me alone, were questions. Who'd sent my mother the clippings? How had they known how to contact her? Who knew about Kyra? What did they want? Why hadn't they reached out yet? Were they even planning to? If so—when? More importantly—how?

Question after question after question.

I wanted to fuck on the balcony amid the warm, humid, sticky nighttime air to escape the unanswered questions momentarily. I wanted to cum in waves as New York City applauded with its unending activity on the streets below. But tonight, no matter how tightly I closed my walls around Ryan's shaft, there was no escape.

I pushed off of Ryan's chest, sat straight up, arched my back, and looked up to the dark, starless sky. I tried to focus, tried to run away from the questions, but yet again, they kept up with me stroke for stroke.

It was frustrating.

Ryan thrust himself up into me. He palmed my breasts. Sat up and took them into his mouth. Ran his tongue over and around my nipples.

This was supposed to feel so fucking good.

I tried again to focus. Tried again to put my mind where my body was. But I couldn't. Someone knew. And that was fucking with me.

Ryan released my breasts and leaned back into the chaise we brought out onto the balcony. I looked down at him. His jaw was tight, his nostrils flared. I bore down with my hips. Closed my walls tighter.

Ryan said, "Fuck!"

One or two more pushes down with my hips and he was going to bust his nut and his condom would be full, while I never even got close.

I climbed off of him, went to the balcony's rail, leaned on it and looked down to the city streets.

Behind me, Ryan said, "What the . . . ? Lisette . . . What's wrong?"

I said, "Nothing."

"So why'd you stop?" His tone was raw. He'd been so close.

"You were about to cum."

"Yeah?"

I turned and looked at him. "I wasn't."

Shock and disbelief flashed in his eyes for a moment. He hadn't expected that response. Every woman came when he was inside of them. That's what the expression on his face said. How the hell could I not have already or at least been close to it?

He nodded and said, "I see." He rose from the chaise and went into the room. He came back seconds later, his condom removed. His expression was cocksure again, as though he'd been unfazed by not being able to get off.

I turned my back to him and looked out into the nighttime, my eyes searching for a person I couldn't find, but had to.

Ryan stepped behind me and kissed the back of my neck. "You are addictive," he said.

I said, "Is that right?"

Another kiss on my neck. "Definitely."

I gave him a "Hmmm," but said nothing more.

"I'd love to see you more."

"I don't think your wife would like that."

Ryan scoffed. "My *wife*," he said. "That's a joke."

"You chose her."

Ryan let out a frustrated exhale, moved to the balcony, and leaned on the rail beside me. "She says that she wants to fix things between us. She says she knows she's been the cause for the distance between us. She's been talking about looking into pills to increase her libido. And if that doesn't work, then seeing a doctor about it."

"Sounds like she doesn't want to lose you."

Ryan shook his head. "It's too fucking late for that."

I raised an eyebrow. He was good. Completely convincing.

I could see how the average woman who didn't know his real story could fall for the bullshit.

"I have a business meeting in Virginia next week," he said. "Virginia Beach. A four-day meeting. I was going to ask you to come, but my wife . . . she invited herself."

I hmmed. "Maybe Virginia Beach will be the remedy. You can fuck her on the beach."

Ryan turned and looked at me. "I want to fuck you on the beach."

"Pretend your wife is me."

"There's no substitute for the real thing."

I shrugged. "Well . . . I won't be at the beach, so you better figure something out." I walked away from him, went into the suite, and grabbed my clothes.

Ryan followed me inside. "You're leaving?"

"Have things to do," I said, slipping on my thong and bra.

"Are you sure I can't have your number?"

"I'm sure."

Ryan frowned. "I want to see you when I get back."

I slipped on my blouse and jeans. "Maybe."

"Is that a maybe that will become a no again?"

"It's a maybe," I said.

Ryan nodded. "Call me next Friday, then."

I slipped on my pumps and grabbed my purse from the chair. I looked at him. Even limp, he was impressive. I said, "Better get rid of the rest of those scabs before Virginia Beach."

Ryan looked down at his chest and shrugged. "Maybe I'll just leave them there for her to find."

My turn to shrug. "Have fun in Virginia."

I turned and headed to the door. As I opened it, Ryan said, "Next Friday, Lisette, call me. We can go out for dinner again."

"Friday's a bad night for me."

"How about Saturday?"

I waited for a moment before I answered. Let him believe I was really giving it some thought. "Saturday might work."

"OK, so, dinner?"

"Maybe," I said, and then walked out.

Next Saturday. He would definitely see me. And then he'd regret ever laying his eyes on me.

32

Aida was fucking up and she knew it.

She was losing her focus, getting caught up physically and emotionally. For the past few days she'd been talking to herself. Telling herself to get a grip, to remain centered. She had a job to do. Set Griffin up, collect her pay, and move on to the next ungrateful bastard she'd be paid to ruin. It was a simple equation.

Unhappy wife + bastard of a husband = *mucho dinero*.

All she had to do was stay in tunnel-vision mode and keep walking with her blinders on.

Griffin was just like the other men she'd fucked over. He was a liar, a cheat. So what if he was sexy as sin, with his wide upper torso, his well-developed arms and chest, a washboard stomach, and a damn near perfect dick? And so what if he knew how to use it in ways that gave her the chills? So what if his macho and arrogant personality was a complete turn-on for her? So what if she loved his style? So what if his eyes and sly smile gleamed with a hint of danger that she couldn't get enough of? So what if she found herself thinking about him and wondering what he was doing at that moment when she did? And so what if she couldn't help but wonder if he'd thought of being with her while he was with his wife? Or if he'd fucked his wife with her on his brain?

None of those questions and thoughts mattered. All that mattered was that Griffin was a disrespectful son-of-a-bitch who deserved what he had coming to him. Damn the great sex and the chemistry that seemed to exist between them.

All week long that's what Aida had said to herself.

All week long she'd insisted that the calls she'd made to him had been for the job. For the setup. For the big payday.

And all week long she'd known that had been utter and complete bullshit.

Aida was falling. Hell—she had fallen for Griffin Steele, and she didn't quite know how to handle it.

She needed to talk to someone, but there was no one. If she told Marlene, she was sure she'd be pulled off of the job, and she didn't want that. She damn sure couldn't confide in Lisette, because she had no doubt she'd lose not only the best money she'd ever make, but she'd also lose the only person who knew and understood just who she was. Someone she considered family. For that reason, there was only one option: She would have to figure this out on her own. She didn't know how, but one way or another, she would.

At least she hoped.

Aida sighed as she caressed Griffin's well-defined chest. They were in the back seat of his Escalade again. She'd just orgasmed sitting on top of him. He'd just finished bucking and releasing into his condom inside of her.

"What's wrong, sexy?" Griffin asked, his index finger trailing along the side of her breast.

Aida shook her head. "Nothing."

"That's a lie."

"How do you know?"

Griffin lifted the corner of his mouth into a sly smirk. "I can tell by your eyes."

"You know me so well, huh?"

Griffin gave her a bad-boy smile and said, "I'm willing to bet I know you better than most."

Aida held his gaze momentarily and then looked through

the tinted window as someone walked by, heading to his car, oblivious to their presence. She didn't know why, but she felt as though there'd been something more to his comment.

Griffin smiled again. "So tell me, sexy, what was up with the sigh?"

Aida shook her head and dropped the corners of her mouth. "Nothing really."

"Mami," Griffin said in a don't-even-try-it tone.

Aida looked at him for another lingering second. Somewhere, Vivian Steele was anxiously waiting for this coming Saturday to arrive. Vivian Steele; she was completely not his type. Unambitious, dependent, soft, attractive yet unassuming at the same time, looked like she didn't enjoy having sex. She was no challenge, which was obviously why the hell Griffin was unfaithful.

Aida couldn't help but wonder what the hell he'd seen in her. He hadn't married her for her money. He hadn't married her for her power or status. So what the hell had he married her for? What *brujeria* (witchcraft) had she performed to snatch him up? She wanted to ask him why her, but of course, she couldn't.

She said, "I was just wondering how a man like you isn't taken already." She watched him intently, wanting to see if her question put him on edge at all.

Griffin never batted an eyelash or took a pause as he answered, "No one has ever had enough strength to take me."

Aida nodded. "I see."

Griffin flashed a devious smile again. "But, mami, I have to be real . . . You are one strong-ass woman."

Bumps rose along Aida's arms. She nodded again and tried to contain her smile. "Is that right?"

Griffin cupped his hand behind her head and pulled her toward him. His lips centimeters away from hers, he said, "That's definitely the case," and then pulled her lips to his.

He kissed her hard, drove his tongue into her mouth, which she'd eagerly opened to allow entrance.

Aida moaned.

So what? she thought. *So what if his kiss is as smooth and hot as he is?* She pulled back. "You're a strong man yourself," she said.

Griffin flashed his sexy smile again. "I try to hit the gym on a regular basis."

Aida laughed.

Griffin did too, then said, "I like you, Aida."

"That's good to know. For a minute I was wondering if it was only my tits and ass you liked."

Griffin cocked an eyebrow. "Oh, without question, I definitely like the tits and ass, but I also like the personality to go along with them."

Aida blushed.

"I feel a real connection with you," he continued. "You get me in a way that no one else has ever gotten me."

Aida said, "You get me too. And there's only ever been one other person who has."

"I hope he's a distant memory."

"She. And she's a very good friend of mine."

"Well, hopefully I get to meet her someday."

Aida smiled. "You never know."

Griffin kissed her deeply again for a few seconds. This time he pulled back. "What are you doing this Saturday?"

Aida looked at him. She knew why he was asking. Vivian had set the trap and told him about her going away to visit the sister-in-law he couldn't tolerate. As she knew he would, he'd said he couldn't go, leaving him the opportunity to be alone for the weekend. She'd been hired for this weekend and it bothered her slightly, because it was a reminder that she was on the job to help Vivian save her marriage, because she couldn't be without him.

She said, "I have no plans yet. Why?"

"I have to go away for a few days for business. I'll be back early Saturday morning. If you don't mind keeping that night free, I'd like to take you out to dinner."

Aida kept her lips tight for a moment.

The time had come.

She said, "We can do dinner, but I want a home-cooked meal."

Griffin looked at her with a curious stare. "Home-cooked?"

"Yes. I want you to cook me a fancy dinner. An authentic Puerto Rican meal."

"Are you serious?"

Aida nodded. "Very."

"What if I can't cook?"

"Something tells me you have skills in the kitchen, too."

Griffin laughed. "I might have some skills."

"Then it's set. I'll come over around eight-thirty."

Griffin shook his head. "Any particular meal in mind?"

Aida shrugged. "Surprise me."

"Damn. Guess I better break out the cookbook."

"Guess you better."

"And you're sure you don't want this authentic meal at an authentic Puerto Rican restaurant? Because I know of some good ones."

Aida shook her head. "No restaurant. I want my authenticity from *el restaurante de Griffin*."

Griffin laughed. "I really love that Spanish shit."

Aida gave him a smile laced with seduction. "You cook me that meal and you'll hear a lot of Spanish shit for dessert."

Griffin clenched his jaw and flared his nostrils. As he did, his manhood jumped.

Aida looked down at it and licked her lips. "Looks like someone likes the sound of that."

Griffin clenched his jaws again. "He and I both."

"Hmmmm."

"You up for round two?" he asked.

Aida smiled. "The real question is . . . could you hang for a round three?"

Griffin nodded. "I have four more condoms in my pack."

Aida growled. "Aye, papi."

Seconds later round two began, and as it did, one word ran through Aida's mind.

Trouble.

She was in for it and she didn't want to do a damn thing to stop it from coming.

33

It's almost time!

My day of retribution. My day of payback.

Oh, so soon, slut. So soon you're going to get everything you deserve and more.

I take a breath and hold it in. I savor it. Pretend it's her last fucking breath. I can't wait until that moment comes. I can't wait until I watch it escape from her lungs and her eyes close for good.

Bitch. I have you so rattled, I love it. Ms. "I am God's gift to the fucking world."

Bitch! Whore! Cunt! Coward!

Waiting is so frustrating. So goddamned painful. But it's oh-so-necessary. I can't wait to see the look on your face when your glass bubble shatters. *I can't wait to look at you eye to eye and tell you all about how I planned everything out. Your death won't bring my Kyra back to me, but I'm still going to enjoy every second of the agony you're going to endure.*

I look to my right. That prick Myles is mumbling again. I'd taken him as he walked to his car after leaving Starbucks. He'd been preoccupied, fishing for something in his laptop case. He'd never even seen or heard me coming up behind him. I tasered his ass, and after he crumbled to the ground like a wet rag doll, I dragged him to my car, duct taped his wrists and ankles, and managed to get him into the back seat of my car before I went to watch that bitch get her surprise visit.

It's his time.

"Not yet," I say. "I have to stick to the plan."

It's his fucking time!

I shake my head, but don't speak this time. Then I leave the bathroom and head into the bedroom, where I have Myles laying face up on a bed, rope tied around his wrists and ankles and fastened to the bed's four posts.

I walk up to him and look down at him as he looks up at me. His eyes are red and wide with fear. "You want to know who the hell I am, don't you? You want to know why you're here?"

He mumbles something that sounds like a yes.

I stare at him and scowl. "I don't know how the hell she put up with you," I say. I sit on the bed beside him. "I couldn't have done it. I wouldn't have been able to stomach being next to you."

I spit on him.

"You're a fucking pussy," I say.

He squirms and mumbles again through the duct tape fastened over his mouth.

I lean down toward him a little. "What was that?"

He mumbles again.

"I can't understand what you're trying to say. You'll have to speak a little clearer." I laugh and then lean toward him more and grab the corner of the tape. "Will this help? Do you want me to take this off?" I tug on the tape.

He nods and says something that sounds like please.

I remove a razor from my pocket. I hold it up for him to see as I unfold it. His eyes grow wider. His fright makes me smile. It makes me think of the fear I'm going to see in Lisette's eyes.

I press the tip of the blade hard against his cheek and drag it down at an angle. He moans as I watch his blood rise up from the two-inch line I've traced.

"I'll take it off," I say. "But if I even think the sound of your voice is too loud, I'll cut your tongue out and feed it to you. Do you understand?"

He nods slowly as his eyes tear up.

I smile again. "Good boy."

I pull on the tape. Slowly. I want patches of his moustache and goatee to come off on the other side of the tape.

"Now, remember," I say, pressing the blade against the corner of his mouth, "watch that volume."

Myles looks down at the blade and then at me. "Wh . . . who are you?" he asks, his voice low and trembling. "Why are you doing this?"

I glare at him. Fear has his forehead covered with beads of sweat. Fear has him taking short, quick breaths.

"Why am I doing this?"

He nods. "Y . . . yes. Why? I don't know you."

"Oh, that's not true, Myles. You do know me."

He shakes his head. "No. We've never met."

"You know me, you pussy," I insist again.

He shakes his head.

"Kyra," I say.

"Kyra?"

"You were married to her, you prick."

He shakes his head. "I . . . I don't understand."

"She was my woman. My completion. You were with her, so that means that you were with me, too."

"Your . . . your woman?" His eyebrows slam together. "I don't understand . . ."

"It was all for your money, you piece of shit! That's all we married you for. But then you presented us with that fucking prenuptial agreement on our wedding day. You asshole! You spineless son of-a-bitch!"

My hands begin to shake as I think back to that day. Back to the moment when Kyra sent me a text telling me about the prenuptial agreement he wanted her to sign.

"Five million dollars for every five years of marriage. You asshole!"

My blood is boiling. My heart racing.

I take the blade and lay it against his Adam's apple.

It's his time!

I want to drag it across. I want to watch it break the skin and watch as blood oozes out. I want to watch his skin grow pale as his life seeps away.

"After all of the time we'd put in with you, we had no choice but to sign it and go through with the fucking wedding."

I press the blade into his skin. Just a little more pressure and it would be over for him.

"I wanted to kill you so that we could collect on our money, but Kyra . . ." I pause and close my eyes tightly for a moment. Talking about her this much is so hard, so agonizing.

It's his time!

I take a breath and then continue. "She convinced me to not do it. She would have been the primary suspect, and if that happened, it would have been too hard to get our money. I didn't want to listen, but she was right. We couldn't kill you. So we had to find another way out."

I pause and glare at him. I'm on fire. On the verge of losing it.

It's his fucking time!

I spit in his face again.

"Lisette was supposed to have been that way out, but the bitch said no. And then she told you about what we were trying to do. And you, thinking that you were a fucking man, tried to kick us out. But we came up with another solution. We got Charles Goodell to do business with you and because of all of the extra income you gained by your new relationship with him, your fucking prenup was negated. We were six months away from collecting our money when . . ."

I stop talking. I don't want to say what I'm about to say. It's a reality that torments me day in and day out.

I press the knife harder against his flesh. Tears fall from my eyes. I can't hold them back. I shake my head.

I was going to wait to kill him. I wanted that bitch to watch him die. But it's too hard. The plan can be altered a little bit. He can die now. There's someone else that bitch can watch die.

I tighten my grip around the blade's handle and stare down at Myles.

He watches me with terrified eyes. "Please," he whispers. "Please . . . don't. I beg you . . ."

I look at him for a long second. It is his fucking time.

I drag the blade across his throat. His eyes open wider as his blood flows from the four-inch gash I make. He tries to speak, but can only gasp and gurgle. He thrashes, trying to break free from the ropes as though something he could do would prevent the inevitable.

"An eye for an eye," I say.

I stand up and step away from the bed and blood. I watch him suffer. I watch him deal with the fact that in another few seconds, he's going to be dead.

"An eye for a fucking eye."

He thrashes again and then goes still. The light is fading in his eyes. The rise and fall of his chest is getting slower. He looks at me as his last breath slips from his lips.

I look back at him for a long moment and then move away, and go back to the bathroom. I turn on the hot water and wash his blood off of the blade. I want it to be clean for her turn.

I turn off the water when the last of his blood washes down the drain. *I told you it was his time.*

I nod. "And soon it will be hers."

34

"It's been awhile. I was really surprised when I got your voice mail."

Back at Barnes&Noble. Early morning. Sitting across from Aida. I'd called her the night before and had gotten her voice mail. I was surprised she hadn't answered. I hate leaving messages, but I left one telling her to meet me in the morning. I'd told Marlene that Aida had nothing to do with what was going on. That anything dealing with Kyra had happened before she'd come into the picture. I did believe my own words, but I wanted to talk to Aida face to face and see for myself that there was no tension in her body language. That there was no worry in her eyes.

I wanted to be sure that she was safe.

I said, "I've been busy."

Aida smiled. "I know. Marlene told me you've taken on a new client."

I nodded. "I have."

"It's been awhile since you've had one. I was beginning to wonder if you'd gotten bored with the job."

Although I'd warned her about the dangers of our profession, I hadn't told her about Kyra. Kyra had been an exception to the rule. She was a freak of nature in the way that a hurricane blowing through the streets of New York would be. I didn't think there'd be another Kyra or another situation similar in any way.

I shook my head. "I wasn't bored. I just needed a break.

Besides, I trained you, so I knew you had things under control."

Aida smiled. She was still a little rough around the edges, but she'd definitely grown in the six months I'd known her. It was a growth that wasn't evident in her height or the way she dressed.

Her eyes.

That's where her growth had been evident. If you didn't know her, you'd never notice, and even if you did, if you looked too fast, you'd miss it. Miss the change in them. The increase in the level of maturity in her gaze. The intensity of the self-awareness and the depth of the scrutiny beneath her brown pupils.

She may not have experienced anything tragic, but in her eyes I could see that the experiences she'd had thus far were shaping her, molding her. I'd exposed her to situations she knew existed, but only at a superficial level. Now she was in deep and, by the gleam in her eye, she was enjoying the depth to which she'd gotten so far.

"So I hear you're working on a new client."

Aida nodded. "Yeah. Setting up a woman's husband."

"Does she want pictures?"

"No. She wants to walk in on us, but she doesn't want us doing anything."

"I see."

Aida's mouth dropped at the corners slightly.

"It looks as though you're disappointed."

Aida shook her head. "Not really disappointed. I just don't really understand her. She wants to walk in so that she can use that to force him to go to marriage counseling."

"I see."

"I mean, what the hell? She's so completely fucking dependant on this guy, it just doesn't make sense to me. I mean how can she be that weak? How could any woman be that fucking weak?"

I raised an eyebrow. It was a question I'd stopped asking a long time ago. It just was.

Aida sighed. "Personally, I don't even understand what the hell he sees in her. She's attractive, but aside from that, she doesn't really have anything going for herself."

I looked at her closely. Her jaw seemed to be getting tighter as she spoke. The muscles in her shoulders and neck becoming more tense.

"I mean, really . . . she's probably the last person I'd really have expected him to be with."

My eyes unblinking and very serious, I said, "This seems to be bothering you quite a bit. His being with her."

Aida shook her head. "N . . . no. It's not."

I closed my eyes a bit. "How many times have you gone out with him?"

She shrugged. "Just a couple. Met him for coffee twice, and had dinner another time."

"Have you fucked him?"

Aida's eyes opened wide and her back straightened ever so slightly. Had I not been waiting for the reaction I could have missed it. But I was waiting.

In our profession, fucking was part of the job sometimes. But only when it was necessary to ensure that the husband slipped on the particular day that was requested, or when requested by the pissed off or very desperate wife.

It's all about the thrill of the chase for men. They go after pussy with all guns blazing, their ears pinned back, the pink of their gums showing as their teeth are bared. Their intensity is high and the fire in their eyes is bright. When they want it, they want it now and they want it bad. They want that release.

But men have short attention spans. And after their load is shot, the fire dims. They'll never turn down an opportunity for more pussy of course, but they won't necessarily go after it with the same zeal.

Fucking was a powerful tool to be used, but contrary to popular belief, not fucking a man was an extremely more potent hand to play.

Put the pussy in the man's face.

Give him a good, long whiff of it.

Let him practically feel its wetness, its warmth around his shaft.

Then pull it away suddenly without reason, without apology as his dick throbs and is on the verge of exploding.

This was a tactic, that, when employed, would make a man go crazy. This was a tactic that men couldn't handle. They had to have it. They couldn't take the almost have.

I'd told Aida about this skill, but as I watched her, I knew that her answer was going to be a lie.

She shook her head and stammered a little as she said, "No."

I looked at her. I'd observed from a distance once or twice and had seen her work. She was good and had learned a lot. But she was also young. And no matter how much I tried to show her the ropes, her youth was a barrier that only time could truly break down.

I accepted that.

I said, "OK."

Her chest collapsed as she tried to discreetly let out a sigh of relief.

I held back a smile.

She quickly took a sip of the Frappuccino she bought. I took a sip of my latte.

"So other than your client, everything else is going well?" I asked.

She nodded. "Yes."

There seemed to be something more to her answer, but

I left it alone. "Has anyone bothered you? Left calls, letters, etcetera?"

She shook her head. "No. Why? Should I be worried about something?"

I looked at her. Thought about telling her about the clippings and my mother's visit, but doing that would have required me to talk about Kyra and what had happened. She'd had no calls, no letters, or strange visits; as I told Marlene—she had nothing to worry about.

I shook my head and took another sip of my latte, which was growing tepid. "No. You're still new to this. Just remember to be careful."

Aida smiled. "I will. And believe me, I am."

I nodded.

"Lisette . . ." She paused and traced a finger around the rim of her bottle. There was a crease in her forehead as her thin eyebrows closed together.

I said, "Yes?"

"Can . . . can I ask you something?"

I watched her and said, "Yes?"

She opened her mouth and then hesitated. Looked like she was contemplating changing her mind, before she said, "Have you ever found yourself getting—I don't know—caught up with any of the men you've set up?"

I looked at her with hard eyes.

She looked down at her Frappuccino.

Had I been caught up?

I thought about Ryan. Like Marlene's ex, Steve. Attractive and incredibly cocksure. He was also smooth and honest. He was married and he left it up to the woman to decide whether she could handle it or not. It was wrong, and made him an ass, but there was a nobility to his infidelity that I liked.

Had I been caught up?

I was intrigued by him. I liked the way he worked his dick,

hence the sex that contradicted my tactic theory. He was away on business, but in a couple of days, he was going to return, and when he did, I was going to set him up because his sister-in-law was paying me to do so.

Had I been caught up?

I looked at Aida as she watched me, her finger circling her bottled drink. In time, she'd figure out how to not get in over her head, the way she was now. This was something I couldn't teach her.

I said, "No. Have you?"

She looked at me for a lingering second and then looked to the right as a woman at the counter by the café complained about her coffee not being hot enough. Aida stared at her for a moment before she looked back at me. "No," she said, her voice strong. "Never. I know better than that."

I stared at her for a few seconds, and then nodded, grabbed my purse, and stood up. "Of course you do," I said. "I have an appointment I have to get to. Call me when your job is finished."

"OK."

I looked at her. Everyone went through certain experiences in life that helped define them. Aida was having hers, as I'd had mine.

Speaking of experiences.

I turned around and walked away. I still hadn't found Myles and that had me upset. I'd called his job, and all I'd gotten was that he had gone away for a few days, and they didn't know when he'd be back. A family emergency, they'd been told.

The excuse had been good enough for the people in his company, but it hadn't been for me.

Something was wrong.

I could feel it.

And it had to do with the someone who was out there. The someone who had yet to make his or her presence known.

I grabbed my BlackBerry and hit speed dial #1 for Marlene.

"Lisette," she answered.

It was quiet on her end. Benjamin must have been napping. "Lisa," I said. "Have you talked to her?"

Marlene sighed. "No. But I did find out that she had an emergency and had to leave the country for a few days. She's supposed to be coming back home on Saturday morning."

"I want you talking to her when her plane lands," I said, my voice no-nonsense.

"OK."

I was about to end the call when Marlene said, "Ummm . . . I hate to tell you this, but Rebecca Stantin called again."

I clenched my jaw.

"She told me what she wants. Is she serious?"

I shook my head as I headed to my car. Rebecca Stantin. She was really starting to annoy me. I said, "Unfortunately."

"What do you want me to do about her? She's pretty insistent about wanting to work with you."

I stood beside my car, my keys in my hand, and looked around in the bookstore's parking lot. Some people were getting into their cars and driving away. Others were just opening their doors, while some were closing them and heading to the store's entrance. I looked at all of them with hard, scrutinizing eyes. Wondered if any of them was the someone I needed to find.

I was on edge and, goddammit, that bothered me.

I exhaled and said, "You think of something to tell her, Marlene. I don't have time for her shit."

I ended the call, opened my car door, and tossed my BlackBerry onto the passenger seat.

Before I got in and pulled off, I took one last look around. *I'll find you*, I thought. *I'll find you.*

35

Saturday night.

My last night with Ryan.

His sister-in-law's night of retribution.

I'd called Shante earlier in the day to confirm that everything had still been in order.

"Everything is set," she'd said. "I stopped by their house and begged Sam to come on an overnight trip to Atlantic City with me and some other girlfriends of mine. She resisted at first, but I, along with my dear old brother-in-law, managed to convince her that she needed to get out and have some fun. Now she's out getting her hair and nails done. I'm going back around six o'clock to pick her up. I'm sure you'll get a call from Ryan before then."

The tone in Shante's voice had been higher than usual, and the speed in which she talked was faster. She was beyond excited for the moment.

I said, "I thought it was just supposed to have been a night out in the city."

"I figured an overnight trip would be better."

The variation in the plan bothered me. "How are you going to get her back to the house if you're supposed to be going to Atlantic City?"

"I'm going to pretend to get a call from another friend, who has an emergency and needs my help. I'll tell Sam that I need to take her home and get to my friend's house right away."

"And if Sam says she can go with you instead of inconveniencing you by having you take her home?"

"She won't. The friend I'll bring up is one she doesn't like."

"OK."

"I'll make sure we're back at her house by one-thirty. I trust that you'll be ready?"

"I will. And I trust that you'll have the rest of the money for me tomorrow."

"Yes. Absolutely."

Everything finalized, I called Ryan about an hour later.

"I'm glad your maybe became a yes," he said, answering the call.

"How was the fucking on the beach?"

"Nowhere near as good as it would have been with you. I'm glad you called. I thought about you while I was gone. If I'd had your number, I would have called you and asked you to come and meet me somewhere."

"It would have been a wasted call."

"At least I would have gotten to hear your voice."

I hmmed.

"So are you free tonight?"

"Nothing's come up . . . yet."

"Good. Have you ever been to the Hamptons?"

"Once or twice."

"Make it a third time and come and see me. I'll cook dinner for you."

"Won't your wife have a problem with an extra house guest?"

"She won't be home. She's going to Atlantic City with her sister. They'll be staying overnight."

"I see."

"Say yes, Lisette. We'll have dinner, some wine, and afterward we can take a late-night swim. I have an in-ground, nine-foot pool."

"Aren't you worried about your neighbors seeing you swimming with someone who's not your wife?"

"The pool is completely fenced in. No one will see anything. We can swim with only our birthday suits on."

"Sounds enticing."

"Say yes," Ryan said again.

I said, "You're sounding desperate, Ryan. It's not very attractive."

It was very unlike him.

He said, "It's not that I'm desperate. I've just been watching a lot of *Turn Up the heat with G. Garvin* lately. I want to impress you with my skills."

I laughed. "I'm not easily impressed."

"I think I'm up for the challenge."

"Others thought they were up for the challenge too," I said.

"The others didn't have the skills I have."

"Is that so?"

"Say yes and you'll see."

I was silent for a few seconds. I wanted to make him think I was really giving his request some thought. As I did, I thought about Aida's question to me.

Had I been caught up?

My answer to her had been the truth, but I had to admit— Ryan was intriguing.

I said, "OK."

"Great! I'll come by and pick you up around seven. Where in the city do you live?"

"I'll drive to you," I said.

"Navigating your way here can be a little tricky. I don't mind coming to pick you up."

"I have a GPS. The navigation won't be a problem."

Ryan sighed. "OK."

I took his address down and then ended the call. As intriguing as he was, I was looking forward to getting the job completed. I needed to be able to focus solely on trying to figure out who sent my mother to me, and I needed to be ready for them—because I had no doubt they were going to make their next move.

I spent the rest of the day getting ready. I went to Saks and bought a new outfit. It wasn't necessary. I just felt like wearing something new. After Saks I called Myles's cell phone and made another pass by Starbucks. As had been the case the previous times, he was nowhere to be found. I couldn't help but wonder, had his disappearance been related to the person who sent the clippings? After all, if this person knew about Kyra, then he or she knew about Myles too.

I'd spoken to Marlene before I confirmed everything with Shante. She still hadn't spoken to Lisa. She was supposed to have called me back later on in the afternoon with a better update. I was now on my way to the Hamptons and she still hadn't called.

I grabbed my BlackBerry and hit the speed dial.

She spoke before I could say anything. "Lisette I'm so sorry I didn't call you earlier, but I had to take Ben to the ER."

"Is he OK?"

Marlene took a breath. "He had an allergic reaction to something and his eyes became swollen and he broke out in hives. I was in the hospital all afternoon with him while the doctors ran test after test trying to figure out what caused the reaction."

She paused to take another breath.

"Is Ben OK now?" I asked.

"Yes. Thank God. The doctors still don't know why he broke out, but they managed to get the hives to go away and the swelling in his eyes to go down. He's sleeping on top of me right now."

"Good."

"With everything going on, I didn't get a chance to call Lisa again. But I'll do it now and call you back."

"OK."

"Any luck with Myles?"

"No."

"Damn. I know you're not one to worry, but his sudden drop off the face of the earth worries me, Lisette."

I clenched my jaw and tightened my fingers around the steering wheel as I drove down Route 27.

Marlene was right.

I was never one to worry.

But this had to do with Kyra, and that connection did have me worried.

I said, "Call Lisa, Marlene. She's the key. And give Benji a kiss for me."

I ended the call and hit play on my iPod. Pink Martini began to play. "Amado Mio." I took a breath and let it out slowly.

Thoughts of Lisa, Myles, my mother, and the newspaper clipping, the person who had sent her, and Kyra ran through my mind, along with their accompanying whos, whats, whens, wheres and whys.

"Amado Mio."

I listened to it. Listened to Chyna Forbes' sweet voice.

I drove at a steady seventy-five miles per hour and focused. I had to get centered. I had a job to complete.

36

Aida was conflicted.

In a few hours she was going to help Vivian Steele back Griffin into a corner and force him to go to marriage counseling because she loved her husband, despite the fact that he slept with other women, and because she was a dependant bitch who was too damned scared to stand on her own two feet.

The day after her work was done, Aida would receive the other half of the $50,000 Vivian was desperate enough to pay. Check in hand, she'd go to the bank, deposit the money, and then head to SoHo to buy a new designer purse from Marc Jacobs. After that, she'd go to Alexis Bittar for a pair of teardrop earrings and one or two knuckle-engulfing rings. Purse and jewelry in hand, her next step would be Te Casan on West Broadway for a pair of sleek black and brown leather boots, and a pair of pixie-like, pointy-toed pumps. She'd then go to Barneys New York on Madison Avenue for some designer tops to match the shoes, and a few pairs of the latest hot denim jeans. Her day would end at Juvenex on West Thirty-second Street, where she'd get a full body scrub.

This excursion was a ritual for her. It was something she did after every completed job. It was something she always looked forward to.

Until now.

Aida sighed and looked at herself in her dressing table mirror. She was drop-dead sexy in a form-fitting, sleeveless black dress that stopped two inches above her knees, and her hair was teased up into a bun so that her neck and shoulders were exposed.

She always went extra sexy for her final night, her final performance. She wanted the men she fucked over to remember her despite the drama and shit they would be going through dealing with their scorned wives. She got off on knowing that they would.

Until now.

Now she was troubled.

She had to set Griffin up. It was what she was being paid to do. She had to set him up and keep moving. But looking at herself in the mirror, she admitted to herself that she didn't know if she could go through with it.

Lisette may have never fallen, but Aida had.

She'd tried to fight the truth, especially after her conversation with Lisette, but the harder she tried to fight, the more the truth refused to stay buried.

She was falling for Griffin like she'd never fallen for anyone before, and the thought of helping Vivian force him to remain with her had Aida's stomach in knots.

Vivian didn't fucking deserve him.

To hell with her looks, she wasn't in his league. Griffin was sexy, successful, and overflowing with swagger. Vivian didn't complement him. She didn't bring anything to the table.

"Why the fuck should I help you?" she asked herself.

She stared at her reflection. Her reflection stared back, with hard stark, unblinking eyes. Eyes that said, "*You know why, bitch.*"

Aida dropped her chin to her chest and sighed.

She knew why. The life she lived was dependent on helping Vivian get exactly what she wanted. She had no choice.

And it sucked.

For the first time, she disliked her job. For the first time, she wished she'd never taken the assignment. Of course, she would have never met Griffin had she not.

She looked at herself. "Meeting him isn't the fucking problem though, is it?" She slammed her palm down on the dressing table. "*Cono!*"

She exhaled and looked down at her watch. She had to get on the road. It was going to take about an hour to get to Griffin's, who, when she spoke to him earlier to confirm their date was still on, had begged her to give him more time and arrive by nine o'clock. He was cooking her dinner. A meal she'd requested. Rice with potatoes and red kidney beans, topped by baked chicken. Griffin said he'd felt a connection with her.

He was a liar.

Aida knew this.

But as he'd made that statement, she felt that she'd seen truth in his sexy, brown eyes.

Aida gave herself a long, hard look in the mirror. She was a home wrecker. Griffin was a man who deserved to have his home wrecked, because, ultimately, he was just like all of the other men she'd taken down. Only she wasn't taking him down. She was helping Vivian, stay with him. Vivian who had no right being with him.

Aida stared.

Her reflection stared back at her and said, "You know what to do."

Aida nodded and then turned around.

She knew what to do.

But could she?

37

"Are you serious? Rebecca, you're . . . you're crazy!"

Rebecca sat up. "How am I being crazy, Kay?"

"Because . . ." Kay Gardiner looked from left to right as though she and Rebecca weren't the only ones in her home. "You just offered to seduce Craig."

"Yeah, and why is that crazy?" Rebecca looked at her friend with a raised eyebrow and the right corner of her mouth closed tight and hitched up.

After her adventure with Cole at the hotel, Rebecca had become more determined than ever to convince Lisette that she could and would be great at setting up an unsuspecting husband. She'd called Marlene numerous times, practically begging for another meeting with Lisette. She was sure that one more face-to-face meeting would have been all she needed to convince Lisette to give her the opportunity. Her confidence was high, and she just knew that she'd take the opportunity and turn it into gold.

Lisette would be pleased, impressed, and maybe even a little jealous of the skill she'd demonstrate. Rebecca just needed that chance.

Unfortunately, getting Lisette to agree to meet with her again was proving to be damn near impossible.

It stung when Lisette brushed her request off and told her to go home as though she were a child. For a couple of days, Rebecca actually began to question the decision she'd made.

Maybe being a home wrecker wasn't what she was supposed

to be doing. Lisette hadn't verbalized it, but her eyes and the brush-off had said it all; maybe she wasn't good enough. She was talking a good game, but when the time came, perhaps she wouldn't have the guts to go through with it. Who the hell was she to think the name she'd taken on—her destiny— was to help other women?

For three days, Rebecca doubted herself, her ability, her belief that doing what Lisette did was supposed to be in her future. But then her soon-to-be ex, Bruce, called, begging her for another chance.

"Please, 'Becca. I need you at my side. The congregation needs to see our holy union. They need to know that Christ can truly fix all things. That Christ can heal all wounds."

Bruce's words and tone of voice seemed genuine, and, for a moment, Rebecca thought about the parishioners. Many of them envied Bruce and Rebecca's partnership. On different occasions, comments were made about their blessed union, and how perfect their paring was. But of course they'd all been looking through a one-way mirror. They never knew about the horror behind the glass. The physical and emotional hell that Rebecca went through. What they saw as perfection had really been the perfect deception.

"I'm sorry, Bruce, but it's over between us, and it's staying that way. And it's Rebecca."

His voice with a harder edge to it, Bruce tried again. "Please, Rebecca. The Lord works in mysterious ways. Sometimes He puts us through trials and tribulations that we don't always understand. I know I was wrong for some of the things I did, but—"

"Some?" Rebecca cut in. "Are you kidding me?"

"I've been praying on it a lot, Rebecca, and I believe the good Lord put me through those things to make me a better man."

"Put *you* through those things? I don't recall me ever

putting my hands on you, or speaking down to you," Rebecca snapped.

"You may not believe me, but it tore me up inside when I wronged you, Rebecca. In some ways I think I hurt more than you did."

"What!"

"Your wounds healed, but mine stayed with me as guilt. And when you left, those wounds got wider. The Lord made you go away to teach me how to be a better man. Give me a chance, Rebecca. You'll see I've changed."

Rebecca could only shake her head at Bruce's words and rationale for the things he'd done. "Bruce," she said, glad that the conversation was taking place over the phone and not in person, "I'm glad you realize the error of your ways, but my answer stays the same. It's over."

"But, Rebecca—"

"I still have the pictures, Bruce. So does my friend. Do yourself a favor and find another woman to be a changed man for, and don't call me anymore."

"You bitch!" Bruce yelled out suddenly. "Do you have any idea what I'm going through right now? Do you know how embarrassing it is for me to walk around now? I'm no longer just Pastor Bruce Stantin. I'm now the *divorced* Pastor Bruce Stantin. I've lost respect in people's eyes. They may not say it, but it's in everyone's fucking eyes. The stigma of being divorced is not a good one for me, Rebecca. Goddammit—you need to bring your ass back where you belong!"

Bruce paused and breathed heavily into the phone. Images of him with his eyes closed to slits, his nostrils flared wide, and his jaw hard, flashed through Rebecca's mind. This image used to make her shiver. Now it just made her shake her head and frown.

"You have a gift, Bruce," she said, her voice as calm as a serene lake on a sunny day with no wind. "I truly believe the people need you and your gift of spreading God's words. But you need help. And I don't think the Lord's help will be enough. Now . . . good-bye. And don't call me again, or I swear to you, everyone will see those fucking pictures. Trust me, the stares you get now will be nothing compared to the stares you'll get after that."

Rebecca hung up the phone as Bruce called her a bitch again.

That phone call erased all doubt from Rebecca's mind, and she knew in her soul that setting up pathetic, weak men was her calling, her destiny.

Darrin had been a test run that she needed to do just for final confirmation. She wanted to tell Lisette all about it, but couldn't get through. Discouragement tried to rear its ugly head again, but one morning, she woke up and realized that if she really wanted to capture Lisette's attention and respect, then she had to truly do the deed.

That's where Kay came in.

Contrary to the shock in her voice, Rebecca knew that having proof of her husband being unfaithful to her was something Kay needed desperately. She was miserable. Her husband, Craig, was and always had been unfaithful to her, but because of the life he provided for her, Kay dealt with the disrespect on a daily basis. She had no say in the marriage. They did what Craig wanted to do. Went where he wanted to go.

Lisette had shown Rebecca how to gain control and Rebecca knew that, without a doubt, she could do the same for Kay.

"It's . . . it's crazy because . . ." Kay paused and frowned.

Rebecca leaned forward in the black leather love seat she was sitting on. She remembered when Kay called her one day to complain about the furniture.

"It's so . . . so manly. It's something a bachelor would have!"

"So tell him to take it back."

"I can't."

"Why not?"

Kay sighed. *"It's his money, Rebecca. I don't really have a say about what he does with it."*

Rebecca put her hand on Kay's knee now and gave it a gentle squeeze. "Kay, Craig is a controlling, cheating son-of-a-bitch, but I know you don't want to leave him because of the life you have. What I'm offering to do isn't for you to leave him. It's simply to give you something you can use to shift the balance of control."

"So you want to seduce him at our barbeque?"

"I know you've seen the way Craig looks at me, Kay. You know it wouldn't really be me seducing him so much as it would be me just giving him what he wants and has probably had in his mind. All I have to do is play up to him when he's alone, and have you walk in on it happening."

Kay shook her head and looked at her. "I'm sorry for asking this, but . . . are you sure you don't just want Craig for yourself?"

Rebecca gave her a disappointed frown. "Come on, Kay."

Kay sighed. "I know, I know."

"Just let me do this, Kay. I promise you'll be able to get rid of this ugly leather and get what you want without him saying a word. I promise you'll be able to do a lot of things after that, because, trust me, letting you do what you want is far less costly than going through a divorce. Just ask Bruce."

"If you're guaranteeing me so much control, why did you leave Bruce?"

"I had a path I needed to follow," Rebecca replied with a glint in her eye.

Kay sighed again. "You're really serious, aren't you?"

"You're miserable, Kay. And this furniture is disgusting."

Kay laughed. "I hate this furniture so damned much! And the marble rhinoceros by the fireplace, and the ugly-ass pictures on the walls. Hell, the only thing that I like is the house itself, and that's only because you can't go wrong with a house in the Hamptons."

Rebecca and Kay broke out in laughter for several seconds.

"So you're really serious," Kay said one more time. It was more a statement than a question.

Rebecca looked at her friend, whom she'd met in aerobics class two years ago and had an instantaneous bond with. "Say yes, Kay, and you'll have this place redecorated before the summer's over."

Kay looked around in her living room. The house she shared with Craig was a four-bedroom, four-bath, 4,523-square foot dream home with cathedral ceilings, a study, a sunroom, and an in-ground pool in the back.

She sighed again. "Can I have a day or two to think about it?"

Rebecca nodded. "Of course." She got the chills. She'd asked for a couple of days, but Rebecca could see in her friend's eyes that she was eventually going to say yes. She stood up. "Just call. I'll be fine with whatever decision you make."

Kay smiled. "OK."

They walked to the front door, opened it, and stepped outside. Dusk was on the horizon. Rebecca looked at her watch. It was nearing eight-thirty. She gave Kay a hug. "Make sure you call me, OK?"

"I will." Kay pulled back, and then said, "Wow," as she looked past Rebecca's shoulder to the right.

Rebecca turned. "What's wow?"

Kay pointed. "That house. It's been sold for months, but other than a guy who comes and cuts the grass and takes care of the flowers, I've never seen another single, solitary person."

Rebecca looked at the house. An attractive black man, wearing a black tank top and blue jeans, was jogging away from his Escalade and heading inside with a black duffle bag over his shoulder. His arms were well sculpted, his chest was thick, and he had a nice ass. "I can't see his face, but I sure do like the body," she said as he slammed the door shut behind him.

"I've never even seen a moving truck over there," Kay said.

"You must have been out the day he moved in."

"I guess. Anyway, there's a *Sex and the City* marathon going on right now. You know how I am about my *Sex and the City*."

"Go watch your show, girl," Rebecca said. "Just make sure you call me."

"I will. I promise."

Rebecca gave Kay a wave and then headed to her car, while Kay rushed inside.

Rebecca couldn't help but smile. She was sure she was going to have actual proof to provide to Lisette soon, and once she did that, she'd be on her way. She couldn't wait for Kay's call.

She dug into her purse as she reached her Lexus coupe, and pulled out her keys. As she did, a Mercedes-Benz pulled into the driveway of the house that was now magically occupied. Music could be heard coming from inside of the car. A sweet, sexy, sounding song. Rebecca stood still beside her car and listened to it for a moment before the music stopped and the Benz's driver's door opened.

Rebecca's heart skipped a beat as Lisette stepped out of the car. "No way," she whispered.

She quickly got into her car and softly closed the door.

"No way," she said again. "No way that she's here right now."

She looked through her slightly tinted window. She was feeling anxious; maybe her imagination had turned the man's guest into Lisette. The sun had almost completely descended, but there was still just enough light for Rebecca to confirm that she hadn't been seeing things.

There was no denying it; Lisette was here!

But why?

"Does it matter why?" she asked herself. "She's here."

Destiny, she thought.

It had to be.

Rebecca smiled and stared at the woman she just knew she'd be working with eventually.

38

Ryan's house.

Eight-thirty.

He'd asked me to get there by eight. He said he had the evening planned out and wanted to stick to a schedule he'd come up with to ensure that we did everything he wanted us to do. He wanted to give me a night I'd never forget.

At one-thirty in the morning, his night was going to be unforgettable too.

I would have been there by eight, but I hit traffic. A two-car fender bender. Had to drive in one lane doing stop and go for several miles. The delay put me behind by half an hour.

I cut the engine, but let my iPod continue to play. I never liked cutting my song off before it ended. As Chyna Forbes sang about things I didn't believe in, I looked at Ryan's house.

It was a stylish home made of red brick, with an arched entry and arched windows, whose vertical blinds were closed, giving no view of the inside. The landscaping was meticulous with perfectly cut grass, and flowers running along the length of the house beneath the windows. It was a beautiful, albeit, boring-looking, house that almost seemed unused.

But that wouldn't be the case tonight.

I closed my eyes for a moment and listened to my song. My favorite part—the breakdown—was coming up. Pink Martini. One day I'd have to see them perform live. Something I hadn't done yet.

The break down began.

Piano rifts accompanied by the chime on my BlackBerry.

I looked at it. Marlene, calling me back.

I answered. "Did you get Lisa?"

"Y . . . I . . . got . . . ette . . . ound . . . ease."

I couldn't understand a word she'd said, but there seemed to have been panic in her voice. "Marlene, you're breaking up."

She tried again. " . . . urn . . . ease . . . ette . . . it's . . . up . . . on't."

I pulled my cell away from my ear and looked at it. I had barely one bar. I said, "I'm in a bad area. Hold on."

I powered down my iPod, opened my door, and stepped out. I put my cell to my ear again. "OK. Try again. What did you say?"

"Urn . . . ound . . . ow!"

As Marlene spoke, the front door of the house opened. Ryan, dressed surprisingly casually in blue jeans and a black tank top, stepped out. He walked toward me, his steps determined, almost hurried.

I put up my index finger as he got close. He paused and remained a few feet away.

Into the BlackBerry, I said, "Marlene, I still can't get what you're saying. Try texting me."

I ended the call and clenched my jaw. I thought about her recounting to me her afternoon with Benji at the ER, and wondered if the hives and swelling had come back.

In front of me, closer now, Ryan said, "Everything OK?"

I looked at him. His eyes were on me intensely. I thought about Marlene and the panic and said, "I don't know." I looked down at my phone. I had two bars now. I thought about calling Marlene back, but then decided against it. I was sure the minute I dialed, I'd lose the bar and have a shitty connection again. "This is a bad area for cell phones," I said.

Ryan nodded. He was sweating as if he'd been working out. "You'll be lucky to get a call out here."

I clenched my jaw again, took a glance at my phone, and wondered if she'd heard me tell her to text me.

"Let's go inside," Ryan said.

I looked up at him. "You go ahead. I'm going to try to make a call."

Ryan flexed his jaw and looked past me to the main road. "I'm telling you, it won't work," he said, looking back at me. "You can use the phone inside. Come on."

I stared at him.

The muscles in his neck were tight as his line of sight went from me back to the road. He'd offered to let me use his phone, but the tone in his voice had a nervous edge to it, and his last statement to "come on'" sounded like an order.

"Expecting someone?" I asked, taking a glance behind me.

"What?" Ryan asked. He sounded irritated now.

"You keep looking to the road. Are you expecting someone?"

Ryan shook his head. It looked like there was more sweat on it than before. "No," he said. "Come on. Let's go inside."

"After my call."

"I said you can use my phone."

I closed my eyes a bit. His stance had shifted. Had become almost predatory.

Something wasn't right.

I adjusted my stance too. "I'll try my phone," I said defiantly.

Ryan looked at me, his eyes dark, his nostrils flaring. Then he looked to the road again.

I watched as he put his eyes back on me.

The night air was warm and thick with tension.

Something was definitely wrong and dangerously familiar.

I thought about the past and being out at night during a rainstorm.

I balled my right hand into a tight fist.

Ryan seemed to lean forward on his toes. It was something people did when they were about to pounce and attack.

My heart beat heavily. Slow, thudding beats deep beneath my chest.

Someone out there said I knew what happened to Kyra.

Ryan's eyes closed. Became dark, angry slits. He looked past me again.

Behind me, I thought I heard the faint sound of music. Salsa.

My cell chimed its special tone indicating I'd received a text message.

I turned my phone upward as I looked down. On the screen in all caps were words that made my Adam's apple rise into the middle of my throat:

LISETTE, IT'S A SETUP! SHANTE HUNT IS THE PERSON LISA GAVE THE INFORMATION TO. TURN AROUND! CALL ME PLE...

I never got to read the rest of the message as searing volts of electricity ripped through my body and went straight through my nerves.

A taser.

I'd felt something cold pressed against my neck a half a second before the pain.

I'd never even seen Ryan move.

My BlackBerry fell from my hand as the muscles became jelly.

My legs, now rubber, gave way beneath me and I fell forward.

Another blast of electricity went through me as I did.

I barely felt the pain from the second wave of electric fire as I faded away into unconsciousness.

39

Aida was in a zone.

The Lebron Brothers were blasting from her speakers. Old salsa.

Aida didn't have much in common with her mother, but one thing she did get from her was her love for salsa. Real salsa. Salsa that started in the seventies. Hector Lavoe, Willie Colon, Ruben Blades, Eddie Pacheco; these and others were the people her mother played in the house daily. Aida didn't know life without the high hats, the trombones, the rhythmic bass, entrancing bass lines, the singers with the voices that fit perfectly. Reggeaton, bachata, merengue—Aida listened to these styles of music too, but none of them moved her the way the old salsa did. The newer salsa was OK, but it didn't have the same passion. When the musicians played and the singers sang, you felt every lick, every note. The words hit the way the writers meant them to.

Aida needed to relax. She was stressed and tight all over from stressing with the decision of doing what she knew she had to do. Griffin be dammed, ultimately, this was about maintaining. This was about her never having to do the nine-to-five.

Aida put the salsa on to get her blood pumping, to get her head right, and cruised down Route 27, slowing only briefly as highway crews cleaned up debris from a two-car accident. The time had come for her curtains to go up as she gave her final performance, while Griffin's went down as his act officially came to a close.

Aida exhaled and lowered the volume of her iPod as she pulled into the driveway of Griffin's house.

"Showtime," she whispered.

She sighed as she cut her engine. She would do what she had to do, but she was definitely going to miss Griffin. She grabbed her purse and stepped out of her car. "Shit," she said, looking up at the house. She hadn't really gotten her before, but looking at the house, she could see why Vivian Steele wouldn't want to let Griffin go. If she was a dependant bitch who had nothing going for herself and could live like this, she wouldn't want to let Griffin's ass go either.

She pulled her cell phone out of her purse to switch it from ring to vibrate and noticed that she had no service. "*Cono!*"

Although she didn't anticipate needing it, she still hated being stuck unable to make a call. She switched it to vibrate anyway and then shoved it back into her purse.

She took a final look around at the home's property. "Goddamned perfect," she said. She looked to her right. Griffin's neighbor's house was just as nice. So was the silver Lexus coupe sitting in the driveway.

She took a final glance at the coupe and then turned and headed toward Griffin's front door. She'd anticipated a hell of a night. Food, wine, sex, and a climax Vivian wouldn't forget, because Aida had decided that there was no way in hell she was going to be naked with Griffin on the bed, and not have him inside of her. It hadn't been what Vivian had requested, but, fuck it, if Aida had to deal with this being her last night with Griffin, then Vivian would just have to deal with him fucking another woman.

Aida stepped to the front door, marveled at how big it was, and then pressed the doorbell. "Showtime," she whispered again.

A few minutes went by without an answer. Aida pressed the bell again, and tapped her foot on the ground as another minute went by. She hated being made to wait. She was about to press the bell again and knock, when the door opened.

"Hey there," Griffin said with a smile.

Aida looked at him. He was dressed in a black tank top, a pair of blue jeans, with black boots on his feet. She hadn't expected him to wear any particular outfit, but she hadn't expected him to be dressed as casually as he was. She also hadn't expected him to be sweating the way he was, either. At least not yet.

"Hola," she said.

Griffin smiled. "I do love that Spanish shit," he said. He stepped to the side. "Sorry I kept you waiting. I was taking care of something."

Aida said, "Sweating like that, I hope it was something good." She stepped past him into the foyer with marble flooring. "Something smells good," she said.

Griffin closed the door behind her, locked it, and then stepped in front of her. "Thanks. Your meal is just about ready."

Aida smiled. "Can't wait to see what you made."

"I think you'll enjoy it. Especially dessert," Griffin said with a mischievous smile

"Dessert, huh?"

"I have something special for you."

"Can I get a hint?"

Griffin shook his head. "No hints. You'll just have to wait."

"You're mean," Aida said, rising up on her tiptoes and wrapping her arms around his neck.

"You haven't seen mean yet," Griffin said. He wrapped his arms around her waist and pressed his lips against hers and kissed her hard and forcefully, driving his tongue into her mouth.

Aida moaned as he pressed his crotch against her. He was hard. Damn hard. As they kissed, she thought about the decision she'd made—to do the job and walk away. It hadn't been an easy decision, but she had every intention of sticking to it. But kisses like the one Griffin was giving put the doubt she'd let go of right back into the forefront of her mind. She reached for his zipper, grabbed it, and started to pull it down.

Before she could, Griffin pulled away.

"What's wrong?" Aida asked.

Griffin clenched his jaw. Aida didn't know why, but he seemed irritated.

He said, "Let's go eat."

Aida grabbed a hold of the top of his belt. "I have a better idea . . . let's go to the living room where you can give me a grand tour."

Griffin shook his head. "As tempting as it is, I don't want the food to get cold."

Aida raised an eyebrow. "Are you serious? We can always warm it up."

Griffin shook his head again. "It won't taste as good as coming fresh off the stove."

"But—"

"I busted my ass over the food, Aida! I want to eat now!"

His sudden outburst caught Aida by surprise. She looked at him. "Whoa," she said, not liking the sudden darkening look in his eyes. "What was that about?"

Griffin clenched his jaw again. "Sorry," he said. "I haven't eaten much today. I'm hungry and getting a headache. I promise the wait will be worth it."

Aida looked at him. His tone had softened, but the look in his eye hadn't changed. If anything, it seemed to get even darker. She said, "OK."

Griffin guided her to the dining room off to the right of the foyer. Based on how the exterior of the house had looked, she'd expected the inside to be decked out, but she was thoroughly disappointed when they stepped into the dining room. It was surprisingly bland and simple. The walls were white and bare. The carpeting seemed low grade and had several red stains. The dining table itself was small, round, and simply set for two with plates, forks, and wine glasses. There were no candles, no flowers—things Aida had expected.

Griffin walked to the table and pulled out a chair for her to sit down.

"Why do you have the blinds closed?" Aida asked. The room was unnervingly dark, as the only light was coming from the chandelier.

"I close the blinds at night to keep people from looking inside."

Aida nodded and sat down. She had an uncle who was the same way. Aida herself didn't like to close blinds. It felt claustrophobic.

Griffin pushed her in. "I'll get your plate," he said. He walked off to the kitchen.

When he left the room, Aida reached into her purse and pulled out her cell phone to see if she had a signal yet. "*Cono*," she whispered. Still no signal.

"You won't be able to use your phone out here," Griffin said, reappearing with a plate of food in one hand and a bottle of wine in the other. He walked to her and set a plate filled with yellow rice, red beans, baked chicken and salad down in front of her.

Aida put her phone down beside the plate. "*Arroz con pollo*," she said. "Now that's authentic."

Griffin smiled, but didn't reply, and went back into the kitchen, returning a few seconds later with his plate. He set it down and then grabbed her glass and filled it with red wine. He said, "I bought this while I was away this week," he said. "The guy in the store described it as a sweet wine with a surprising kick. It made me think of you."

Aida looked at the filled glass and smiled. "Sweet with a kick, huh? That's how you think of me?"

"Most definitely."

Aida smiled.

"Take a sip. Let me know if they were right."

"Aren't you going to join me?"

"Of course." Griffin went to his chair, sat down, and filled his glass. "I was looking forward to tonight," he said. He raised his glass. "Here's to a night you won't forget."

Aida smiled. "A night that we both won't forget."

"Here, here."

Aida took a healthy sip. "Wow. This has some serious kick for real," she said.

Griffin looked at her. "But is it sweet?"

Aida drank some more. "Very. It's good. A little strong, but good. You didn't drink any."

Griffin put his glass down and grabbed his fork. "I want to get some food in my stomach first. Hope you enjoy."

Aida took one more sip, put her glass down, and grabbed her fork. "I have no doubt that I will," she said.

She stuck her fork in the rice, and as she did, a wave of dizziness came over her. She blinked her eyes a few times.

"Are you OK?" Griffin asked.

She blinked several more times and opened her eyes wide, the dizziness worsening. "Y . . . yeah. I didn't eat much today, so I guess the wine is just getting to me."

She tried to lift her fork to her mouth, but couldn't, as the fork suddenly seemed to weigh two hundred pounds.

She suddenly felt warm all over, as though she were cooking from the inside. Her vision was becoming blurry as the room began to spin slowly.

"Shit," she whispered.

What the hell was happening to her? She'd drunk on an empty stomach before, but nothing like this had ever happened.

She lifted her head and looked at Griffin. He was blurring in and out of focus, staring at her, his arms criss-crossed against his chest.

Something was wrong.

"W . . . what . . ." Aida started to say slowly.

"Yes?" Griffin said, his voice faded, distant.

The spinning of the room increased in speed. "Wh . . . what have you done to me?"

Griffin rose from the table, and as he did, two people appeared beside him. Two women.

Aida looked at them. Tried to focus on their distorted faces. One person she didn't recognize at all, but the other . . .

Something about her seemed familiar.

Aida squinted, trying to force her image to remain in one place.

Slowly, the woman started to come into focus. Not much, but just enough for Aida to say, "I . . . I know you."

She felt nauseated, feverish, dizzy, weak. She tried to speak again, but couldn't.

She knew her. She was sure of it.

Aida felt her body slumping sideways.

She tried to right herself. Tried to keep from falling. Her life depended on it.

She knew her.

She tried again to rise as her body slumped further to the side.

Don't fall, she told herself.

Her head throbbed as the room spun out of control.

She raised her head again. Caught a glimpse of the blurry form, the person she recognized.

Vivian Steele.

Griffin's wife.

But she wasn't supposed to be there. That wasn't part of the plan.

Aida fell from the chair to the floor.

Before she passed out, she saw Vivian smile.

40

"Oh my God! Oh my God! Oh my God!"

Rebecca's heart was pounding as she took short, quick breaths.

"Oh my God!" she said again.

She'd watched in paralyzed shock as the attractive brotha in the black tank top put a taser to Lisette's neck and shocked her twice, and then threw her unconscious body over his shoulder and carried her inside.

The scene still hadn't registered with Rebecca when a woman emerged from the house, got into Lisette's car, and drove it into the garage, which had another car inside.

Rebecca shook, and after the woman rushed back into the home, Rebecca grabbed her cell. Lisette was in trouble. She had to call the police. But as she went to dial, she saw that she had no signal.

She cursed and made a move to get out of her car to run to use Kay's phone, but before she could, another car pulled into the driveway.

Rebecca sat immobile and watched as a young female got out of that car and took a look around. At one point, she thought she'd been spotted. It seemed as though the female had been looking right at her. But then she turned around and headed to the front door, where she knocked and was let in by the same man who'd attacked Lisette.

About ten minutes later, another woman emerged from

the house, got into the female's car, and pulled it to the side of the house where it couldn't be seen from the main road.

"Oh my God!" Rebecca said again.

She was still inside of her car, afraid to move in case someone came out again.

Lisette was in trouble and it looked like the young female was too.

Rebecca looked down at her cell phone again. Still no signal.

She took another quick series of breaths. She had to move. But what if someone saw her get out of the car? What if they saw her go to Kay's door?

All of Kay's lights were off, save the upstairs bedroom. And what looked like light was really just illumination from the television as Kay was watching her *Sex and the City* marathon.

"Oh, God," Rebecca whispered again.

She couldn't believe this was happening.

Lisette was in trouble while she'd been here determined to prove to Lisette that she was good enough. Determined to show that she could help women the way Lisette had helped her.

Help.

That's what Rebecca had to do.

Somehow, she had to help Lisette and the younger female. But how?

She looked toward Kay's house. The TV's illumination was still the only light being given off. "Damn."

She wanted to go, but if she knocked on the door, Kay would turn on the lights to come downstairs. If the people who'd taken Lisette saw that . . .

Rebecca shook her head.

She couldn't chance it.

But what could she do?

"Think, Rebecca. Think."

She looked at Kay's house again. Still nothing but the damn TV.

She grabbed her cell and took another look at it, knowing there would still be no signal, but hoping for a miracle anyway, which she didn't receive.

"Think, Rebecca."

She breathed in and out deeply. Her heart was jackhammering deep inside of her chest.

Lisette needed help.

"Come on, Rebecca . . . Think, damn it!"

And then it hit her.

She grabbed her purse from the passenger seat, reached into it, and wrapped her hand around something she always had with her, but never thought or hoped she'd have to use.

A 9 mm–caliber pistol.

After all she'd been through with Bruce, she swore she'd never allow herself to be in a position in which a man could ever take advantage of her again. She took self-defense classes and also became licensed to legally possess and carry a firearm after months of extensive training on the firing range.

The moment she'd purchased the weapon had been a frightening yet powerful one. She was the owner of something that could kill and that was scary, almost terrifying. But at the same time, she was also the owner of something that could keep her from ever being harmed again, and that was an almost invincible feeling.

Rebecca closed her hand tight around the gun.

Lisette was in trouble.

Rebecca was there.

It had to be destiny.

She closed her eyes. She didn't know exactly what she would do, but she had to do something.

She removed the 9 mm from her purse and held it in her lap. It suddenly felt so heavy. She said a silent prayer and asked God to protect her and give her the strength to do whatever it was that He would direct her to do.

"My steps will be yours, Lord. I trust in you to guide my hand."

She clicked the safety off, opened her eyes, then reached up and pressed the button to disable her interior light.

She took one final breath, held it for a long second, then let it out and opened her car door and got out slowly. Crouched low, she took another breath as her heart pounded.

Destiny, she thought.

"My steps will be yours, Lord. I trust you to guide my hand," she whispered again.

Rebecca moved toward the house, not knowing what she would do, just knowing that she would do something.

41

Shante Hunt.

The someone who'd been out there.

She'd set me up.

Before Marlene's text I'd known something was wrong. I'd heard it in Ryan's voice. I'd seen it in his eyes. He was going to attack me just like Steve had. His stance told me that. But I was ready for him, because I swore I was never going to be caught off guard again. And then the text came through and for the briefest of seconds I fucked up and looked down.

Now I was naked, my wrists and ankles tied to four posts of a bed, while my song played from somewhere in the room Ryan had taken me to.

My muscles were still weak from the volts of electricity I'd received. I slowly looked to my left and right. Eight candles were lit on night tables on both sides. Four on each side.

"That's a beautiful song."

I lifted my head as much as I could and looked down toward the foot of the bed. A woman I'd never seen before was standing in front of a dressing table, which also had eight candles spread across it. Along with the candles was a small shelf system. My iPod was plugged into it.

"I had another song I was going to play," the woman continued, "but we took this from your car and since you have it as the only song rated with five stars, I figured I'd play this one instead."

She closed her eyes, swayed her head from side to side, and began to hum off tune and off rhythm.

My heart beat heavily as I watched her in the eerie glow. I tried to pull my wrists and legs free from my bindings, but they were tied tight.

"I learned how to tie knots in Girl Scouts," she said. "You're not going anywhere. At least, not yet."

The knots tight as hell, I struggled again anyway.

The woman laughed.

I stopped after another few seconds of futility and looked at her again. She was still humming. I wanted to tell her to shut up, to stop disrespecting my song. Instead I asked, "Who the hell are you?"

She smiled again. "I bet you've been wondering that since your dear old mother came to see you."

I closed my eyes slightly at the mention of my mother.

"I was there watching you," she said. "You were so shocked. So knocked off of your fucking game. You looked around that parking lot so many times trying to find me." She paused and laughed. "You looked like a fucking bobblehead doll. It was hilarious. At one point I drove right past you. The thought of running you over crossed my mind, but instead I slowed down. I wanted you to see me, but of course you didn't."

She paused again and rocked her head from side to side as the breakdown in the song came. "Goddamn, this really is a sexy-ass song," she said. She opened her eyes then and looked at me. "Who am I? That's the fucking million-dollar question isn't it? Who am I? Why would I go through the trouble of paying a down-on-his-luck gigolo one hundred thousand dollars to play your ass? Who, by the way, did an exceptional job, don't you think? Maybe we should bring him in here so that you can tell him how good he was."

She turned her head toward the opened doorway.

"Oh, Ryan . . . you can come in now. Lisette has something she'd like to tell you."

I turned my head and looked at the doorway as Ryan appeared in its frame.

I looked at him as he looked at me.

A gigolo.

Hired to play me.

I clenched my jaw and tightened my fists as he walked into the room with a smile.

"Tell him, Lisette," she said. "Tell him how good he was. How convincing. Do you know he wanted to be an actor? But he went to jail for rape and attempted murder, so his acting career died after that. But of course his dream never died. But everyone deserves a second chance, right?" She turned and looked at Ryan, whose eyes were still on me. "You had a lot of fun didn't you, Ryan?"

Ryan smiled, came toward me, and got down on one knee beside me. He trailed his index finger up from the inside of my ankle to just below my pussy. "I had a lot of fun," he said, forcing two fingers inside of me.

I squirmed and tried to close my walls. He laughed and drove his fingers deeper, before pulling them out and slipping them into his mouth. He leaned forward and licked the side of my face. "A lot of fun," he said again. He stood up and backed away, smiling at me the whole time.

"Fuck you, you fucking coward!" I said.

Before I realized she'd moved, the woman I'd never met before came over and slapped me viciously across my mouth. "No!" she yelled. "Fuck you, you whore!" She slapped me again. Two times. "You cunt! You bitch!"

She breathed heavily as she glared at me. In the candlelight's glow, her eyes were demonic. It gave me the chills.

I gritted my teeth as pain shot through my lips. I tasted my blood as it trickled.

She looked down at me and smiled, and then walked back to the sound system and replayed my song. "Who am I?" she said again. "Who. The. Fuck. Am. I? Ryan . . . do you know?"

Ryan shrugged and shook his head. "I couldn't care less who you are. Just as long as you pay me the rest of my money."

The woman laughed and said, "I know that's right. Maybe we should ask your sister-in-law." She looked toward the doorway again. "Shante," she called. "Can you come in here? Lisette has an important question to ask you. Oh, and bring our other guest with you."

I was breathing heavily as I looked toward the room's entrance again and watched as Shante Hunt appeared with a limp and naked Aida in her arms.

She looked at me and smiled and then pushed Aida inside to the ground.

Aida.

I looked down at her as she lay on the floor on her side, her eyes open and staring up at me. Her lip was split and bleeding badly, as was her nose and a cut above her right eye.

I stared at her as she stared at me, unmoving. I was certain she'd been drugged. I held my breath and looked at her chest. It took a few seconds in the dim glow, but I saw it rise and fall. I exhaled slowly. She was still alive.

I looked at Shante, who was standing beside the woman. "You bitch!" I spat. I looked to the woman. "What the fuck do you want?"

The woman put her hand to her chest, and in a horrible French accent, said, "Moi?"

I struggled with my bindings, again to no avail. "Fuck you!" I said. "Fuck both of you!"

The woman rushed toward me again and wrapped her hands around my throat. "Shut your mouth, bitch!" she said, squeezing.

I thrashed, trying to make her loosen her grip, but couldn't get her to.

I gagged as she squeezed harder. I could feel my head getting light.

"You cunt!" she seethed. "You fucking whore!"

She applied more pressure.

I tried again to twist my head from side to side to get some relief. A wave of dizziness came over me as I began to see spots.

The woman squeezed and cursed me more.

From the corner of my eye, I saw Aida watching, her eyes wider than before.

I was going to die. I could feel its imminence coming.

And then the woman let go suddenly and slapped me again.

I coughed and gagged as I took a labored breath of air.

"Are you paying attention?" the woman said, looking over at Aida. "This is what happens when you think you're too fucking good."

Aida remained silent and unmoving.

The woman looked from her to me and watched me for a long, intense couple of seconds. "Back to the million-dollar question," she said, her voice suddenly calm. She went back to my iPod and replayed the song.

"I want to tell you a story," she said, picking up a razor blade and unfolding it. "Five years ago, two women met in a club. They talked, they kissed, and before they parted ways, they were completely devoted to one another. It was one of those rare connections you hear about in storybooks. You know, love at first sight. It was fucking magical.

"Anyway, these two ladies, who were so in love, began running scams together. They would take turns meeting, seducing, marrying, and then divorcing men for their money and possessions. It was a very good scam, but it wasn't perfect. The men they met weren't filthy rich, but they had just enough in their bank accounts. The women were able to live fairly well, but they kept looking for that big score, which they eventually did find when they met a pathetic man with more than enough money in the bank, named Myles Rogers."

She stopped talking and looked down at me.

I watched her, my heart racing, my mind grasping what she was telling me.

She must have seen the recognition in my eyes. She smiled a wicked smile. "You're getting it now, aren't you, you trick," she said with soft vehemence.

I stared at her but didn't reply.

She played with the blade in her hand and continued.

"So, these two women—these two soul mates—they decided that the more attractive of the two would go after millionaire Myles. God, he was so pathetically easy and gullible." She paused and looked up toward the ceiling, obviously reminiscing, and then looked back at me. "He believed their entire made-up story. Everything was going perfectly for these two women until Myles did something neither one of them had anticipated. Do you know what that was, Lisette?"

She watched me intensely as she walked toward me, her fingers continuing to dance around the hilt of the blade.

I remained silent and still, my heart hammering.

Steve had taken away my control in a way no other man had before. Kyra had broken me in a way I'd never been broken. But as bad as both occurrences had been, one thing had never happened. I'd never really felt fear. Not true fear. Not like what I was feeling as Kyra's lover approached me with a look of promised death.

Standing by my thighs, she stood still and continued with the story that I knew all too well.

"On the day of the wedding, Mr. Myles presented his bride-to-be with a prenuptial agreement that stated she would get five million dollars of his money after five long, fucking years of marriage. She'd get an additional five million after ten years. Well . . . let me tell you, Lisette, the ladies weren't happy. When they pulled these scams, they always had to remain apart and see one another on the side, because obviously they had the role of the good wife to play. But the longest they'd ever had to go seeing one another like secret lovers had been for nine months.

"One of the ladies wanted to call the whole thing off. She couldn't handle the length of time required to get that kind of money. She was content to pull a few more scams and wait for the next big score. But the other female, the one who'd been playing the role, she talked about how much time and effort had been put in. That Myles was the here-and-now opportunity, and that if they'd just stick it through, they'd be able to live in love for the rest of their lives."

She paused and closed her eyes for a few seconds. When she opened them, tears began to fall from them slowly.

She continued.

"But after two years, the prospect of lasting another three became too hard for the ladies, and they began to rack their brains for a way out. Now at the same time, a woman named Shante ran into an acquaintance of hers who she'd met at the gym, named Lisa. On this particular day, Lisa had the biggest smile on her face Shante had ever seen. Now, Shante was very used to seeing Lisa with a frown and a beaten demeanor, so naturally she was curious about Lisa's change in mood. So she asked her why she'd been so happy. With no one around, Lisa explained how a woman helped trap her husband, who'd been abusing the hell out of her, so that she could get out of her marriage.

"As luck would have it, Shante, who ran in the same circles as the woman, just happened to be friends with one of the women who'd been running the scam on Myles. Well, one day, in casual conversation, Shante happened to mention to one of the ladies the story of Lisa and her savior, and about how that savior had given Lisa evidence of her husband doing things that no husband should do that she was able to use to get out of the marriage without any fuss from her bastard of a husband."

She paused and sat down beside me.

"Lisette, it was as if the heavens had opened up. Do you want to know what happened next?"

She looked at me.

I clenched my jaw and closed my fists as my stomach twisted.

"I said, do you want to know what happened next?" she asked again.

I looked at her. I didn't want to respond, but knew that I had to. My body shook with each beat of my heart. Reluctantly, I said, "Yes."

She scowled, then leaned toward me and placed the cool, sharp edge of the blade against my warm cheek.

I took a breath and held it as bumps rose on my skin.

Her mouth low beside my ear, she said in a whisper, "The women got the savior's information, and the next day they called her for help. But guess what?"

She pressed the blade into my cheek and began to drag it down slowly.

I closed my eyes. A moan escaped from my lips as I felt my flesh tear.

"You know the rest of the story, don't you, you bitch?" she said, pulling the blade away.

Tears fell from my eyes as I forced my body to stay still.

"I've been planning this for six months, cunt. I hired your friend over there to play dual roles. He was Ryan to you, but Griffin to your easy protégé. I promised him money and a lot of sex. You whores didn't disappoint.

"Then I talked to people from your past—you weren't well

liked by the way—and got the information about your mother and about how she'd left you. I had Shante deliver the papers to her. I bought this house under a false name and kept it maintained just for this night. I've been watching your every move. Your meetings with Shante. Your dates with Ryan. Your searches for Myles. By the way, I think you should know that he's dead. Your associate, Marlene, would have been here tonight too, but luckily for her, she got a pass because of her son. I have a weak spot for kids. But you . . ." She leaned over me and looked down at Aida. "You won't be so lucky. You wanted to follow this bitch. Well, now you can follow her straight to hell." She came back in and held her face inches away from my own. Her breath was hot and stale. "You took Kyra away from me, whore. You took my soul mate away. I've painstakingly waited for this fucking moment. An eye for a fucking eye. I'm going to kill your little star over there first. I want you to watch her die. And then it'll be your turn."

She wiped the blood—my blood—from the blade off on my breast, cutting it a little, and then stood up.

My cheek stung as blood flowed.

Six months.

She'd been planning revenge.

All because of Kyra.

I looked at Aida. Her eyes were wide with fear. Whatever drug they'd given her still had her immobile. I'd told Marlene that she'd been safe. That she had nothing to do with any of this. I looked at her as she stared at me.

I was horribly wrong.

Blood ran. My heart galloped. I felt cold with fear, but mostly hot with hatred. Hatred for Ryan. For Shante. For Myles's death. For Kyra's lover who held all the cards. Most of all, I felt hatred for Kyra.

The bitch just wouldn't leave me alone.

I looked at Aida. Told her I was sorry with my eyes. Told

her to be strong. And then I saw something that surprised me. Her fingers closed ever so slowly until she was giving me a thumbs up sign.

In the six months that I'd known her, she'd been taking weekly kickboxing lessons from me. If Kyra's lover thought Aida was going to go down easy, she had another thing coming.

42

Music was coming from upstairs.

Rebecca was crouched low at the side of the house. Her heart was beating so hard, she could hear it. Her 9 mm was gripped tightly in her hand, which was becoming slicker with each passing second.

Lisette was in trouble.

She'd been repeating that in her mind like a mantra.

Lisette was in trouble.

On wobbly legs, she'd moved from her car and hurried quickly to the front of the house where she flattened her back against the home's red brick, just below the living room window. She didn't think it would have been, but she carefully—as quietly as her trembling hand would allow—checked to see if, by some miracle, it was unlocked.

Of course it wasn't.

She moved slowly along the base of the house, checking three other windows before going to the side of the house. That's when she heard the music coming from above her.

She moved away from the house a few inches and craned her neck upward. Although the blinds to the room were closed, she could see light flickering. Candlelight?

She flattened her back to the house again. Music and candlelight were for romantic evenings. But she'd seen Lisette get tasered and her car taken away and hidden in the garage. Then the younger female's car had been taken. Rebecca didn't know what was going on, but she felt in her bones that whatever the purpose for the music and candles had been, a romantic evening wasn't it.

She took a breath, then wiped her slick palms on her black slacks before reaching into her pocket and pulling out her cell phone. She looked at it.

One bar!

She exhaled. She had one bar. Quickly, she dialed 9-1-1 and hit the talk button to send the call, and put it to her ear. She took a slow, deep breath as she waited for the call to go through and connect with the police. But as she breathed out, a beeping sound went off in her ear.

"No," she whispered.

She pulled the phone away and looked at it. Her heart dropped. The call had never gone through as she no longer had service.

She whispered, "No," again and then held the phone up and moved it from side to side, hoping that she'd get lucky and come across a spot in which the phone would get service again. But that didn't happen. She sighed and put the phone back into her pocket.

Suddenly she heard someone yell out.

It sounded like Lisette's voice. Sounded as though she were cursing. Then she heard another voice—another female—cursing and yelling back.

A chill crept up Rebecca's spine.

Lisette was in trouble.

Somehow she had to get inside.

She swallowed and headed toward the back, being careful to avoid any twigs lying around. She was no expert, but she'd seen enough thrillers and horror movies to know what not to do, and what to avoid. In the movies, the actors always did great jobs of portraying fear, stress, and angst. As Rebecca made her way to the back of the house, she knew that none of the actors, no matter how many times they rehearsed, could come close to walking and breathing with the anxiety that was running through her.

Rebecca moved slowly and as swiftly as she could, and made her way to a back door. She didn't think her chances were good, but she lightly wrapped her fingers around the knob. She was about to turn it when she paused. She had ADT wired throughout her home. If someone opened a window or door, a chime went off, followed by a programmed voice, letting her know which window or door had been opened. Rebecca looked at the doorknob. What if they had ADT or something similar?

She pulled her hand away from the knob and wiped her palm on her slacks, the nervous and anxious sweat having built up again. She tried to peer in through one of three crescent-shaped windows, but saw nothing but darkness.

She swallowed again. Her throat was as raw as her nerves. She reached into her pocket, grabbed her cell phone, and prayed to see a signal, but her prayers went unanswered.

"Damn," she whispered, putting the phone away.

She looked behind her, not because she'd heard anything, but just because. She was on edge, nervous. Crickets rubbed their legs together in the grass, giving off an eerie whine. The stale, humid air hovered over and around her as though it were draped over her shoulders. Rebecca peered into the darkness of the backyard. An idle thought passed through her mind: if this were a movie, when she turned back around to face the door, someone would be there waiting, their face grotesquely disfigured or hidden behind a hockey mask. She'd have time to let out a scream before something pierced through her midsection or came down and spilt the top of her head.

Rebecca flexed her fingers around the butt of the 9 mm and held it at her waist, ready to fire as she turned back slowly to face the door. No one ever used a gun in the horror films, and if someone was there, she wouldn't scream. She'd just pull the trigger.

But no one was there.

Rebecca looked at the knob. *Lisette is in trouble*, she thought. She wrapped her fingers around it again, squeezed it as her heart drummed on speed beneath her chest, and turned. Or at least tried to.

Rebecca exhaled a breath of both relief and disappointment as the knob didn't budge, and then moved away from the door. Seconds later she was at the side of the garage. There'd been no way for her to sneak inside, which meant there was only one way in.

She moved toward the front again and looked across toward Kay's house. Her lights were still off and now the illumination from the television was gone too. She thought about running across and ringing Kay's bell to tell her to call the police, but as the thought ran through her mind, she thought also about Lisette and her screaming match a few minutes ago. Rebecca didn't know what was going on, but she knew it wasn't good, and as much as she wanted to, she knew that she couldn't risk anyone seeing Kay's lights go on and her front door open.

Rebecca took a breath and held it as her 9 mm seemed to vibrate in her hand. She'd fired the 9 mm many times, sending bullets center mass and straight through the heads of paper targets a few feet away. She was a damn good shot. Her instructor even bought her a T-shirt one day that read "Born to shoot" on the front, and the words "Test me" on the back.

Rebecca closed her eyes.

Lisette was in trouble and she was there.

She'd shot paper targets before. Tonight could be different.

"My steps will be yours, Lord. I trust you to guide my hand."

There was only one way inside the house and Kay's lights were off.

Rebecca inhaled and exhaled and then moved to the front door.

She had an idea.

She just prayed it would work.

43

Aida did her best to keep her breathing as even as she could. Whatever drug she'd been given had almost worn off completely and although they tingled and felt a little weak, she could pretty much move her limbs.

She took a very slow breath. Vivian Steele was walking around the bed to which Lisette was tied, and heading for her with a blade she'd just used to slice a deep gash in Lisette's cheek.

Aida tried not to, but she shivered. She couldn't believe what had happened. Didn't want to believe it. One minute she'd been dressed and having wine, and the next, she was naked and hurting from wounds to her face. She was also hurting between her legs. A chill ran over her as she tried not to think about what had been done to her during her time of unconsciousness.

Griffin was a gigolo. Not a womanizer who traveled. A convicted rapist. Griffin. The man she'd fallen for. Almost broke protocol for. A man who despite saying she'd be done with after her job was complete, she still had doubts as to whether she could or would.

A tear snaked from her eye as she thought of the number of times he'd been inside of her raping her, not fucking her. And he'd raped Lisette too as Ryan.

She looked at Lisette lying helpless on the bed, bleeding badly from her knife wound. Aida had given her the thumbs-up. She wasn't exactly sure how or even if they'd be able to escape from the unbelievable horror they were experiencing, but, win or lose, Aida would get blows in for both of them. If she was going to go, she'd go down swinging.

Aida was a fighter. Always had been. She'd fought on the playgrounds at school. She'd fought in the streets of her neighborhood in the Bronx. She'd fought to break the cycle her grandmother, mother, and sister had all been prisoners of. She'd fought to do things her way, and her fight had been rewarded when Lisette first approached her.

Win or lose.

Do or die.

Aida took a breath.

"Make sure you pay close attention, Lisette," Vivian said, coming toward her. "The things I do to her, I'm going to do to you, only worse. I promise. But before I do that . . ."

Aida turned her head slightly and averted her gaze upward. She could only see Vivian from the waist down. She watched as Vivian paused beside Griffin, or Ryan, or whoever the fuck he was.

"...let me take care of this small business matter first."

Aida watched Vivian's legs turn toward Griffin. Seconds later she heard a gurgling sound and then watched in shocking dread and disbelief as Griffin fell to the ground. He was bleeding profusely from a gash across his throat. Aida clenched her jaw as he covered his throat and tried desperately to keep his blood from flowing out.

"You didn't really think I'd give you the other half of the money, did you?" Vivian said, stepping over him. "You're a fucking whore too, just like they are. But hey—at least you got to bust your nut one last time."

Aida made eye contact with Griffin while Vivian laughed. He was staring at her as his life drained and pooled around him. She stared at him and thought about the sex they'd had in his Escalade, and over the phone. She thought about the few dates they'd had, the Mexican restaurant he'd taken her to.

Vivian was right.

He'd been damn good.

So good that as she watched him dying, she felt nothing but contempt. The motherfucker had gotten what he'd deserved. An eye for an eye.

Griffin stared at her, his mouth hanging open, his eyes open. For a brief moment, Aida was sure he'd seen the satisfaction in her eye. And then he went limp and made no more sounds.

"Now . . ." Vivian said.

Aida averted her gaze upward in time to see Vivian turning to face her.

"Back to you, you junior whore." Vivian took a step toward her and then she suddenly stopped. "What was that?"

Shante said, "Someone's knocking on the door."

"Fuck!"

"Wha . . . what should we do?"

Vivian growled. "What do you mean 'what should we do'? Go and answer the fucking door and get rid of them."

"What if it's the police?"

"The police have no reason to be here."

"But—"

"Goddammit, Shante. Get the fuck down there now!"

Aida's heart beat powerfully in her chest as bumps rose from her skin. Someone was there.

She couldn't see Shante's legs but she heard when she quickly left the room.

With the speed of a snail, she turned her gaze back to Lisette, who was staring at her, her eyes alert with hope. Minutes before, Aida had been determined to fight to her last breath. Death at that point seemed imminent. But what had started with three was now down to one. And that one was now cursing in frustration. Her determination still there, still as strong, death was no longer an option.

She looked at Lisette.

Lisette looked at her.

They nodded.

And then Aida sprang to her feet, while Lisette screamed out for help.

44

"Can I help you?"

Rebecca forced the most genuine smile she could and said, "Hi. I don't mean to trouble you but I could really use your help. My power went down in my house and I really need a phone."

She stared at the woman who'd opened the door. It had been from a distance before, but she knew from her outfit—a pair of blue jeans and a white top—that she'd been the one who'd moved the cars into the garage.

She continued to keep the smile plastered on her face as her nerves jangled. She was leaning to her left against the frame of the door with her right hand behind her, clutching her 9 mm. The darkness in Kay's home had given her the idea of a power outage sans rainstorm. It had been a stretch, but it had been the only thing she could think of to help her get into the house.

She widened her smile as Shante looked back at her with a suspicious gaze. "I promise I won't take up too much of your time."

Shante shook her head. "Sorry, but our phone's not working either. The power's out here too."

Rebecca shifted her head to the right and tried to look past Shante, who quickly shifted to the left to block her view. "But your lights are on," she said.

Shante said, "The lights are, but the phone's out. Sorry."

"That's weird," Rebecca said, flexing her fingers around the grip of her 9 mm. She was a horrible liar.

"Yeah, it's a weird house. Anyway, I was in the middle of something, so . . ." She started to close the door.

Rebecca quickly slid her foot against the bottom of it. "What about a cell phone?"

"Look, I don't own one."

"What about the man of the house? I saw him walking around earlier."

Shante clenched her jaw and drummed her fingers against the wood of the door. She was agitated and nervous as she took a quick glance behind her. "He doesn't own one either," she said, looking back at Rebecca, her voice sharp and biting.

Rebecca stared at her intensely. Lisette was in trouble and by the panicked glint in Shante's eye, and the drumming of her fingers, Rebecca knew that something was going on right at that moment.

She gave Shante a hard glare.

Shante returned it in kind.

And then a scream for help erupted from upstairs.

Lisette's voice.

Shante turned her head momentarily and in that brief moment, Rebecca didn't hesitate.

She pushed against the door, knocking Shante back, and brought her pistol from behind her back and pointed it at her. "Don't move!"

Shante's eyes grew wide.

"Back up!" Rebecca ordered as Lisette called out for help again.

Suddenly there was a crashing noise. Rebecca looked up toward a set of stairs at the end and to the right of the foyer.

That was a mistake.

Before she knew it, Shante rammed her shoulder into her,

sending her crashing back into the wall. Rebecca grunted and air escaped from her lungs as the 9 mm fell from her hands.

Shante dove for the gun. Rebecca quickly made a move for Shante, throwing herself down onto her. The gun, which had been in Shante's grasp slightly, went sliding down the foyer.

Rebecca grabbed Shante's hair as she tried to scramble for the 9 mm.

Shante screamed out, "Bitch!" and tried to pry Rebecca's hands from her hair with one hand, shoved her other hand in Rebecca's face, and lashed out at Rebecca's thigh and midsection with her feet.

Rebecca had always been attractive, but she'd never been an attractive women who shied away from physical contact, and even though it had been a very, very long time since she'd been in a knock-down, drag-out rumble, she tussled as though it were something she did on a regular basis.

She tightened her grasp around Shante's hair, refusing to let go, and bit at Shante's hand in her face.

Shante screamed and contorted her body wildly, trying to get Rebecca off of her. Rebecca rammed her knee into Shante's side and pulled at her hair even harder.

Shante screamed out again, swung out, and knocked Rebecca off of her just enough for her to stretch out and wrap her fingers around the gun. Quickly, Rebecca was on her again, her hand clamped over Shante's. They wrestled on the ground, both fighting to possess the weapon, while upstairs more crashing could be heard.

Shante was strong, Rebecca would give her that. She was giving her all she could handle and more, but Rebecca had been too determined and also too scared, and that fear gave Rebecca the edge.

She drove her knee into Shante's stomach, then used her elbow and hit her in her face. For a split second Shante released the gun, and that split second was all Rebecca needed.

Acting purely on instinct, she took control of the 9mm, shoved it into Shante's chest, and squeezed the trigger.

Shante cried out and then within seconds, her fight ceased. Rebecca, breathing heavily, backed away and pointed the 9mm at Shante, ready to fire again. But that wasn't going to be necessary.

Shante was dead.

Rebecca breathed deeply as her heart beat heavily. Her hands trembled violently as the reality of what she'd done hit her.

She'd killed someone.

Before she could prevent it from happening, she doubled over and vomited. When she was finished, she wiped her mouth with the back of her hand and then sniffed as the scent of something caught her nostrils. She turned quickly, looked toward the end of the foyer, and saw smoke coming from upstairs.

She stood up with her 9 mm gripped tightly in her hand and ran to the stairs.

45

I could do nothing but watch.

As Aida rushed the woman whose name I still didn't know. Kyra's lover. She killed Ryan. No. Not Ryan. Griffin. I'm sure that wasn't his real name either. She killed him without a thought, without hesitation, in cold blood. She was going to do the same to Aida and then come back to me to finish the job she'd started.

I pulled against the ropes tied around my wrists, hoping that if I couldn't break free from the bindings, then maybe I could use the bindings to my advantage to break one of the bedposts.

I pulled. Hard. Felt the rope dig into my flesh. Felt it burn as I eased and then pulled again. I pulled relentlessly. Tried to be superhuman. But as hard as I tried over and over and over, nothing happened. And so I was forced to just watch and hope that Aida could kick the bitch's ass.

I watched.

As Aida grabbed Kyra's lover by her wrists and shoved her back into the dressing table.

I watched.

As that bitch bent her wrist and tried to angle the razor blade down so that it sliced Aida's hand. And when her attempt had been unsuccessful because Aida's strength was too much for her, I watched her lift her knee and drive it into Aida's stomach. The move had been just enough to cause Aida to let go, and when she did, I watched as she brought down her hand with the razor. Fortunately, Aida had moved just enough to the side so that the blade only caught her on the arm.

Aida cried out, but her adrenaline pumping, she quickly blocked the next attack with her left forearm and then threw a right cross straight to the bitch's chin. The bitch cried out, but refused to let go of the blade, and swung out to keep Aida from advancing.

"Bitch! I'm going to kill you!"

In a wild rage, she charged at Aida, who sidestepped her and stuck her foot out, catching her at her ankle, causing her to stumble. As she fell forward, she swung out again and caught Aida on her thigh.

Aida yelled out as blood flowed from a gash the blade produced, but refused to let that stop her. She threw herself into the bitch, and I watched as they came crashing to the floor beside me.

Two things happened then.

One good.

The other bad.

The good: the blade finally fell from her hands.

The bad: the night table with the four candles toppled over, sending the candles to the ground, where one of the candle's flames set afire the bottom of the curtain hanging by the window.

I watched.

As Aida, who had the advantage by being on top, hit the bitch twice in the face, one of her blows bringing blood from her nose.

Kyra's lover yelled out and reached her hands up and grabbed strands of Aida's hair. She pulled down hard, causing Aida's chin to go up toward the ceiling, and then twisted her over.

While all of this went on, I watched smoke begin to fill

the room as the fire on the curtain grew bigger and began to spread.

I watched.

That's all I could fucking do.

Aida and Kyra's lover continued to go at it.

Blow for blow. Kick for kick. Scratch for scratch. Bite for bite when possible. Wrestling, twisting, grunting.

A gun shot suddenly went off from downstairs.

I turned and looked toward the door for a moment, and when I turned back, the bitch was still on the bottom, but had the blade in her hand again. In a swift motion, she dragged the blade across Aida's stomach.

Aida cried out as Kyra's lover pushed her to the side.

"Bitch! You fucking whore! Now it's over for you!"

Kyra's lover got to her knees and raised her hand.

Aida was on her side, her hand over her wound, which was much more than a flesh wound.

Fire burned.

Smoke as thick as cotton hung around us.

I coughed and watched as Kyra's lover brought the blade down, going for Aida's neck.

I watched.

As blood and brain matter spewed from her forehead suddenly, and her body slumped to the side, her arm, blade in hand, coming down at Aida's side.

I watched.

As Rebecca Stantin rushed into the room and screamed my name. "Lisette!"

Rebecca Stantin.

There.

It didn't make sense to me. But I said, "Untie me! Quickly!"

Rebecca moved to me and fumbled with the ropes. "The knots are too tight!"

"Grab her blade!"

Rebecca nodded, and moved to Kyra's lover's dead body.

I glanced at Aida. Blood was flowing from her stomach, but she was breathing.

Rebecca came back and began cutting the ropes.

I coughed, the smoke burning the inside of my lungs, and stinging my eyes. "Hurry!" I said, my eyes still on Aida. The fire was getting worse, spreading now across the room.

Rebecca worked frantically and cut the rope tied around my right wrist. She moved to my left, cut it, and then took care of the binds around my ankles.

I rolled from the bed and moved to Aida, pulling her away just as flames crept toward her. "Help me!"

Rebecca moved and together we lifted Aida by her arms and carried her out of the room, which was quickly becoming engulfed in flames. We made our way down the stairs and out of the house where we collapsed on the front lawn.

"We . . . need . . . help," I said, coughing.

Rebecca got up and ran to the neighbor's house and banged on the door. When the owner opened the door, she raced inside without saying a word.

I looked at Aida, who looked up at me with eyes dazed and bloodshot. She was bleeding and shivering, but despite the obvious pain she was in, she gave me a smile. She coughed and said in a whisper, "Is there something . . ." She coughed a few times and continued. ". . . something about your past you . . ." Another series of coughs. "You want to tell me about?"

I shook my head and did the only thing I could. I laughed.

Rebecca returned a moment later with blankets in her hand. "The police, EMT, and fire department are on the way." She draped a blanket around me and then covered Aida.

I looked at her and said, "What the hell are you doing here?"

She raised her eyebrows. "Proving to you that I'm worthy."

I nodded and looked back to the house where Kyra's lover, Shante Hunt, and their hired gigolo were burning up.

I had to give it to Kyra's ex.

She'd done her homework and had put in a lot of overtime. It had been one hell of a plan. I was almost envious. Almost.

But as good as her plan had been, there'd been one major flaw. It was the same flaw that Kyra's had fallen victim to.

They'd chosen the wrong bitch to fuck with.

I looked back to Aida and Rebecca, their faces and bodies bruised and covered in blood and soot.

No. I stand corrected.

They'd chosen the wrong bitches to fuck with.

Future

46

Three Months Later . . .

"So you're really going to do this?"

"It's time. Besides,you're stepping down. Someone's got to take your place."

"I'm not really stepping down. I just want to take some time. I want to focus solely on Ben, Michael, and me."

"I understand."

"And you're sure that you can leave the field to come behind the desk? Because I'm telling you, it's nowhere near as exciting."

I put my hand to my face and ran my fingers up and down my three-inch scar. It was a constant reminder of how exciting life could get.

Kyra was dead.

So was her lover, Vivian Johnson—not Steele—along with Shante Richards—not Hunt—and their hired gigolo, Jermain Reese—not Griffin or Ryan. Their identities were confirmed after their autopsies were conducted. All three of them had priors on their records.

Hurt, but always thinking on my feet, I used the information Vivian had given me about Jermain, and told the police that both Aida and I had been kidnapped. That they'd planned to rape me after they had their way with Aida, who informed them that they had indeed done just that.

Rebecca's side of the story was that she'd been visiting her friend next door and was leaving when she heard screaming coming from the house. At first she was going to ignore it, but then she heard another scream, and this time it sounded like someone said the word, "Help!"

Curiosity getting the best of her, she went to the neighbor's house and knocked on the door until Shante answered. She was asking if everything was all right when another scream for help came from upstairs. Next thing Rebecca knew, Shante was attacking her, trying to drag her inside. Fortunately for Rebecca, she took self-defense classes and was licensed to carry a firearm for protection. She didn't want to do it, but Shante had been trying to kill her, so Rebecca had to shoot her. She was going to call the police, but more screaming came from upstairs and so did smoke. Without giving it a second thought, Rebecca rushed upstairs and found me tied up and Aida on the ground bleeding and about to be cut again by Vivian. She hadn't meant to shoot her in the head, it had just been a lucky shot. She untied me and then the two of us carried Aida out. Rebecca called 9-1-1 after that.

The three of us wanted our identities to remain private, so before the media arrived on the scene, the EMTs took us away to the hospital, where we gave the police our stories and answered all of the questions they had. We were three women, three strangers, who'd survived a harrowing ordeal.

No one doubted us and Rebecca never had to worry about using her gun.

After the fire was put out, the police searched the home looking for any other kidnap victims. They didn't find any, but they did find Myles's body wrapped in a body bag and stuffed in the trunk of one of the cars in the garage. The discovery of Myles's body allowed them to close the case for Kyra Rogers, who'd gone missing months ago.

I said, "I don't need the excitement right now."

Marlene said, "I think a break from it would do you some

good. Who knows, maybe you can take that time to find someone."

I shook my head.

She would never give up.

As if she'd read my mind, she said, "It can happen, Lisette. Right now your song is just a song. There's no real meaning behind it."

My song.

"Amado Mio."

It was playing from my new iPod in the living room. Vivian tried to ruin it for me with her off-key and off-rhythm humming, but she'd failed. We had nothing in common, but through good times and bad, "Amado Mio" and I were joined at the hip. We would last longer than any marriage between a man and woman would.

I said, "I don't do love, Marlene."

She sighed. "I know, I know. I'm wasting my breath."

"Yes. You are."

"One day," she said, breath wasting and not giving a damn. "One day I'm going to win this argument."

I smiled.

She was ever the optimist.

"Anyway, how's Aida? I called her, but her phone went directly to voice mail."

Aida.

I'd watched and approached her nearly a year ago because I'd seen in her things I'd only ever seen when I looked in the mirror. Most women would have caved after going through an experience like the one she'd gone through. But like me, she wasn't most women. She'd been beaten and scarred, but she was now mentally stronger than before. That made her one hell of a force to be reckoned with.

"She's in Hawaii on assignment."

"Really?"

"A woman wants her husband taken down at his family reunion."

"Ouch," Marlene said.

"She wants to humiliate him in front of everyone before she leaves him."

"Are you sure Aida's up for this? I mean, I know I've asked before if she was OK before, but what she went through . . . I don't know . . . I just don't see how she can't be traumatized."

"Aida is fine," I said. "She took what happened, processed it, accepted it, and learned from it."

"You make her sound like a robot."

"Not a robot. Just someone who understands the possible consequences of the business she's in."

"But—"

"She's fine, Marlene," I said. "I wouldn't have let her get into anything if she wasn't."

"I know. Well . . . what about Rebecca?"

Rebecca.

Of all the places in the world, she'd been at her friend's house that night.

She told me all about how she'd seen me go down and about how she'd gone around the house searching for a way inside, until she eventually had to knock on the front door. A move that eventually saved my life along with Aida's.

Of all the places.

Despite the cold shoulder I'd given her and the messages I hadn't returned, her desire remained strong. Rebecca wanted to be a home wrecker not for the thrill or the control, but because she wanted to truly help those who, for one reason or another, couldn't or just didn't know how to help themselves. Her ex-husband had his mission in life, and thanks to me, she had hers. All I had to do was give her a chance.

She'd killed Shante.

She'd killed Vivian seconds before Vivian could kill Aida.

Of all the places.

With her resolute determination, her will, and her 9 mm pistol, she saved my life. Not being sentimental, but I would always owe her for that.

I said, "Rebecca is better than I thought she'd be."

"I still can't believe her friend lived right next door," Marlene said.

"Of all the places," I replied.

In the background, Marlene's doorbell rang.

"Sounds like you have company."

"Michael's here to pick me up. He's taking me out to eat at a Japanese restaurant for dinner and then we're going to the movies."

"Steve's weekend?"

"Yeah."

"Enjoy."

"I will. Do you want to come?"

"Good-bye, Marlene."

I ended the call, shook my head with a smile, and put my phone down.

My song was replaying.

As Chyna Forbes sang, I closed my eyes and thought about what was to come. Marlene was stepping down. I was going to take her place, not because of what had happened, but because it was time. The fire that burned inside of me hadn't gone out, but it had dimmed.

I realized that one day talking with Aida and Rebecca over coffee at Barnes & Noble.

They were both telling me about the new clients they had. Aida had her family reunion to crash and Rebecca's friend Kay had finally reached her breaking point with her husband. The fire in their eyes and the excitement in their voices had been high. They were looking forward to the game play, the manipulation. Things I used to crave.

Until that day.

That day I realized that I needed something different. I needed a new challenge.

I took a breath, held it, and then exhaled slowly.

I thought about Marlene, Steve, Kyra, Myles, Aida, Vivian, Shante, Ryan/Griffin, Rebecca, and all of the others in between.

My life.

From beginning to end, it was one hell of a story. It would make one hell of a movie too.

"Amado Mio."

I listened to the melody, the piano in the breakdown. I enjoyed the hot water's caress over my skin.

I imagined a scene where a woman sitting at a bar in a hotel slams down her cell phone and curses about her unfaithful husband to a coworker, sitting on a stool beside her. A female coworker. One with telling eyes, sexy lips, and a body made for sin.

The coworker would complain to the female about how her husband was probably off fucking his secretary at that very moment.

The female would watch her frustrated coworker with a disapproving gaze, and after a few minutes, she'd ask one simple question: "Why don't you just set him up?"

"Amado Mio" would be playing from speakers above them.

My life.

It would be one hell of a movie.

Home Wrecker would be the title.

ORDER FORM
URBAN BOOKS, LLC
78 E. Industry Ct
Deer Park, NY 11729

Name: (please print): _____

Address: _____

City/State: _____

Zip: _____

QTY	TITLES	PRICE
	16 ½ On The Block	$14.95
	16 On The Block	$14.95
	Betrayal	$14.95
	Both Sides Of The Fence	$14.95
	Cheesecake And Teardrops	$14.95
	Denim Diaries	$14.95
	Happily Ever Now	$14.95
	Hell Has No Fury	$14.95
	If It Isn't love	$14.95
	Last Breath	$14.95
	Loving Dasia	$14.95
	Say It Ain't So	$14.95

Shipping and handling - add $3.50 for 1st book, then $1.75 for each additional book.

Please send a check payable to:

Urban Books, LLC

Please allow 4 - 6 weeks for delivery

ORDER FORM
URBAN BOOKS, LLC
78 E. Industry Ct
Deer Park, NY 11729

Name: (please print):_____

Address: _____

City/State: _____

Zip: _____

QTY	TITLES	PRICE
	A Man's Worth	$14.95
	Abundant Rain	$14.95
	Battle Of Jericho	$14.95
	By The Grace Of God	$14.95
	Dance Into Destiny	$14.95
	Divorcing The Devil	$14.95
	Forsaken	$14.95
	Grace And Mercy	$14.95
	Guilty & Not Guilty Of Love	$14.95
	His Woman, His Wife His Widow	$14.95
	Illusions	$14.95
	The LoveChild	$14.95

Shipping and handling - add $3.50 for 1st book, then $1.75 for each additional book.
Please send a check payable to:
Urban Books, LLC
Please allow 4 - 6 weeks for delivery

ORDER FORM
URBAN BOOKS, LLC
78 E. Industry Ct
Deer Park, NY 11729

Name:(please print):_____

Address: _____

City/State: _____

Zip: _____

QTY	TITLES	PRICE
	The Cartel	$14.95
	The Cartel#2	$14.95
	The Dopeman's Wife	$14.95
	The Prada Plan	$14.95
	Gunz And Roses	$14.95
	Snow White	$14.95
	A Pimp's Life	$14.95
	Hush	$14.95
	Little Black Girl Lost 1	$14.95
	Little Black Girl Lost 2	$14.95
	Little Black Girl Lost 3	$14.95
	Little Black Girl Lost 4	$14.95

Shipping and handling - add $3.50 for 1st book, then $1.75 for each additional book.

Please send a check payable to:

Urban Books, LLC

Please allow 4 - 6 weeks for delivery

ORDER FORM
URBAN BOOKS, LLC
78 E. Industry Ct
Deer Park, NY 11729

Name: (please print): _____

Address: _____

City/State: _____

Zip: _____

QTY	TITLES	PRICE

Shipping and handling - add $3.50 for 1st book, then $1.75 for each additional book.

Please send a check payable to:
> **Urban Books, LLC**

Please allow 4 - 6 weeks for delivery